A WOMAN

A WOMAN

SIBILLA ALERAMO

Translated by
Rosalind Delmar

With an introduction by
Richard Drake

UNIVERSITY OF CALIFORNIA PRESS
Berkeley and Los Angeles

University of California Press
Berkeley and Los Angeles, California

Introduction, Copyright © 1980
by The Regents of the University of California.
English translation, Copyright © 1979
by Virago Ltd., London
Italian edition UNA DONNA published
by Giangiacomo Feltrinelli Editori, Milano, Copyright © 1950

First Paperback Printing 1983
ISBN 0-520-04949-7

Library of Congress Cataloging in Publication Data

Faccio, Rina, 1876-1960.   (pseud. Aleramo, Sibilla)
    A Woman.

    Translation of Una donna.
    I. Title.
    PZ3.F118Wn   1980   [PO4815.A3]   853'.912   80-17123

                                Printed in the United States of America

                              5 6 7 8 9

The paper used in this publication meets the minimum requirements of American
National Standard for Information Sciences—Permanence of Paper for Printed
Library Materials, ANSI Z39.48–1984. ∞

INTRODUCTION

For a book that sent shock waves through the European literary establishment and, since its original publication in 1906,
has gone through seven editions along with highly acclaimed
translations into all the principal languages of Europe, *A
Woman* by Sibilla Aleramo (1876-1960) has remained curi-
ously obscure in America. Hailed in its day as the Book of Gen-
esis in the bible of feminism, Aleramo's lightly fictionalized
memoir presented a kaleidoscopic series of Italian images — the
frenetic industrialism of the North, the miserable squalor of
the country's backward areas to the South, fin de siècle Italian
politics and literary life — all set in the framework of a drama
admiringly characterized by Luigi Pirandello as "grim and
powerful." For some other Italians, *A Woman* touched a raw
nerve, and many critics reacted to Aleramo with extreme
hostility. However, whether one liked Aleramo's novel or not,
the book was an iceberg in the mainstream of Italian literary
life, impossible to get around without careful inspection.

On the whole, foreign reviewers liked *A Woman* better
than Italian reviewers did. Georg Brandes's preface to the 1909
German edition assured the novel a wide readership in central
Europe, and with the publication of Stefan Zweig's glowing
article about Aleramo in the *Neue Freie Presse,* the young
Italian novelist acquired a very powerful ally indeed. A year
earlier Mary Lansdale's English translation, *A Woman at Bay,*
had brought Aleramo to the attention of an admiring Anglo-
American audience. Spanish, Swedish, Russian, and Polish

translations soon followed, but, as usual in the case of Italian writers, the real international breakthrough for the author of *A Woman* came with the appearance of the critically applauded French translation in 1908. Not since the nearly unanimous celebration of Gabriele D'Annunzio (1863-1938) in the 1890s did French critics write so approvingly of an Italian author's work. A good deal of ill-disguised cultural and male chauvinism was present in the French praise of Aleramo, however: supercilious amazement at the thought of an Italian writing such a brilliant book gave way to positive shock over such an achievement by a woman. While irritating, French persiflage in no way detracted from *A Woman*'s triumph, from what the critic and novelist Edouard Rod called the book's "almost terrible sincerity." No one, certainly not the reviewer for the immensely influential *Mercure de France,* could deny the importance and obvious worth of a novel that boasted the most complete female character in Italian literature.

This anonymous reviewer's assessment touches close to the heart of the book's historic significance. *A Woman* may have been "a scream of pain," as another French critic put it, but above all else the novel declared that Italian women had passed into literature. Similar declarations on behalf of women were being heard all over Europe and the United States. Over a period of centuries, the male imagination had created and developed a mythology of women. Now the truth would have to be written, and written by women themselves. For the Italian part of the story, *A Woman* was a heroic start toward that distant goal, but Aleramo paid for it by a lifetime of anguish, doubt, recrimination, and guilt. The new translation by Rosalind Delmar is to be welcomed for the opportunity it affords a generation of readers, especially interested in the social and cultural issues raised here, to appreciate a classic too long neglected by Americans.

I

The making of Sibilla Aleramo was, in the beginning, the work of Giovanni Cena (1870-1917). A poet and a novelist whose *Gli ammonitori* (1904) would win the ecstatic praise of Maxim Gorky and gain him a wide international reputation, Cena wielded a powerful influence in Italian literary life as editor in chief of the *Nuova Antologia,* beginning in 1902. He had met Aleramo in 1899 when she was Rina Pierangeli Faccio, editor of a Milanese feminist journal, *L'Italia Femminile.* At twenty-three she was ravishingly beautiful, with literary gifts that any aspiring writer might envy. She was also suffering acute depression over a loveless marriage to a man who had raped her at fifteen and later had gotten her with child. Scarcely more than a child herself, Rina sustained a double shock from this brutal attack: not only were her romantic sensibilities about love violated and permanently injured, but the ensuing marriage plunged her, a Piedmontese by birth, into the primitive world of the Italian Marches. In 1887 her father had moved the family from Milan to Porto Civitanova on the Adriatic coast, near Porto Recanati, where he managed a glassworks. Enlightened and iconoclastically progressive by late-nineteenth-century Italian standards, he imparted his advanced views to the adored Rina. Even after the removal to Porto Civitanova, she continued to live on an oasis of northern Italian culture and values. Marriage to the man who had raped her, one of her father's local employees, deprived her of this parental shelter, and direct exposure to provincial mores chilled her soul.

Since childhood, Rina had been an indefatigable letter writer, and now writing as a craft and occupation took her mind off the provincial torpor of married life in Porto Civitanova. At first she wrote fiction, short stories describing unhappy heroines whose misery reflected the author's own emotional state. These stories, echoed the literary conventions made inescapable by the international triumph of D'Annunzio in the 1890s, but the literary success that D'Annunzio achieved with such facility eluded young Rina, as it did most writers who attempted to reproduce the inimitable decadent-romantic style of *Il piacere* (1889), *L'Innocente* (1891), and *Il trionfo della morte* (1894), then being hailed in their French translations as harbingers of a Latin renaissance. Even in her journalism, a line of work in which she enjoyed immediate success, contributing light society articles to several provincial newspapers, the hyperbolic, florid style of D'Annunzio was evident.

This D'Annunzian affectation underwent total, though impermanent, eclipse in 1898 when she encountered the work of Guglielmo Ferrero (1871-1942), a sociologist who had not yet discovered that his true gift was for history. His *L'Europa giovane* (1898) was *the* book of Rina's young life. In the previous year her depression had become so deep that she had attempted suicide. Narrowly escaping death, she feared the onset of madness. Her mother had gone insane in 1893 and lay entombed in a Macerata asylum. This was a fate that seemed all too likely for Rina herself, and indeed family life in Porto Civitanova, at least in the violent Pierangeli household, gave every promise of leading straight to the madhouse.

Ferrero's book helped to rescue her from this life-threatening despondency by galvanizing her active and powerful mind around critical social issues, especially socialism and feminism. The young Italian sociologist, a student and colleague of the positivist thinker Cesare Lombroso, explained in *L'Europa giovane* that peculiar cultural and hereditary factors tended to transform Latin marriages into prison sentences for women. This was an image of which Rina could take an empathic view. The maddening phenomenon of compulsively philandering husbands, as likely as not to come home with venereal disease, who at the same time were pathologically jealous of wives whose freedom of movement might make prisoners in maximum-security jails feel superior, was here set forth in the language of common sense and in the light of science. She would have learned of Mona Caird's work through Ferrero as well. Caird had written extensively on the problems besetting family life, but her special concern, evident, for example, in the novel *The Daughters of Danaus* (1894) and in *The Morality of Marriage and Other Essays on the Status and Destiny of Women* (1897), was the loveless, forced marriage in which the woman had been compelled to bear a child without her consent. One need not merely imagine Rina's eyes opening wide as she read these pages in *L'Europa giovane,* because in chapter 11 of *A Woman* she described how the contents of Ferrero's book reinforced her ideals and gave vivid expression to her own increasingly desperate longings.

Feminism provided her writing with a focal point, hitherto lacking, but it was, even at this early date, a feminism reflecting her own personal situation rather than a program for social reform. Programmatic feminism was essentially a socialist monopoly in Italy, echoing from afar the orthodox Marxist argument of August Bebel's *Woman and Socialism* (1879), translated into Italian in 1891, that the problems of women would be solved when the economic problems of society were solved. Anna Kuliscioff, the companion and colleague of the man who founded Italy's Socialist party in 1892, Filippo Turati, affirmed in a famous lecture entitled "The Monopoly of Man" (1890) that "economic independence was the first condition of civil and political rights." Bebel and Kuliscioff asserted in their work the basic Marxist point, that is, the primacy of the substructural mode of production in comparison to which questions like feminism were superstructural manifestations.

Theoretical consistency would never be Rina's strong point, and Marxist dialectics played virtually no role in shaping her fin de siècle feminist position. She was interested in a dimension of the women's problem for which the mode-of-production theory alone could not possibly account: the peculiarly oppressive character of the cumulative cultural heredity in Mediterranean countries. English and American women lived in capitalist countries, too, but at the same time they enjoyed rights and honors of which few Italian women had any inkling. After reading *L'Europa giovane,* Rina became one of the few.

Beginning in 1898 her journal and newspaper articles showed increasing concern for feminist issues. Always writing at home in Porto Civitanova, she defined her feminism at this time as a proposal for "the radical abolition of all those usages and prejudices which, with barbaric hypocrisy, now make of woman an unconscious and miserable slave, almost irresponsible for her own acts." Rina held herself up in these indignant pieces as "the destroyer" of the traditional contempt regarding women, but her feminism appeared more radical than it really was. Close readers of *L'Europa giovane* would find in Rina's feminist articles some of Ferrero's own reservations about the direction that the more shrill feminists were taking. It was Ferrero who had uttered dark prophecies about the evolution of a "third sex," similar to worker bees—"imperfect females whose sex organs are atrophied and due to this sterility become active, intelligent, courageous and superior to many men." In fact, the title of his essay on feminism was "The Third Sex," but an alternative title might just as easily have been "The Varieties of Maternal Experience." Ferrero argued that a childless woman in the job market would remain, whatever her profession, "a caricature of a mother." He did not mention Freud anywhere in *L'Europa giovane,* but the idea of sublimation was clearly on Ferrero's mind when he wrote "The Third Sex." By seeking perfect equality with men, feminists encouraged the displacement of maternal instincts, and as a result society was being subjected to more and more women "with brain of fire and heart of ice." Eventually the family would disappear entirely—it would have to if the feminists won and implemented their program. For all of his liberalism and advocacy of women's rights, Ferrero feared such a drastic prospect. Rina shared that fear. Although in 1898 she wrote some impassioned pleas on behalf of a public life for women, these feminist articles were aimed at tranquilizing middle-class public opinion on the real meaning of feminism in Italy. In other words, she argued that the liberation of women would not destroy the family but, on the contrary, would give it new life. The enslavement of women, not their freedom, threatened both the family and society. This was essentially a conservative argument, although the emphasis fell on what would be for Italian sensibilities a shocking means to attain a traditional end. Now she had hold of a lively issue, and her career sped forward. The progressive humanitarian left, that fin de siècle intellectual circle served by Ernesto Teodoro Moneta's *La Vita Internazionale,* found her eminently sensible. Moneta, almost a prototypal moderate socialist of the period, presided over Lombardy's Peace Society and promoted campaigns against dueling, alcoholism, and the oppression of women. Ever on the lookout for writers who shared his views on the political and social issues of the day, he made in Rina a pleasant discovery. Moneta published a number of the young author's feminist articles in 1898 and 1899, giving her a tremendous boost toward national prominence.

She took another large stride in this direction later in 1899, first by contributing articles to Emilia Mariani's *L'Italia Femminile* and then by becoming that journal's director. In the same year, following an argument with Rina's father, signor Pierangeli was dismissed from the glassworks. He then moved with Rina to Milan, hoping to start a new career as an exporter of fruit. For Rina this was much more than a simple geographical move; the relocation was a return to life from her cheerless sepulcher in Porto Civitanova. No longer did she have to mail her articles from that nether world to the real world. Now she lived in the real world, actively participating in literary life, the only life that ever did or ever would have any lasting meaning for her. Directing *L'Italia Femminile* was hardly all play atop Mount Parnassus, however; she learned soon enough that not all the serpents nested in Porto Civitanova. Milan had at least one snake in the grass, right in the editorial office of *L'Italia Femminile,* named Lamberto Mondaini. She haughtily rejected the "decorative director" role that Mondaini envisioned for her while he, as executive editor, would handle the real work and exercise all authority.

After three months of ceaseless struggle with Mondaini, Rina resigned in January 1900, but not before making a number of new literary contacts. The most important of these were Guglielmo Felice Damiani and Giovanni Cena, both writers who contributed poems to *L'Italia Femminile* and who became her lovers. First Damiani and then Cena, enveloped in an aura of poetry, captivated Rina. Next to such men, signor Pierangeli, with all his talk about the prices of apples and oranges, seemed in his wife's eyes to be even more of a provincial lout than before. Life with him in Milan was torture enough, but when late in 1900 he announced that the family would move back to Porto Civitanova, she went limp at the thought of resuming their former lifeless existence. Rina did go back, but away from Milan, with its writers, intellectuals, and artists, she felt hopelessly marooned. The old fears of insanity and suicide resurged in that "dull, semi-barbaric land." Even the love she bore her son and the passion she brought to her journal writing could not protect her from a sickening sense of dread. It seemed as though at twenty-five, while in full possession of health and faculties, the lid had been nailed shut on her coffin.

II

A Woman is an artistic rendering of Rina Pierangeli Faccio's escape from the graveyard of her fears to freedom. The symbol of that transition was a name change: Sibilla Aleramo. Her lover, Cena, thought up the name, and she took it to signify the beginning of her "second existence." Upon leaving her husband and child, Rina, now Sibilla, moved close to Rome, where for some months she vainly attempted to acquire both a legal separation and custody of her son. It soon became clear that neither goal would be achieved, and only then did she perceive the full magnitude of her act. It was one thing to walk out on a witless husband, but to leave a small child was quite another, particularly for that time and place. An Italian mother abandoning her little boy? Such liberation as this was nearly as tragic as the slavery that had preceded it. Her steely resolve, implacable in its disregard for all consequences, required some explanation, and Sibilla Aleramo would be explaining it, in one way or another, for the rest of her life.

The autobiographical character of Aleramo's writing, always a prominent feature even in the 1890s, became and remained obsessive after she deserted her family. In the voluminous diaries that she kept from 1940 to 1960, Aleramo often remarked on the incalculable but certainly disastrous psychological consequences of her desperate action in 1902. It was obviously the turning point of her entire existence. She gained freedom, but lost peace of mind; and the anxieties arising from that loss increased rather than diminished as the years and decades passed. Her notorious love affairs and scandalous books provided either temporary escape or confessional expression, but total absolution was denied her, as she herself very often mourned.

Hardly had Aleramo left home than she began to write about why it had been necessary for her to leave. *A Woman* took shape around this necessity. Cena had quickly supplanted Damiani as her lover and intellectual guide, as the man who added "a warm light of hope" to her life. Eventually she went to live with Cena, and their romantic relationship would last for seven years. From him, her "initiator," Aleramo learned the meaning of love and intellectual companionship. Although Cena was writing the novel *Gli ammonitori* in these years, he had already acquired fame as a poet with *Madre* (1897) and *In umbra* (1899). A man of striking physical unattractiveness, the gnomish Cena gloried in the love of his radiant mistress. She inspired in him a fresh poetic outburst, and in the sonnet "Sibilla" he sang of his love for her, at the same time envisioning himself as Pygmalion to her Galatea: "I discovered her and called her Sibilla."

To contemporaries their life together seemed to be taken from a page out of *Vie de Bohème;* but actually the truth was considerably different. In November 1939 Aleramo wrote an autobiographical fragment, entitled "Cena," which described these years. Later published in *Dal mio diario: 1940-1944,* the essay was a record of a relationship "much more serious than a marriage." Cena, Aleramo remembered, had influence and reputation, but no money; she herself was conspicuously deficient in all three. Their shabby apartment on Via Flaminia near the Piazza del Popolo was hardly more than a writing studio and an editorial office where they both labored on the *Nuova Antologia* and, in odd hours, on *Gli ammonitori* as well as *Una donna*. Almost from the beginning of their affair, Cena had urged her to stop wasting time and energy writing ephemeral articles in favor of "narrating my life up to the present." However, it is almost miraculous that she ever got any work done on her book in this apartment, for, despite much high-flown talk about liberation, Aleramo played the traditional woman-of-the-house role, cooking and cleaning while at the same time performing "anonymously and gratuitously" the functions of a factotum on the biweekly *Nuova Antologia:*

correcting proofs, reading and criticizing manuscripts, writing summaries and reviews under the pseudonym "Nemi." One of her jobs in 1904 was to copy by hand the entire manuscript of *Gli ammonitori* for the publisher. History is silent on the question of whether Cena returned the favor for *A Woman,* but this silence attains a revealing eloquence. The most overworked and exploited housewife might have less ground for complaint than the liberated Aleramo did; as she herself acknowledged in 1939, the Cena-Aleramo household was a bizarre setting for a feminist author.

In 1904, though, she would not have traded her writing desk in Rome for all the luxuries that her now affluent husband in Porto Civitanova could have provided. The disgust and humiliation that his memory engendered in Aleramo's mind made a pair with the guilt and remorse she continued to feel over her son. Outraged and troubled, she tried to put these feelings down on paper, to analyze them, to trace their origins in her personal history and their shattering consequences in her present life. Few books have been written in such pain, and no one can read *A Woman* without being affected by the author's distress.

Cena aided her through the entire literary process, from outline to published book. She never forgot him for this, or forgave him, either. True, "he had made opportune observations, indicating . . . where it was necessary to abbreviate and to develop," but Cena was also responsible for a decision that she regretted for the rest of her life. He prevailed upon her to change the ending of *A Woman.* She had originally closed the book with a candid confession of all her motives in leaving home, including the love affair with Damiani. However, Cena sensed correctly that the moral force of *A Woman* would be diminished if public attention were distracted by the all-too-familiar device in Italian fiction of an adulterous triangle. He strongly urged her to end the novel on a lofty moral tone, revealing the "naked relentless conscience of a woman facing

herself, with a duty toward herself." Aleramo yielded to her
lover on this point with extreme reluctance, remembering
in 1939 that "by mutilating the truth" she had experienced
a sense of committing a sin. In her old age she preferred to
believe, with her usual spite toward ex-lovers, that Cena was
only interested in protecting his male vanity because he wanted
no one to know his mistress had loved anyone before him. In
reality, however, the enormous success of *A Woman,* together
with its continuing worldwide appeal, suggest that Cena the
critic never gave any writer better advice than he did his reluc-
tant protégée.

III

Aleramo did not write another book for thirteen years. In
1919, a second "novel," *Il passaggio,* appeared, and in this
work she carefully retold the story of how and why she had left
her son, this time with a strict adherence to remembered truth.
"It was not for the love of another man that I liberated myself,
but I did love another man," the author confessed. With Cena
safely in his grave since 1917, this confession, if she had cared,
could not injure him, and at the same time it set the record
straight. Setting the record straight had by then become the
sole aim of her art, and if she failed to develop into a great
autobiographical writer, it certainly was not for lack of trying.
During the last forty years of her life Aleramo tried to do little
else, but from the 1906 publication of *A Woman* to 1919 she
was still searching for her authentic voice.

The period from 1906 to 1910 was a strange interlude in
her career. The international success of *A Woman* gratified
Aleramo, but she did not then think that her personal life was
sufficiently meaningful to serve as a literary subject indefinitely. The little writing that she did during these years, in the
form of newspaper articles for *La Tribuna,* was related to the

most proud and decent efforts of her life — working with the
poor, first in one of Rome's most wretched quarters, the Tes-
taccio, and then in the Agro Romano, just outside the capital.
Gaetano Salvemini described the malaria-ridden, illiterate,
and despised *guitti* of the Agro Romano as "the most miserable
and oppressed peasants in Italy." A social outcast herself now,
Aleramo turned to them as her own people, working tirelessly
with Cena and with the then-famous humanitarians Dr.
Angelo and Anna Celli, to combat the ghastly working and living conditions of those nomadic workers. Her life became
utterly absorbed in this philanthropic labor, as she helped to
establish schools, to teach in them, and to solicit funds for
their support. In later years Aleramo remembered this period
as "the long, long apostolate" when she was a "missionary" in
the service of suffering humanity. It was an achievement she
remembered with deserved pride.

While living this way, all thoughts of literature had to be
put off, but Aleramo was nothing if not a writer. She seems to
have left the Agro Romano for the same reason Thoreau left
Walden Pond — that there was more than one life to live.
Thoreau, however, produced a book from his experience;
Aleramo did not from hers. That she was deeply concerned
about her "long silence" is revealed in Cena's increasingly desperate letters to her in 1909 and 1910. They had slowly been
drifting apart, and he dreaded the end that was so plainly in
view. Cena, agonizingly certain that another man had replaced him, knew his Sibilla. Toward the end of 1910 he
explained in a letter to her how clearly he understood what was
going on, that, in effect, she felt the need of "new sentimental
experiences" for her art. But could she be sure, he asked a little
cruelly, that her "inactivity" depended on the scarcity of such
experience. It would seem that men who are scorned do not
lack a certain degree of hellish fury, and Cena lashed out at his
former mistress-disciple in the only way he knew was sure to
hurt — by impugning her literary talent. Less than a year later,

after everything had ended between them, Cena expressed, in a letter dated 31 May 1911, his regret that he had contributed to her "excessive self-evaluation." It was a pity: a good writer with a heart to match had been ruined by the immoderate praise of those who had loved her best.

On the subject of Sibilla Aleramo, Cena always stood out as the most subjective man in Italy, initially as a protector and then as an enemy; his statements about her require a careful winnowing of fact from either loving or spiteful fancy. He was surely right, none the less, to stress the importance of the dramatic changes in Aleramo's life around 1910, when she turned thirty-four. This was the beginning of a "third existence," a much more radical departure in terms of art and conduct than anything she had experienced in 1902. For seven years after leaving Porto Civitanova, Aleramo had been scarcely less than a devoted wife to Cena. The traditional structure of Italian family life, minus the ceremonial symbolism, had been preserved in their relationship. However, after 1910, until nearly the end of her life, she became notorious in Italy as a Messalina, a voracious devourer of men.

But not just any man: an artistic pedigree or promise was the surest means of arousing her amorous interest. Beginning in 1910 with the young poet Vincenzo Cardarelli (the pseudonym of Nazareno Caldarelli, 1887-1959), Aleramo established and embellished an erotic reputation that in time became the new subject of her writing. Cardarelli, illegitimate, impoverished, and handicapped by a malformed left hand, had moved to Rome in 1906 and labored at odd jobs before finding work as a reporter on *Avanti!* Circulating in the city's fashionable left circles, he met Cena and Aleramo, and then wrote a story about Aleramo's exertions in the Agro Romano, "Conversazione con Sibilla Aleramo," which appeared in the socialist newspaper on 26 September 1909. The young man soon became enmeshed in what he would eventually represent to Cena as "our triple situation." From wishing to be regarded as Aleramo's "younger brother," Cardarelli expressed the bold desire to become "more than a lover" to her.

Right from the start, however, she gave him much more than he bargained for, as his published letters to her fully disclose. Cardarelli was proud to be the lover of a beautiful and famous woman, but at the same time he felt eclipsed by her, living "silently in your shadow." The other image that came to his mind in describing their relationship was hardly more reassuring: "your fire is made to destroy . . . not to warm a poor unquiet soul like mine." She possessed a killing force, and this, together with his gnawing guilt over Cena, drove Cardarelli wild with jealousy and grief. What a pathetic contrast to the breezy self-confidence of his early letters is the later plea regarding Aleramo's treatment of Cena: "My friend, this is not literature, it is life." Did she not perceive the distinction between the two realms? Did her "blind terrible ingenuousness" mislead her to that "egocentric and repulsive" extent? In September 1910 Cardarelli lamented that her love had fallen on him like a death sentence. A month later he compared himself to Dante looking at Lucifer in the *Inferno:* "I did not die and I did not remain alive."

Making allowances for a certain unavoidable element of romantic posing in all of this, we can still appreciate the young man's fright and his haste to withdraw from an involvement that he had grossly misjudged. Correspondence between Cardarelli and Aleramo continued for several years, but in 1911 the romantic phase of their relationship ended, a conclusion presaged on his part with a precocious 1910 whimper: "I did not suck at my mother's breast to merit so much evil from life." Incidentally, this declaration did not prevent him from bombarding Aleramo for years with petulant requests for money (*anche poco* — "even a little") and literary favors. Could she not introduce him to some wealthy woman of her acquaintance who might be interested in supporting an impecunious poet? he queried on one occasion in 1914. It was a pitiful start for a major Italian writer, but Cardarelli eventually gave abundant proof that he was worth the trouble Aleramo took on his account, although she personally became completely and permanently disgusted with him.

In the autumn of 1911 Aleramo abandoned the two "miserable rooms" on Via Alessandria which she had shared with Cardarelli and moved from Rome to Florence. No writer living in Florence during those years could possibly avoid Rosalia Jacobsen, the reigning *salonnière* of the city, who gathered in her home the artists and writers of *La Voce,* the cultural journal directed by Giuseppe Prezzolini (1882-). *A Woman* would have been entrée enough into this prestigious salon, but on 9 April 1911 she had gained fresh notoriety when her article "Apologia dello spirito femminile" appeared in *Il Marzocco,* a Florentine literary journal. This was certainly the most significant piece of writing she had done in five years. To begin with, Aleramo emphatically and in some heat broke with her "feminist" past in the interest of what she now called "true feminism." Why were women's books generally so inferior to books written by men? she asked. Why was it that even on the women's question the best work in the world — *A Doll's House* by Henrik Ibsen — had come from the pen of a man? Why had all the greatest geniuses in philosophy, music, art, and literature been men? These were hard questions to which Aleramo no longer proposed to give the easy answers of conventional feminism, a movement she now described as "a brief adventure, heroic in the beginning, grotesque at the end, an adventure of adolescents, inevitable and now superceded." By this time it seemed absurd in her mind to argue that women had merely lacked the opportunity to think, to compose, to paint, or to write. Women had done all these things for centuries, but they had never done them as women. The feminine personality had been missing from these enterprises, Aleramo claimed: "Woman, who is different from man, copies him in art." The cultural legacy of women had therefore been extremely meager, and until women took possession of themselves, trusting to their feminine intuition instead of trying to imitate masculine rationality, men would continue to create the world, "women no."

In support of her theories about culture and women, Aleramo referred to Henri Bergson's *Creative Evolution,* particularly to his exposition of intuition and rationality, the two modes of human intelligence. She accepted these categories and then staked out intuition as the province of women while conceding rationality to men. By 1913, when Aleramo wrote "La pensierosa" for *Il Marzocco* (14 January 1914) — an article that became as famous as her previous one for that journal — her persuasion of a profound mental difference between men and women had grown stronger; even more insistently than before she lamented the sad truth that every creative attempt by a woman really had been imitative rather than an act of self-discovery. Aleramo drew attention to the "peculiar energies" of women. As for herself, yes, she could write like a man, "strong, precise, disinterested"; she could follow his "dialectic" and reflect his "representation of the world"; but in so doing she denied her primary gifts as a woman, "intuition, poetry, the marvelous." Women artists would experience true liberation and become genuinely creative only after they abandoned the path of abnegation, when at last they had the courage to express their "own vision of life."

These two *Marzocco* articles are documents of unusual significance in Aleramo's development as an artist. They express her disdain for "social feminism" and her acceptance of "individual feminism" as the only intellectually honest position for a female artist. She had been moving in this direction for a long while. Nietzsche, for instance, had been one of her favorite writers since the turn of the century, and now the open, exultant celebration of the individual, elect personality over the common herd became a fixation with her. Both Cena and Cardarelli had complained of these tendencies in

Aleramo, but the Florentine *Voce* group, especially Giovanni Papini (1881-1956), encouraged them. In 1912 Papini took over as director of *La Voce,* and in the same year he and Sibilla had a brief but torrid affair, a "rapid idyll," as she later called it. His autobiographical *Un uomo finito* (1912) became a model for other *Voce* writers — including Aleramo — of art as an intensely personal testament (*esibizione di sé*), with literature produced as the distilled essence of a diary. There was less originality in this autobiographical mania of the *Voce* movement than any of its members cared to acknowledge, but the impulse to tell all did give rise to some important books. Besides *Un uomo finito* there were Scipio Slataper's *Il mio Carso* (1912), Piero Jahier's *Risultanze in merito alla vita e al carattere di Gino Bianchi* (1912), and Ardengo Soffici's *Giornale di bordo* (1915).

Aleramo conceived *Passaggio* under this literary influence, and the rest of her life's work followed an identical autobiographical pattern. Although she had done the same sort of thing in *A Woman,* she had not done it on principle. Whereas *A Woman* was a powerful story told as realistically as her talent and then as Cena would allow, *Passaggio* and the other books — novels and poetry — that followed had a completely different purpose: to reveal the romantic life of a passionate artist. This accounts for the odd disjunction in style and scope between *A Woman* and the other, vastly less successful, books that she wrote, beginning with *Passaggio.*

Actually the first published specimen of her truly "sibylline" works was the short story, "Trasfigurazione," subtitled "An Unmailed Letter," which she wrote in 1912 and published in 1914. The letter was addressed to Papini's wife, and it requires very little imagination to envision his discomfiture upon taking in Aleramo's revelations about "we three." Papini, like Cardarelli, had quickly felt the sting in a Sibyl's love, and on 30 June 1912, after the initial erotic impulses had spent themselves, he tried to put her off with admittedly tardy regrets about the wife and two children "toward whom I have complete responsibility." This tactic has never worked yet in getting rid of a truly determined mistress, and even apart from that Aleramo was more than a dialectical match for the brainiest man in Florence. She explained to him in a letter on 22 July that he should not be shocked by her rashness. Did not Papini himself write that "madness is more human than wisdom?" What did all his talk about the "twilight of philosophy" and the call for virile, reckless action mean if in his own life he chose prudence as a guide? It was not long after this that Papini began to grow extremely conservative, finally converting to Catholicism and developing a high tolerance for the Fascist regime; this drastic change may well have come about at least in part, as a result of his acutely distressing affair with Aleramo. It was one thing to talk about anarchy and free love over a glass in the Caffè delle Giubbe Rosse, the favorite haunt of the *vociani* in Florence, but in practice these ideas had intolerably disquieting results.

Papini was a disappointment to Aleramo, as all men had been and would continue to be. To forget him she traveled, first to Corsica and then to Sorrento, where she met Maxim Gorky, had an affair with the young author Vincenzo Gerace (1876-1930), whose novel *La grazia* had just been published, and through Gerace gained entrance into Benedetto Croce's Neapolitan circle. She became fascinated by Croce's house, "an immense library," but not by the man himself, for his icy intellectuality admitted of no compromise with the "female principle." He took no notice of Aleramo, and many years later she wrote accusingly in a diary entry that the hugely influential critic had never once condescended to write so much as a page about any of her books. In late 1912 and early 1913, however, she seemed more concerned about impressing Gerace, who dubbed her "the pilgrim of love." It was an enduring epithet, summing up her Donna Giovanna public image. Arising from the facts of her life, that image had nothing artificial about it, and for two generations of young Italian writers an affair with Sibilla Aleramo was worth, in terms of publicity and reputation, at least a major literary prize.

It was perhaps inevitable that love's pilgrim should meet her male counterpart, Gabriele D'Annunzio, though it surprised their contemporaries when the meeting of such powerful romantic legends failed to produce a legendary love affair. For one thing, the Divine Sibilla and the Napoleon of Italian Literature met in Paris sometime during December 1913, while she was rebounding in great distress from an affair with the futurist painter Umberto Boccioni (1882-1916), who had thrilled her earlier that year with impassioned descriptions of the aesthetic revolution that he, Filippo Tommaso Marinetti, Gino Severini, Giacomo Balla, and Luigi Russolo were leading in Italian art. She must have felt hopelessly passé around such a dynamic figure, charged as he was with the avant-garde energies then emanating from Paris. Boccioni had gone there in the summer of 1911 and through Severini had met Picasso, Braque, and other leading cubists; now he was in the midst of combining cubist techniques with futurist theory and producing brilliantly original works in painting and sculpture. Although Marinetti, the chief of futurism, was to pay Aleramo what he intended as a stupendous compliment, praising "the strange virility" of her genius, Boccioni himself quickly grew weary of the demands she made on his time. Aleramo imagined that when he urged her to go to Paris it was for her aesthetic education; this may have been partly the case, but the main purpose in Boccioni's mind was to get her out of Milan so that he could attend to "the thousand and one things I have to do." Only in 1914 did the truth and then the force of Lord Byron's words on women in *Don Juan* hit her: "Men have all [the] resources, We but one — / To love again, and be again undone."

D'Annunzio, who called Aleramo his "attentive sister" (she later repaid the compliment in a piece entitled "Brotherly

D'Annunzio"), charmed her, but their relationship remained, for both of them, gratifyingly platonic. The last thing on earth that the romantically overindulgent, fifty-year-old poet needed was another woman in his life, especially a poor one. He could not fail to enjoy her conversation, however, since so much of it dealt with his own transcendent genius. Discipleship has its own rewards if the master be powerful enough. D'Annunzio had arrived in Paris at the end of 1910 and now stood at the center of the city's literary life. He knew everyone who mattered in the cultural capital of Europe, and he helped Aleramo enter the intellectual *haut monde*. Her letters to Boccioni are filled with admiring references to Guillaume Apollinaire, Charles Péguy, Auguste Rodin, and Emile Verhaeren, but meeting D'Annunzio himself was the most memorable event of her Parisian stay, which lasted from November 1913 to March 1914. While living in Provence that spring, she wrote to Boccioni about D'Annunzio: "In truth, it is one of the most beautiful episodes of my life."

Aleramo returned to Milan in June 1914, only to be rudely and definitively rejected by Boccioni. When World War I broke out later in the summer, she remained lost amid her broken dreams of love, maintaining a precarious equilibrium by working on *Passaggio* and finally finding solace in the arms of the twenty-two-year-old painter Michele Cascella, who had been introduced to her by the poet and future priest Clemente Rebora (1885-1957), also in love with her. By the summer of 1915, after Italy's May entry into the war, she had published her first poems in *La Grande Illustrazione* and was writing moderately patriotic pieces for the *Marzocco*. Nevertheless, the war did not appreciably change the tenor of her life: love, its laments, and the effort to turn them into literature preoccupied her still.

For instance, Aleramo's most important love affair during the war years occurred with another of her multitudinous young poets, Dino Campana (1885-1932), and to read their voluminous published correspondence from the period 1916-1918, one would never know that there was a war going on. Born near Florence, Campana had exhibited a rebellious nature and been susceptible to painful nervous disorders since childhood; after abandoning his university chemistry studies in 1907, he had led a strangely disordered vagabond existence in Europe and Latin America. He had lived this way, from hand to mouth, for years, spending two months in a Belgian jail and a brief period of detention in a Tournay mental ward between jobs. Then in 1912 Campana returned to the University of Bologna in an unsuccessful attempt to resume his work in chemistry. A transfer to the University of Genoa in 1913 proved no more rewarding. Meanwhile, the frustrated scholar had been writing poems about his travels and fantasies. In 1914 his *Canti orfici* appeared, having been extensively rewritten after Ardengo Soffici, one of *Lacerba*'s editors, had lost the first manuscript. Partly modeled on Walt Whitman's *Leaves of Grass, Canti orifici* sold poorly but enjoyed an impressive critical success.

Aleramo came to hear of Campana through the *Voce* circle, of which the journal *Lacerba* was a futurist offshoot. Interestingly, in his first letter to her, on 22 July 1916, he asked, "Do you know Walt Whitman?" Indeed, she did: "I have loved Walt Whitman, as few others. And I have for a long time." How gratifying it was for him to receive from her shortly afterward some Whitmanesque verse entitled "Per Dino Campana":

> I close your book
> I untie my hair
> O savage heart
> Musical heart.

By the end of July, Aleramo was describing him in the language of another writer they both admired — Nietzsche — as "my beautiful blond beast."

Toward the end of her life, Aleramo wrote in her diary that Campana was probably the young man she had loved more than all the others, certainly the one she had loved most "desperately." She had turned forty in 1916, ten years had passed since the publication of her first and only book, and feelings of guilt over "an evil of fifteen years ago," when she had abandoned her son, continued to bedevil her. Boccioni died in the war that year, but the bitterness of his deception lived on in her heart. Aleramo looked to "Dinuccio" for surcease from these too numerous sorrows, and for a brief time love worked its old cure. His loving kiss, she wrote, made her "the richest, strongest, and most beautiful creature" in the world. Alas, the idyll had scarcely begun when it ended, the victim of Campana's acute neurasthenia. He had been ill for a long while but still hoped that his "adored Rinetta" had arrived in time to be the eternal feminine inspiration for his life and poetry. Aleramo soon discovered, however, that although they could enjoy the most delightful relationship by post, in person the two artists were killing each other from "each other's evil." Moreover, Campana periodically erupted into fits of uncontrollable violence, and in early 1917 they separated.

In his few and evermore intermittent lucid moments, he begged for a second chance, but Aleramo's reply of 30 May was typical of her responses to these woeful requests: "Oh Dino, Dino, it is now too late. I cannot stand it anymore." Over him she had wept the tears of a child who is beaten and lost, *"ma non più."* Throughout the remaining months of 1917 Campana's letters to her became by turns plaintive ("Sibilla, why do you want me to die so far away from you?"), cryptic ("Your [sic] for ever [sic]" in English on a postcard, and on the same day the single word "Sibilla?" on a postcard), and finally horrifying (". . . but come and drink the blood of my knees, come divine one among women"). The last letter was dated 17 January 1918; the return address on the envelope read "The

Asylum of S. Salvi, Florence." On 28 January the authorities transferred Campana to the psychiatric hospital of Castel Pulci near Florence. He died there, insane, in 1932.

IV

Thus did Aleramo pass the war and the Russian Revolution; amid similar "personal distractions" she would essentially miss the rise of fascism, the appearance of Hitler, the outbreaks of both the Spanish civil war and World War II. That she hardly thought about these events in a serious intellectual way became a source of deep shame and embarrassment to her after 1946, when she formally joined the Communist party, embracing with an ardor she customarily reserved for young poets the promise of a social ideal. On 6 November 1949 Aleramo attended a speech in Rome's Teatro Quattro Fontane, where the speaker commemorated the Russian Revolution. Later the aged author wrote in her diary, "What was I doing in the fall of 1917?" Sadly, she could remember nothing at all about the world war or the Revolution. Completely absorbed by the tragic experience with Campana, Aleramo had never written a word about Caporetto or the Petrograd Soviet; nor, she confessed in the same diary entry, was her memory any clearer on the Fascist takeover of Italy. Living in Paris at the time of the March on Rome, in October 1922, Aleramo did sign Croce's anti-Fascist manifesto a few years later, but even then she had no strong political convictions or interests. Personal events had excluded public events from her memory, for which she was, in 1949, "dismayed and disgusted."

The works that she published after 1919 bear out her own retrospective analysis. Between 1919 and 1921, three new Aleramo books appeared: the novel *Passaggio;* a book of poems, *Momenti;* and an anthology of previously published articles, *Andando e stando.* It was all Sibilla and Sibilla's world of love affairs and broken hearts. The critics and the public had been waiting a long time to see what the author of *A Woman* would do for an encore, but after reading *Passaggio* most people would have preferred to go on waiting indefinitely. The unmitigated failure of the novel caused Aleramo "the greatest disillusionment" of her literary life, and there was not much of a market for her poetry either.

What had gone wrong? For one thing, she was repeating herself in *Passaggio,* but this alone would not have been damning; if it were, the vast majority of writers would be in hell. More serious for an Italian writer was her irresistible attraction to D'Annunzianism, something she had been flirting with since the beginning of her career. D'Annunzio's most famous novels dealt with his love affairs or his fantasies about love, and he analyzed these subjects in a style of rococo preciosity and extravagant hyperbole which required unlimited literary mastery to be used effectively. He possessed the skill to make that style work in an eminently personal way. Whatever people may have thought about the overall quality of his books, nearly every Italian writer of the age, from Pirandello down to the lowliest hack, regarded D'Annunzio as the literary maestro, the Paganini of the Italian language. How the admiring Pirandello himself escaped from that nearly institutional D'Annunzian influence in Italian literature from the 1890s to the 1930s is an interesting and crucial story in his own artistic development, but Aleramo did not escape. Indeed, she became in literature what she had long since been perceived to be in life — the female D'Annunzio, now writing like him though never possessing his easy mastery of all literary forms. Despite what she may have intended by her theoretical call for a feminine literary revolution in "Apologia dello spirito femminile" and "La pensierosa," the practical results in her own case hardly amounted to more than imitation D'Annunzio.

How distant, in tone and in feeling, all this was from *A Woman.* That book had been motivated by a struggle for freedom and had attained a rare sublimity of expression. Perhaps it is only from such a struggle that a great book can issue. Surely with Aleramo the attainment of freedom itself eventually gave rise to a very different kind of literature, the highly mannered ruminations of Echo pining away from unrequited love for Narcissus. *Passaggio,* her play, *Endimione* (dedicated to D'Annunzio and whistled off the stage during its one 1924 performance in Turin), her epistolary novel, *Amo dunque sono* (1927), and her last novel, *Frustino* (1932), all belong to that mysterious "sibylline" realm of self-mythification, with close affinities to the worst qualities of D'Annunzian fiction: the decadent-romantic combination of the erotic with the spiritual, the deliberate mystification of the reader through the employment of peculiar syntax and enigmatic phrases, and the perversion of Nietzsche's celebration of the *Superuomo,* modified by Aleramo to include the *Superdonna.* These self-pitying tales of love's anguish have none of *A Woman's* strength or restraint. Equally disappointing from a feminist point of view are Aleramo's total identification with men and her cloying dependence on them for her art. The heroines of these books only possess life insofar as a romantically attracted man confers it on them. Moreover, the female characters, aside from Aleramo's own heroic persona, are drawn to specifications that have an ironically misogynist prejudice: it would be difficult to find in the work of another twentieth-century writer a more depressing gallery of jealous, evil-tempered women.

After a while these "Songs of Myself," Italian style, stopped paying the rent, and by the early 1930s we find Aleramo doing translations out of economic desperation. Meanwhile, she had come to terms with the Fascist regime. Although Aleramo was genuinely drawn to the vitalism she found in Fascist doctrines, there can be little doubt about the main motive behind her frankly partisan political writing during the 1930s: the need for money. For years the sick, aging, and impoverished author had campaigned to gain a state pension.

In 1928 she beseeched D'Annunzio to speak for her to Mussolini, but by then the poet had no power and little influence on
the regime, hidden away as he was in his fantastic mausoleum,
the Vittoriale, on the Lago di Garda. Next Aleramo tried to
help herself by publishing pieces that would attract favorable
government notice. In *Gioie d'occasione* (1930), the formerly
pro-socialist writer confessed to an inexpressible delight in gaz-
ing at a group of Fascist *squadristi* on a train, thinking of them
as masterful specimens of "this our vigorous and mystical
race." That same year her article "La Donna Italiana" was
published; in it, the one-time feminist praised Mussolini for
having reawakened "the female masses to their precise and
sacred function as reproducers of the species." Mussolini himself received praise as "this enigmatic, most lucid statesman"
whose wise measures had produced "the spiritual type of
Italian woman."

Aleramo's campaign for state support succeeded in 1933,
though not, she later recorded in her diary, without the decisive intervention of Queen Elena, who personally paid for some
of the sick writer's medical bills at the Quisisana Clinic in 1935.
On 11 August 1933 Aleramo explained to a friend that her
pension amounted only to 1,000 lire a month. Apparently, the
Fascists did not consider her a very big catch. Still, small as the
sum was, Aleramo had to earn it. Her infamous hymn to Mussolini, "Visita a Littoria e Sabaudia," in *Si alla terra: nuove
poesie* (1935), demonstrated the truth of the adage that the
man who pays the piper calls the tune. Three years later *Orsa
minore* appeared, and in this collection of articles Mussolini
loomed as "the gigantic miracle-worker" whose voice expressed
a "mystical fulfillment of faith and love."

Aleramo took money from Mussolini's government until
the fall of fascism in July 1943. On 25 January 1953 she lamented this regrettable fact in her diary; it was something that
"disturbed" her profoundly. "How lucky was poor Gabriele to
die in time," she had written during the summer of fascism's

fall. Aleramo, on the other hand, had lived to see the ghastly fruition of her "blind terrible ingenuousness," to recall Cardarelli's phrase. Sitting alone in her desolate apartment on Via Margutta, burning old love letters for fuel, listening, terrified, to the explosion of bombs in the distance and sometimes not in the very far distance, Aleramo recorded her impressions of Italy's calamitous finale under fascism in a book eventually published with the title *Dal mio diario: 1940-1944*. It is, in part, a fascinating record of her conversion to Marxism, and, since an ideological shift toward the Marxist left characterized in a large way postwar Italian intellectual life, *Dal mio diario: 1940-1944* has a historical importance that transcends Aleramo's biography.

The diary also described her love affair with, as far as she was concerned, the last of the young poets, Franco Matacotta (1916-1978), who, in a neat twist of fate, had come to her in 1936 for information about Campana, the subject of his university thesis. Instead of merely accumulating anecdotal material for a research project, he had ended up getting involved in a decade-long affair with a woman forty years his senior. As Aleramo remarked in the diary, she with her "enormous experience" and he with "his delicate years" made an unusual pair. Fausta Cialente recalled in the preface to a later Aleramo diary, *Diario di una donna: inediti 1945-60,* that people had become used to her maternal love affairs with very young men. However, Cialente added, when in her sixties Aleramo fell in love with the extremely youthful looking, twenty-two-year-old Matacotta, it was a case of being "faced with a grandmother and her grandson."

Matacotta became a Communist during the war, and, as usual with the men in Aleramo's life, he had an enormous influence on her. For Italy's young intellectuals Marxism was the only remaining ideological possibility in the 1940s; fascism had failed terribly, and all of bourgeois Italy seemed to them compromised by that failure. The Communist party beckoned to the young like an El Dorado in the surrounding wasteland of

Italian political life. People like Ignazio Silone, who attempted
to debunk the myth of the Communist party by pointing
toward its soft underbelly, where it was connected to a totali-
tarian Stalinist regime in Russia capable of signing the Nazi-
Soviet Pact of 1939, found themselves denigrated as "empiri-
cists," accused of being small-minded and intent upon examining only isolated facts instead of appreciating the big picture, in which facts tended to dissolve at the dialectical vanish-
ing point. Insofar as Aleramo was concerned, her own "feminine principle" militated against the possibility that she would
ever undertake an empirical investigation of the facts; with
relief and abandon she took the leap with Matacotta to El
Dorado. In 1946 Aleramo applied for party membership, con-
tending that at heart she had always been for the people, for
men as well as for women, and that, therefore, if her request
were granted, it would represent "the crowning glory of my life
as a woman and a writer." On 10 January 1946 she fittingly
described herself in a diary entry as "a catechumen."

In the postwar epoch an exciting new career opened up
for her. Through the warm friendship of Palmiro Togliatti,
the Communist party became home and family to Aleramo,
enabling her to overcome a final male "betrayal," this time by
Matacotta, who at thirty had had the temerity to desire a wife
and family. She wrote quantities of ideological verse for Communist publications, hardly any of it worth much as art even in
the judgment of the Marxist critic Carlo Salinari, who liked
her as a comrade but thought her poetry trite. More successful
were her public readings and her campaign for literary recognition. In 1948 Aleramo won the 300,000-lire Versilia prize for
poetry, which ended at last her extreme poverty, although she
felt outraged and humiliated that her prize was 200,000 lire
less than the Viareggio prizes won at the same time by Elsa
Morante and Aldo Palazzeschi. She still suffered from a feeling
of neglect, a sense of being undervalued. It was easy for women
to write now, at mid-century, but fifty years earlier to write
well and worthily of Italian life a female author faced forbid-

ding obstacles. She, Sibilla Aleramo, had faced those obstacles and had overcome them, but she might as well have done it in a distant and unknown land insofar as her countrymen were concerned. These melancholy thoughts, together with declining health, caused her to weep "for the weight of so much living, for the incredible mass of living that weighs on me." Aleramo even contemplated suicide, but when her young friend Cesare Pavese fatally poisoned himself in 1950, she wrote in her diary: "The only liberty that communists do not have is that of suicide." There was too much work to do in the world for that, and she kept on with hers for the party, writing, lecturing, and traveling nearly to the end, which came on 11 January 1960.

Aleramo had been afraid to die: "Yes, *I am afraid*," she wrote on 27 December 1959. With the last conscious flickering of life in her body, she fought off the fear the way she always had, brandishing pen and paper. After all was said and nearly done she went on writing. Aleramo could not conquer death, but to face it undismayed and to record her pain in those last solemn pages of the diary was a kind of victory, the best that she could ever hope to win.

V

On 14 January 1960 the poet Eugenio Montale eulogized Sibilla Aleramo in the *Corriere della Sera,* declaring that her firmness and sense of dignity "had been her true force and secret." Such sentiments were in keeping with the many in memoriam tributes to the deceased author. Aleramo herself had explained her force and secret a little differently, however. She had taken up the fundamental romantic position, "to live first, then to write" (*prima vivere poi poetare*), but her actual writing resulted both directly and indirectly from one experience in particular: her abandonment of her son. The books dealt almost entirely with her love affairs, and she did not have

to undergo analysis in order to realize that these affairs were
motivated "by the perpetual nostalgia for my son." She deeply
regretted that none of her lovers ever got her with child. In
1940 Aleramo ruminated over the irony of how the only child
she had ever conceived was by a man who had raped her and
then become her despised husband. The trauma of that sexual
initiation could only be erased, she thought, by a child conceived in love, "a masterpiece of my flesh, my heart and my
spirit." A cruel fate denied her this recompense: "And thus was
my poetry generated. And the thousands of pages that I wrote
to describe myself, to explain myself. Until today. A fury of
incessant self-creation. Moments, days, years."

In 1933, a few years before falling in love with Franco
Matacotta, often described by her as "my son," Aleramo saw
her real son, Walter, for the first time since 1902. The boy had
been six at the time of his mother's flight. Ever since, she had
thought about him, wondered what he was like growing up
and then what he had become as a man. Their long-antici-
pated meeting was nothing like what she had expected. Walter
was just an ordinary businessman, on the verge of middle age
and not very different from the husband she remembered leaving. After her husband's death in 1947, she saw more of
Walter and his children, but these events did not precisely con-
stitute a homecoming. For one thing, hearing herself addressed
as "grandmother" was not a pleasant sensation. Even worse
was Walter himself, now in his fifties and a Republican, no
less. Her little boy had disappeared, and when Matacotta
proved to be "the last of my great errors," all of the little boys
were gone as well. "I am a widow of love," Aleramo wrote in
1946, and shortly afterward declared herself free to love the
world, "which is also a child."

A Woman is not an easy book to introduce, any more
than the author herself is, but Sibilla Aleramo's story begins
here. It is, whatever its social message, a book about a woman.
In it Aleramo succeeded, more completely than she ever would
again, in relating her personal story to universal concerns, to

the lasting interest of readers all over the world. That must be one definition of a masterpiece, if not the most exalted one. The most persistent question about Aleramo, in her lifetime and especially now when *A Woman* is being hailed, properly, as one of the outstanding feminist books of this century, remains, Why did she not produce a body of work in the image of her first success? Why is *A Woman* the sole exception in a career not noted, until the very end, when her creative powers were gone, for an abiding interest in broad social, economic, and cultural issues, least of all from a consistent feminist point of view? In answer it might be enough to quote her favorite author, Walt Whitman:

> Do I contradict myself?
> Very well, then, I contradict myself
> (I am large, I contain multitudes).

But Aleramo herself had an answer for the people who raised that question, and it was one she fired off in a fury of indignation in 1942:

> What did they want of me?
> Those who know nothing really of that which has been my life.
> Those who do not know what a miracle is represented by that which I have produced, little or great as it is: a miracle, given the immense difficulties amidst which, *always,* I had to struggle: not only economic, practical, but also, and more, moral and spiritual.

These people wanted masterpieces from her, but she had only one to give.

Wellesley College   Richard Drake
January 1980

PART I

ONE

I had an active, carefree childhood. If I try to live it again in my memory, rekindle it in my conscious mind, I always fail. I see the child I was at six, at ten years old, but it is as if I am dreaming her. It is a lovely dream, delicate and vibrant as a piece of music, clothed in light. The least recall to present-day reality can dispel it. But it leaves me with a sense of enormous joy.

For a long time, in the darkest periods of my life, I looked back to my earliest years as if they had been perfect, completely happy. Now, with less anxious eyes, I look back and can see that even then I was troubled, that even as a little girl I never believed myself entirely happy; though never wretched either — I'm sure I always felt independent and strong. I was the eldest child and confidently asserted the authority this gave me over my brother and two sisters. My father made it obvious that I was his favourite, and I was aware of how much he wanted me to improve and progress as I grew older. I was healthy, graceful, and intelligent — everyone told me so — and I had games, sweets, books, and a piece of garden all to myself. My mother never denied me anything. Even the friends I played with unquestioningly accepted my leadership.

The only thing that dominated me was love for my father. I took my love for my mother for granted, but for him I felt boundless admiration, and I was aware of this difference in my feelings without every trying to explain it. *He* was my model; everything that made life seem worth living belonged to him, and I believed without doubt that his charm had been given him by the gods. There was no one who could equal him; he knew everything and was always right. When I walked beside him along the city streets or in the countryside beyond the city walls, holding on to his hand for hours upon end, I felt extraordinarily elated — nothing else could possibly matter. He told me stories about my grandparents (they had died just after I was born) and about his childhood and the wonderful things he had done; he told me that when he was only eight he had seen French soldiers arriving in Turin, "before Italy was unified." What a glamorous past! When I looked up I could see him, tall, slender, and agile, his proud head held high, the smile of a young conqueror on his lips. At these moments the future seemed filled with promises of adventure.

He supervised my homework and my reading, although he never demanded much effort of me. When my school-teachers came to visit us they seemed amazed at his knowledge, and often treated him, I thought, with profound respect. I was one of the best pupils in the school. Occasionally I suspected that this was because I was in some way a privileged child. Even in my first year I observed differences between my clothes, the food in my lunchbox and those of my friends; I began to work out what sort of families they came from — workers oppressed by the harsh rigour of factory life, or shopkeepers who had never had an education. When I went home I could see my father's name and status inscribed on a polished plate beside our door.

I was born in a small, impoverished town where father was a science teacher. When I was five he quarrelled with his employers and lost his job, so he went to work for a brother-in-law, the owner of a large business in Milan. I realised that he could not have been very satisfied with this new situation because he still spent all his free time in an untidy little room where he kept all his equipment for experiments in physics and chemistry. I was convinced that only in that room did he ever feel really happy. My father taught me so many things!

Although as a child I was rarely impatient, I was intensely

curious, and this sharpened my appetite for living. I was never bored. Sometimes when mamma went out to visit her friends in the afternoon I would refuse to go, staying at home instead to loll in an armchair and read any book I could lay my hands on. I found many books incomprehensible, but some were like wine to my imagination, transporting me into a different world. Occasionally I paused as I tried to find words for the confused ideas my reading had suggested; sometimes I spoke these words out loud, as if reciting lines of verse welling up from an unknown source; and then I would blush, just as I blushed in that same armchair when I experimented with languid poses, making believe that I was a beautiful, seductive woman. I doubt if I was able to tell what were my real feelings and what was fantasy. Father greeted all manifestations of the poetic spirit with an indifference verging on contempt: he claimed that such ideas were beyond his understanding, and although Mother sometimes recited verses of out-dated lyrical poetry or passionately declaimed fragments of old epics, she never did so when he was there—and I always thought his judgments more trustworthy than hers.

Even when he flared up in one of his tempers I believed that he was in the right—although they terrified us all and threw me into a state of unutterable anguish. Mother, suppressing her tears, would flee to her room. She often seemed humiliated and discouraged when Father was there. All the same, it was he, not she, whose authority we children respected.

Yet I do not remember them having any serious quarrels in front of us: only occasional complaints or bitter criticisms or angry questions. Usually, Father's tantrums seemed provoked by our naughtiness or a servant's carelessness, but even so mamma seemed to feel responsible and she would hang her head as she listened, as if suddenly exhausted. Or else she would smile. How I hated that smile and the way it deformed her beautiful, resigned mouth!

I wonder if at times like these she remembered that in the past things had been different.

She rarely talked to me about her childhood, but from what she did say I formed a picture far less interesting than the one my father's memories conjured up. Her father had been a white-collar worker, and her family had lived in very modest circumstances. Like my father's mother, her mother gave birth to many children, most of whom now lived abroad. I gathered she had grown up in poverty, without much love, a family Cinderella. She had met papa at a ball when she was twenty. Once she showed me a picture of him as he was then: he still looked a boy, with a sweet, handsome face. Only his eyes betrayed his indomitable will. It was the year before he left university. As soon as he graduated he accepted a teaching post and they married.

Within a year of the wedding I was born. Whenever my mother talked to me about the two small furnished rooms they had first lived in, her face, normally so pale and aloof, became radiant. I couldn't understand why she didn't look so enthusiastic and happy all the time. Nor could I understand why she cried so easily when it was obvious that Father couldn't stand the sight of her tears, nor why, if ever she plucked up the courage to express an opinion, it was always different from his. Why did we children fear her so little and obey her so seldom? Sometimes she lost her temper with us just as Father did, but in her it always triggered off violent sobs, as if she had held back her tears for too long. Father's irritation might be excessive, but always seemed natural; Mother's outbursts against us or the servants always seemed to contrast painfully with her normal gentleness — like convulsions which took her unawares and which she instantly regretted.

I saw my mother's eyes glistening with unshed tears so many times: they stirred up in me an almost uncontrollable sense of unease, a feeling which was not pity or pain or humiliation but rather the terrible frustration of realising that I could not respond properly, could not prevent happening what was about to happen. Yet I had no real idea of what that might be. When I was eight I became aware of a strange anxiety: perhaps I didn't have a "real" mother, the sort I had read about in books, who gave their children superabundant happiness through their love, and the confidence of constant protection. This fear gave way two or three years later to the realisation that I couldn't give my mother all the love I would have wished to give her. It must have been this fear which held me back from examining the reasons for the constant feeling of distress in our household, and prevented me from demonstrating my spontaneous affection. For I wanted so much to throw my arms around my mother in the hope that I would be understood and to promise that when I was older I would look after her, thus sealing the same pact of mutual tenderness and support I had sealed with my father so long ago.

I could tell that she admired me, although she never told me so. She was as proud of me as once she had been of her husband — she thought we had the same iron will. All the same she didn't approve of the education he so ardently wanted for me. She was worried for me, fearing that I would grow up devoid of emotions, fated to live only through my intellect. Yet she lacked the courage to argue openly with him about it.

Yet I didn't feel that Father made any real attempt to understand me either. At times I felt completely alone. Then I withdrew into daydreams, the secret mainstay of my inner world.

I was beginning to learn the meaning of shame. A hidden life grew inside me, parallel to my everyday existence but quite different from it. In my first year at school I started to think about my character and realised that it was made up of different elements. There, I was angelic, even exemplary — a girl with a tranquil face and timid smile, always attentive. But once outside the school gates I took a deep breath as if trying to fill my lungs with every molecule of the air around me, and danced off down the street, babbling nonsense, entering our house like a whirlwind; and all the other children would have to stop their play and prepare to submit to my autocratic demands.

Yet I forgot them all when the time came to do my homework, and went alone to my room or into the garden, returning happily to my books and to the challenge of intellectual effort. It was sheer pleasure: competition with my schoolfriends and desire for prizes never entered into it.

After that mamma would come to me, and before I went to bed we would recite together a short prayer in our dear Northern dialect I loved so much: "Oh Lord, help me to grow strong and to be a consolation to my parents." Then I would be left in the dark next to my sister, who was already asleep. And I would feel such a sense of calm and contentment, beyond the merely physical, that it was as if in that moment, lying constrained by darkness, silence, and stillness, I was more free than I had been throughout the entire day.

I liked looking into the darkness. It held no fears for me because my father had told me that I would find witches and bogeymen only in fairy tales: like the devil, they didn't exist. I would think about the events of the day, remember Father's seductive smile, Mother's hands as they moved in a gesture of annoyance, my own irritability with the younger children and their stupidity, and I would speculate on what the next day would bring: exam results, outings, new books, new games, new friends, new teachers to be turned into allies.

I prayed every evening because my mother wanted it. I prayed to God . . .

When I was in my second year at elementary school I heard someone refer contemptuously one day to another girl who sat near me in class as a "Jewess." She turned white, but didn't reply. After a while she burst into tears, and when the schoolteacher found out what had happened she was very angry. I was astonished by this incident because I had never heard of differences in race or religion. But something my schoolteacher said astonished me even more. She argued that all religions were worthy of respect because they all brought men nearer to God; the only people who should horrify us were the *atheists,* and even they deserved our pity. Immediately I thought of my father. I was sure he was an atheist. He often talked about atheism, and he never went to church. Did that mean that as far as my teacher, my friends, everyone was concerned he was an object of pity?

I still worried about this as I lay in the silence of my bedroom three or four years later. Father was now more open with me about what he considered a time-honoured lie. He told me that before there were men on earth other creatures had lived here who were similar to us, and that they had been preceded by other animals and by plants and that before any of these had existed the earth had been a desert. He told me that our earth was only a small point in space, similar to the stars we saw in the sky, and that those stars were really other worlds which might be inhabited by other beings. He told me all these things so naturally that it never occurred to me to doubt him.

All the same he never explained, and nor did I ask, why it was that we existed on this earth. The answers in the school catechism seemed more satisfactory. We existed because there was a God who made us, watched over us from on high, and took us to heaven if we were good. Our lives were merely a passage.

Yet people seemed to attach so much importance to this passage! Although no one took the idea of hell very seriously, everyone seemed afraid of hurting themselves or falling ill and dying. I was prepared to agree with papa that hell didn't exist: no angel or tempter had ever stood at my shoulder—if I was good it was because I wanted to be, if I felt guilty it was because I had done something wrong. Even so . . . my mother, my father, my teachers, the workers in the streets, everybody in fact, even the rich and powerful, worked day and night to earn money which they then spent on food which they ate so that they wouldn't die. Yet days passed, and weeks and months, and they did die; and the same would be true of myself and my brother and my sisters.

It was a worrying thought, but I could feel sleep creeping over me. I would have the same useless thoughts again tomorrow night. Would I ever find an answer to them? As I lay half asleep mysterious words crowded into my ear: "eternity," "progress," "universe," "consciousness".... They danced together until even their sounds became confused. I thought back to the troubled expression on my teacher's face. I wondered if mamma went to church on Sundays because she really believed or because of her strange fear of other people. And then I remembered an evening in May, the one and only time I had ever been to hear a sermon. I remembered an altar shimmering with lilies and wax candles, a monk waving his arms imperiously in a pulpit as his voice descended on the kneeling congregation, telling them about the miracles some saint had been able to perform: everyone seemed to believe him. As he finished, an organ started to play, accompanied by an invisible choir which intoned an anthem like a pure stream of silver from on high. I shivered to hear them, and shivered once more whenever I remembered this experience. I felt unutterably sad that I didn't know how to pray; I felt painfully aware of my own isolation. But this feeling quickly vanished. After all, why should I complain? I might be young, but I didn't want to be deceived. I would understand everything one day, when I was grown up.

I could hear my sister breathing evenly in the bed beside me. What was she dreaming about? Was it the crystal doll's house I had promised her if she left me more space in the bed? I had no idea how I would find it for her.... But when I was older — *then* I would be more loving towards my brother and my sisters. I would stop making them cry so much, and Mother would become more cheerful...

In the meantime I must sleep; I was tired. I wished for a puff of wind to come and blow me to the top of one of the mountains I had seen on holiday that summer. I had loved them so much. I was sure I could hear their bells in the distance calling to me . . .

TWO

One morning, just as I was wondering what my parents would decide about my education after I had finished elementary school, my father suddenly arrived home from work an hour early. A clerk followed him, carrying a trunk on his shoulders. Father picked me up for a moment and looked into my face; then he said to Mother, who was watching him anxiously, "Well, that's over with . . . I've finished with him. At last I can breathe."

For some time now the brothers-in-law had been finding it increasingly difficult to get on with each other. Their personalities were so different that they constantly ended up in conflict: as soon as one took an initiative the other applied the brakes. Office routine bored my father, too, and he felt that his salary was too low to give him adequate compensation. That morning a trivial incident had sparked off a violent argument, which brought their partnership to an end.

At thirty-six Father was starting his life all over again. Just as the last time, his thirst for new excitement and independence was driving him on.

That morning he took me out for a long walk. I have a confused memory of the vast Piazza d'Armi lying veiled in autumn mist while my father talked and talked, almost to himself, and I grew silently more and more elated. America . . . Australia . . . Oh, if only he would take us around the world! He hinted at less adventurous possibilities too — going back to teaching, starting a business — but always away from Milan. Until then I had loved the city without really thinking about it, but from that moment I found it unbearable. A host of new enchantments lay in wait for me elsewhere, and Father was beginning to take me into his confidence. I seemed to have grown in years and in importance. All my plans for future study simply melted away. Why, I might be called upon to go out to work in order to support the family! As I gazed up into Father's face he must surely have seen the light of enthusiasm sparkling in my eyes.

But when we returned home Mother was like a lost soul. I couldn't understand what she had to fear. She was still a young woman: she was younger than papa; she had strong, healthy children. . . . And I could tell that Father wanted her to be more courageous!

A few weeks later a man who wanted to build a chemical plant in the South asked Father to be the factory manager, but even that didn't reassure mamma. It was true that Father would be taking a big risk if he accepted the job: he had no experience of that kind of work. It was the cheery confidence of his smile that had seduced the man who was putting up the capital, and he offered Father an excellent contract which would allow us to spend the next few years in a sunny climate. Father had never been one to look very far into the future. For the moment he felt happy just to be taking a risk. He paid no attention to Mother's anxieties and agreed that we would leave in the spring.

Oh, the sun, the sun! There was so much dazzling sun! In this new landscape everything sparkled; the sea was a broad band of silver, the sky an endless smile above me, which wrapped me in its infinite blue embrace and made me see, for the first time, how beautiful the world could be. The green meadows of Brianza and Piedmont, the Alpine valleys I had glimpsed as a child, with their placid lakes and charming gardens, were as nothing compared to this immensity of space, this abundant miracle of water and sea breezes. My eager lungs inhaled all

that clear air, all its salty savour: I ran along the beach under-
neath the sun, defying the waves and feeling that at any
moment I might change into one of the great white birds I saw
skimming the foam before they disappeared over the horizon.
After all, wasn't I really just like them?

Oh, how happy I was that summer! How I rejoiced in my
beautiful, carefree adolescence!

I was twelve. In our village (dignified by the locals to the
status of a town) there was only an elementary school. A
schoolmaster was brought in to give me lessons, but was
quickly dismissed because he was unable to teach me more
than I already knew. So I chose a large room in our enormous
new house as my study, and stayed there during the noonday
heat, leafing unenthusiastically through the fat textbooks on
botany, physics, and foreign grammar which Father had given
to me. If I went out on to our balcony I could look down at the
people who habitually loitered in front of the chemist's shop
and the bar in the square below: there were peasant women
whose lives seemed weighed down by intolerable burdens, and
unkempt youths who wrangled with each other in their sono-
rous, incomprehensible dialect. Beyond the square the sea
glittered. And just before sunset I was able to pick out in the
distance the sails of fishing boats making their way back to
port. As they gradually drew near they glowed red and yellow,
following each other into the harbour, and the babble of fishermen's voices carried right up to me; I could hear the rhyth-
mic chanting of the men who dragged the boats ashore.

If I went out, I would run to the huge building site by the
railway line where the new factory was springing up with incredible rapidity, and where Father was almost always to be
found. Sometimes he found me little jobs to do. I carried them
out anxiously, exact to the last detail. "You'll help me later on
as well, won't you?" he used to ask. "Would you like to be my
secretary when everything is ready?" My old shyness was now
struggling with a new sense of independence and boldness.

Father may only have been trying to compensate me for the education he had brought to an end, but unnoticed by anyone else I was developing a pride of my own. I felt that I was now in contact with real life, and believed that the things I saw around me were far more complex and absorbing than anything I could read about in a book.

The building workers were handsome and sun-tanned peasants who had come from the surrounding countryside looking for work. There were girls, too, who scaled the scaffolding like acrobats, balancing buckets of lime on their heads. They smiled when they saw me, and I felt a sort of comradeship for them, overridden by a strong sense of curiosity. When I went home I recited their romantic-sounding nicknames to the younger children and wondered if I would ever dare order them around the way I did the maids.

Father was totally suited to his new job — firm and decisive, full of energy, always involved in his work. Sometimes after our evening meal we would walk with him along the main streets of our village. The local people watched us from their doorsteps with a mixture of admiration and fear; they thought my mother a picture of the Madonna come to life, and we heard women's voices following us, murmuring blessings on her children. Small and delicate in her unpretentious clothes, she thanked them with a gentle smile. At times like these even she seemed happy, and she watched her husband with a respect verging on veneration, as if she were discovering anew how fascinating he could be.

I remember a photograph of myself taken a year later, when I started to work regularly in the factory office. I was wearing an odd assortment of clothes — a straight-cut jacket with lots of small pockets for my watch, pencil, and notebook, over a short skirt. My hair fell in curls over my forehead but had been cut short at the back, making me look like a young boy — at my father's suggestion I had sacrificed my glossy pigtails with their golden gleams. My odd appearance reflected clearly the way I thought of myself: no longer a girl, but as yet with no proper sense that I was a woman. I thought of myself as a conscientious worker, and drew confidence from the importance of my job. Just to feel useful was a source of endless satisfaction, and carried out my father's orders with absolute loyalty and fierce devotion. I was as absorbed as he was in all the factory's problems, and was never bored by my task of entering figures in a ledger for hours upon end. But watching the labourers at their work or chatting to them in their brief breaks was like looking in on some fascinating game. There were over two hundred workers. One group came from Piedmont, and they kept the furnaces going day and night. The rest, local men, moved constantly about the yards, and in and out of the sheds. It was clear that not all the men liked me, yet when they saw me appear suddenly, with my rather severe expression, it seemed nevertheless to give them some sort of pleasure. They conveyed this by consciously moving more briskly, creating for a moment the illusion that they gladly accepted their work.

Father terrified them, and they believed that I was more reasonable than he, so by naïve flattery they tried to get into my good books, hoping that I might use my influence with him on their behalf. But I knew that it would be useless to try to relax his rigorous discipline, and in any case, like him, I considered it necessary. All I ever tried to do was to get them to accept him, even attempting to persuade them by using my own obedience as an example. Perhaps Father was aware of this. On the short walk between the factory and our house he talked to me with a note in his voice which only I ever heard — a tone not especially affectionate or gentle, but calm, relaxed, and untroubled. "Let's try things this way, or that . . ." he would say, "then let's raise the wages a little." He seemed to be asking for my opinion, and I was acutely aware of how happy it made me to be asked to help solve his problems. For both of us the factory had taken on the power of a monster in a fairy tale:

it demanded our total commitment, it steadied our nerves even though it made us dizzy with fear and excitement, and it dominated us completely even though we believed that we were its masters.

When I went home in the evenings I felt as dissatisfied as I had been as a child coming home from school. I felt I didn't really belong there, and allowed my sense of isolation to show through my obvious contempt for the others. I was like a young man recently come of age who is full of arrogant complaints about the servants. My voice had the same superior ring as I pointed out how thoughtless my brother and sisters were, how they neglected their homework, and how mamma lacked the calm authority which might have made them more disciplined. The servants must have told hair-raising stories about me. I was never seen with a needle in my hand, was rarely at home, and showed no interest in helping with the housework.

Then there were my tantrums: they could only be compared to my father's. Perhaps I was too highly strung and these eruptions marked some slight relaxation of my nervous tension, or perhaps they were simply the sign of adolescent crises. Wherever they came from, they were as much a mystery to me as to those around me. My only way of dealing with them was to leave the house, hurl myself into a mad race along the beach, and draw in great gulps of air, to return calmer, having erased the memory of my own anger. But in the process I would also have forgotten my mother's distress during my scenes.

My mother! I can hardly believe how much I neglected her. At this stage of my life I hardly thought about her at all. From the moment we arrived in that place she started to go into a slow decline, but I have no recollection of its stages. From the outset she suffered from a crippling timidity which even prevented her from going alone or with her children to the beach or into the fields. The district offered no other form of relaxation. The local middle-class women, ignorant, lazy, and superstitious, rarely left their homes. The peasant women worked harder than their husbands, and most of the community lived by and from the sea, huddled together in shacks only a hundred metres from the water's edge.

She had no interest in the factory either, and so found no distraction in its problems. Personally I was quite pleased about this because I was not sure that she would have approved of everything that I did there, but it also made me feel, even more than in Milan, that her tastes and interests were totally alien to those of my father and therefore to mine. I also sensed that this difference was at the root of the bad feeling between them, the mutual dissatisfaction which they were not always able to hide. Not that I let this perception disturb me: I evaded such worrying thoughts and never tried to work out what lay behind them. Perhaps I was afraid to find out things I was too young to understand, but I did observe one small incident which made me begin to realise that perhaps my father didn't love my mother as much as he did me.

It happened towards the end of our first winter there. Mamma, papa, and myself had been invited to the provincial capital to have dinner and then go to the theatre with the factory owner and his wife, who had paid us a visit during the summer. As the sun began to set the time to catch the train drew nearer. When father came home I was dressed and ready, and in no time he was ready too. But Mother hovered in front of the mirror, doubtful about her evening dress, which she had not worn for a long time. She was passing the powder-puff across her face over and over again, when father, irritated by the delay, appeared once more in the doorway to their room.

I can still see the room, the mirror, the window through which seemed to filter not the glow of sunset but the sea's reflection, gray and troubled. And I can still hear, quivering in the air, a phrase hurled like a knife: "Must I conclude, then, that you are nothing but a flirt?"

Half an hour later in the train I was shivering still, unable either to criticise papa or to defend mamma. Then suddenly I saw her face, turned towards the compartment door, running with tears. Was she re-living that bitter moment? Or remembering many others like it? Or was she distressed because I had witnessed the insult? I began to think of her, for the first time, as a sick woman, melancholy and weak, who didn't want to be cured or even acknowledge that anything was wrong. In the books I had picked up at home I had read about love and about hatred; I had observed our neighbours' friendships and antagonisms; I thought that I knew a lot about life. But I could not explain to myself why our family life was so miserable.

Months passed. Mother became increasingly sad. Father's concern for her diminished; their walks together became rarer. And I, although no longer a child, went on living my life as though nothing threatened it. Why? I can't explain my blindness simply by my continuing absorbed admiration for my father. Perhaps Mother was too ashamed of her illness, too pained by it, to want to confide in me, young as I was and devoted to the man who hurt her so. Or perhaps she had decided to leave explanations to the future, relying wearily and ambivalently on the arrival of some providential opportunity.

Even though, at Father's insistence, she no longer went to church and so gave sanctimonious women cause for gossip, she was so well-bred and so polite that the local people respected and liked her all the same. Perhaps from the very beginning they had concluded that she must be unhappy with a husband like my father and a daughter like me — for in no time my father had aroused obdurate hostility locally. He was the only rich man in the neighbourhood, apart from the owner of the factory, who mainly lived in Milan, and a count who owned nearly all the land in the area but rarely appeared there (when he did appear, with his wife laden with jewels like some pagan idol, men and women would bow down as they passed until

they almost touched the soil). The middle class comprised professional men, including a handful of lawyers who fomented
long lawsuits in which they ensnared the small farmers who
were already bled dry by taxes. Together with a few priests and
police officers, they were the leaders of our community. But
Father never gave any sign of having noticed them. Worse
than that, he rejected out of hand a dinner they proposed to
give in his honour, and refused to become chairman of some
ancient and pompous local institution which needed funds.
Such behaviour was unheard of — as unusual, and almost as
offensive, as his systematic refusal of the gifts people brought
him. I often saw women leaving our doorstep distraught and
bewildered because he would not accept the chickens they had
hoped might soften his attitude to their sons.

It was the working people who were the most attractive
members of the community, for all their lethargy and lack of
education. At least they seemed to have a certain instinctive
goodness. Their only complaint against "the director," as they
called him, was that his standards of discipline (greatly exaggerated by word of mouth) were unprecedented.

At first my father responded to this general antipathy by
laughing at it. But as he gradually came to know the local
workforce he grew bitterly resentful. He was most incensed by
the prevailing hypocrisy, and the more isolated he became the
more implacable were his judgments. He exaggerated the difference between this almost oriental people and his fellow
northerners. They seemed to press in on him; he felt surrounded by squalor. Perhaps he was unconsciously reacting to
the fear of being assimilated or seeing his children assimilated
into the community, but as a result he was finally unable to be
objective. He so overestimated his own superiority that his contempt developed into provocation. At first he wanted to
employ only Piedmontese workers in the factory — to found a
kind of colony. The owner refused to let him — for economic
reasons, but also from prudence. Nevertheless, all the skilled

craftsmen were from the North, and they and their families lived in an isolated group, much distrusted by the indigenous workers.

I, too, used to measure the distance between ourselves and the "others" and found it enormously exciting. When I hurried home from the factory with my red cap pulled over my short hair I could hear people talking about me as I passed. There were the usual idlers outside the bar who watched me, grinning. I seemed to arouse their curiosity, yet also to deprive them of their usual pleasure in seeing the local girls pass by, timid, cautious, yet flattered by their interest. These men made me detest the place. I only liked it for its extraordinary natural beauty, of which I never tired. I became infected by a strange nostalgia for Milan — strange because I had left the city without a pang — which I only ever voiced in letters to my girl friends. When I looked back to my own north country, now veiled by memory, it seemed desirable and full of magic. I longed for the inexhaustible city and the thronging crowds which gave it such vitality. I would try to recapture it in its most typical moods, summoning up sharp images, making believe that I was still there, a little girl, holding my father's hand as we walked in fog or dusty sunlight. These memories of my childhood city were shot through with a sense of unutterable regret, so intense that sometimes as I reminisced I trembled uncontrollably.

Papa took me to Rome and Naples as a reward for my first winter "in service," and this desire for the city, where "life" really existed, blazed up inside me again. For the first time in two years I moved among crowds and met people whose faces were marked by intellectual activity and lively intelligence. I felt a child again: insignificant, ill at ease, but eager to learn from everything and everyone around me. I suspect that this experience had a much greater emotional impact on me than did any art gallery or wonderful landscape. My letters to my mother and the diary of our journey which Father encouraged me to keep were full of naïve observations, ecstatic comments, and childish criticisms, but the intensity of my emotional response continually showed through.

That holiday was the crowning point of my triumphant adolescence. I remember it only indistinctly, bathed as it is in too vivid a light. The images I recall are piled on top of each other, like the syllables of a new word which might hold the key to existence. I made them a part of myself, gravely, yet with surprise; I could feel a new warmth snaking through my veins, a languor for which I could find no cause, a longing for tenderness and for wider horizons . . . yet in the present I felt only lethargy; did all this mean that I was about to enter a new phase in my life?

THREE

It was our third September in the town. The bathing season
had been and gone, no different from the ones before. As far
as I remember I divided my time between the exhausting pleasure of swimming ever longer and more daring distances, and
reading too much, which tired my brain and left me with a
vague feeling of discontent.

I remember nothing special from that summer about
what I felt for my mother, brother, sisters, or friends, nor even
my father. But one evening we gave a sort of party for summer
visitors and local families. It must have been Father's idea.
Three rooms of the house were taken over and decorated with
plants and lanterns. About forty people came: women from
Rome and Naples, their eyes gleaming with amusement at our
provincial ways; soberly dressed men, watching my father curi-
ously as he played host; some clerks from the office; and the
local school teachers with their families. Young and old danced
to a small band. As the eldest daughter I had to join in,
although I did so reluctantly because dancing gave me a head-
ache. I felt I was being singled out by the boys, and their hesitant approaches amused me. In the interval between one
dance and the next I caught myself watching my parents.
Father, an enthusiastic and excellent dancer, seemed a young
man again, his good humour catching everyone's attention. As
his tall figure wove its way through the couples he once more
symbolised for me simple, joyful energy. I wondered if my
mother was happy that evening. Wrapped in a dress of black
lace glittering with seed pearls, she brought back memories of

years past, of evenings when I had watched her leave for the theater on my father's arm, timid but proud in her elegant clothes. She was still graceful; that evening she looked no more than thirty.

Yet her behaviour made me suspect that she had now completely lost her self-confidence, although I couldn't imagine why. It was only by making a huge effort that she was able to follow the games and conversations. Whether this was equally obvious to papa and our guests, I could not tell.

I got up just before eight the next morning. Passing Mother's room and thinking she was still in bed, I knocked to see if there was anything I could do for her. I heard her wearily call me to come in. Father was still asleep: I could see his face turned towards the door. But her face was indistinct among the pillows and the bedclothes, and so I closed the door and went to have breakfast with my brother and sisters.

Some time elapsed. Then a cry, followed by many more, and a great shout from the square below, made me leap up from the table. Before I had time to reach the window the noise shifted to the foot of the stairs and I ran back towards the door, followed by the maid and the children. I could hear shouts of surprise and alarm, and feet shuffling as if people were carrying something heavy. The maid, hurrying to the staircase, screamed, then turned back quickly to shield us from the sight, and hustled us into the dining room. But I saw my mother's body being carried by two men. It was white, half-naked. Someone had thrown a cloth over it, which, dangling down, accentuated the limpness of her arms, feet, and hair. A crowd of people followed behind. I thought I was going mad.

But I wasn't mad. It really was my mother. Her eyes were closed, her face white as death, and there were red stains along one arm and down her side. Father came out of the bedroom. He wasn't fully dressed and seemed utterly bewildered. As he clutched his forehead his face filled with fear. After that I remember nothing because I fainted.

When I revived I heard a babble of women's voices discussing what had happened. They had seen a white figure on our balcony and in the sunlight had mistaken it for one of the children. Although they signalled to it to go back, the figure leaned forward, then let itself go, plummeting to the ground.

The doctor came. I went with him into the bedroom, where mother lay motionless on the bed. Father, completely distraught, was standing beside her, wringing his hands. When he saw me he let out a great sob, the first I had ever heard from him, and then collapsed on to a chair, pulling me between his knees and burying his face in my shoulder.

I was overwhelmed by an unbearable sense of loss. The strength of Father's emotion filled me with terror; I had a secret foreboding that this was only the first of many such dreadful moments. I didn't want him to let go of me. For the first time in my life I wished I could close my eyes and disappear. I could think of nothing to say—could not even ask whether she was still alive.

She was alive. Miraculously, her head and body had been unhurt. Only her left arm was broken. She was unconscious for three days, and afterwards refused to say anything about what had happened. One evening Father pleaded with her on his knees to talk to him about it, but she would not. All she would say was, "You must forgive me, forgive me..." We were all together in the room. Father wept, and to this day I don't know which was the more heart-rending—his tears or my sick mother's faint speech, coming as if from the dead.

I wanted to believe that she had done it in a fit of madness, though even this thought frightened me. Father, subdued and trembling in the darkened room, sounded passionately sincere when he asked her what had provoked such despair. She gazed at him silently. I had the strange feeling that she was waiting for an explanation from him ... Yet I was convinced that he had no idea what he had to reproach himself for.

She was in bed for two months, wracked by a fever which

threatened cerebral congestion, present as never before, yet absent too as if she had finally renounced us. An ominous atmosphere spread through the house, something different from our anxiety about her continuing illness. Hard as we tried to resist this mood, it continued to grow. The younger children were not so aware of it — they simply lived through the sadness. But I noticed, at first uneasily and then with alarm, that although my mother was slowly growing stronger, there was a peculiar insistent sluggishness about her, that there were gaps in her memory, and that she reacted with either excessive affection or hostility to those around her. However, I kept myself busy running the house, working a few hours a day in the office, reading, and writing letters. I certainly made no effort to examine these new perceptions or try to resolve the conflicts they produced in me. I felt sorry for my father and watched over my mother with vigilant care, as if by doing so I might be able to charm away her new symptoms, so afraid was I of her illness. By that time I was certain that I loved them both, but now I had developed a new anxiety. Gradually I convinced myself that from now on I was alone with my feelings, quite separate from these two people, and though I cared about them and pitied them, I felt I did not know them, and certainly that I did not dare pass judgement on them.

By the end of the winter Mother's recovery was almost complete. Only the arm she had broken was still weak. It had had to be re-set twice because of the incompetence of the surgeon, and she couldn't move her hand properly. Constantly fatigued, and old before her time, she seemed more demoralised and crushed than ever. Tears came to her eyes every time my youngest sister kissed her crippled hand. She seemed to have returned to us a child, a frightened child, trapped in the memory of her own mistakes.

Father had mastered his distress as soon as she was definitely out of danger, and seemed to regain his self-control. But he began to be absorbed in long, silent meditation and, not daring to interrupt him, I too would sit and think. I thought about the past and for the first time tried to explore it for clues which, linked together, would offer some explanation of the present.

I began to realise that the conflicts between these two people I loved so much were of a completely different quality from the arguments I sometimes had with my father. They seemed to have deeper roots, and to come from something inevitable and invincible. It threw new light on some of my own antagonism to certain people and the things they did. Once upon a time Father must have loved that poor creature very much, and now, in his silent isolation, he must be recalling a past of which I knew nothing. But I felt sure that by now their happiness existed only as a memory. Furthermore, I could no longer believe that my parents would learn to find new strength in loving each other or that they would re-establish family ties.

Although Father was very considerate, even affectionate, with Mother and controlled his temper, he accepted her persistent melancholy with a certain resignation. As for her, she seemed weighed down with shame, heartbroken, yet longing for reconciliation.

One day, when the house was full of sunlight, they stayed closeted together for more than an hour in the little room where Father now slept alone. When they emerged Mother's face was flushed, and she was smiling the misty smile of a young girl. I hadn't seen her look like that for a long time. She stared at me as if she didn't recognise me. But Father looked miserable and refused to meet my eyes.

During the following weeks I was often to feel disturbed by the sight of my mother resting wearily against my father's shoulder. I was sure he was avoiding me. Indeed, he seemed to be avoiding us all, gradually making hs escape from the house, almost without anyone being aware of it.

That spring dragged past. Sometimes in the cool twilight

I felt overcome by a need to weep in anguish, to break down. Where had the carefree days of childhood gone: Why was Father cutting himself off from me? Couldn't he tell how I was suffering? Didn't he love me any more? Oh, I was sure he didn't. I seemed to be losing confidence in him, in myself, in life altogether.

But slowly youth and optimism reasserted themselves. I went on with my work and wrote long letters to my friends, expressing a new found asceticism. I flirted naïvely with the Piedmontese workers — perhaps to offset my irritation with local people and local things.

And I was changing physically. My features and movements were now less awkward. My face grew brighter, more expressive. It was my father who first made me examine myself anxiously in the mirror. One evening I heard him say to himself, in joy and amazement, "She's going to be a beauty . . ." I didn't really believe it, but it gave me unutterable pleasure.

Others also noticed my transformation. There was a handsome young man who came from the village and worked in the office alongside me. I enjoyed his company and made friends with him. When we were left alone in the breaks between one job and the next we would argue cheerfully and exchange jokes. Before that spring he had always treated me with respect, even if he had often been mildly sarcastic. But now he began to pay me compliments. At first, his new attitude amused me. He told me the local gossip and repeated everything his friends said about me. One of them, he claimed, was in love with me and wanted to carry me off. This was common practice in those parts, where rape would be followed by marriage. I treated it as a joke and dropped hints about my father, whose name easily struck terror. But afterwards I was annoyed to find myself meeting the eyes of my self-styled lover.

The young man in the office also told me that the priest had made several references to our family from the pulpit, and had claimed that my mother's troubles were a judgement from God. He swore that some of the old ladies made the sign of the cross whenever I passed. They called me an "imp of Satan" and thought me a strange, even dangerous person possessing mysterious qualities. The men, on the other hand, admired me, according to him, and he was determined to make me aware of their flattery. It seemed to give him pleasure just to tell me about it. I didn't know whether to feel complimented or insulted by his stories. Yet he seemed sincere, and because he was the first person to recognise my feminity, I was prepared to excuse him for forgetting his place — after all, I was the boss's daughter and his social superior. I tried to turn everything into a joke, to show him that I didn't attach too much importance to what he said. Sometimes I would suddenly change the subject. He wasn't very well-educated and had rather conventional attitudes: I would deliberately lure him into discussions where I could quickly put him at a disadvantage. Then I would laugh, a high, pealing laugh, so girlish that his face lit up with childish amazement and he ended up laughing with me.

An old woman who came to help mamma with the housework was another victim of my caprices. We often chatted together and she would say that when I was older and a wife and mother, I would look back at my present job and smile. Calmly I assured her that *I would never marry*, that I would never be happy unless I could go on working, and that furthermore all girls should do the same as me, for marriage was a mistake — Father said so. The old woman was indignant. "And what would happen then? The world would end with no more children born, don't you understand that?"

I was speechless. Years before my mother had talked to me about the mysteries of the female body, but she hadn't explained the relations between men and women. Even if he wanted to abolish marriage I was certain that Father still wanted children to be born. I was sure that he didn't want the end of the world. But as yet I felt no special responsibility for the future. I was still determined never to marry.

Although Mother was there when I argued with the old woman she never joined in. She was increasingly self-absorbed, as though she had withdrawn to live in an internal desert. Towards the end of spring, Father suggested that she and I should go to Turin for a month to stay with relatives. I felt such a weight of responsibility at the thought of going alone with her: my constant fear was that she might be driven to commit some wild or destructive act yet again, and since I still wasn't sure that I loved her as much as I ought or wanted to, I felt helpless in the face of her unhappiness and bowed down by my own sense of enormous regret.

But we went, and on holiday she seemed in fact calmer and more hopeful as well as physically more active. As for me, I found that to be unexpectedly back in my childhood haunts helped to dispel some of my more obscure fears and gave me new courage.

Then once again it was summer. I was fifteen. Another colony of bathers arrived. They met each day on the beach, inviting us to join in their games. Everyone was curious about me; men of all ages watched me wherever I went. I daydreamed, first about one boy, delicate and teasing, then another, still pubescent with a strong agile body and curly hair, reminding me of bronzes I had seen in museums. But none of them made my heart beat faster or inspired me to flirt with them. I constantly wondered whether I was falling in love, but I treated it as a source of amusement, as something which gave new flavour to this life I was now living so fully. For hours upon end I cradled myself in the waves under the hot sun, enjoying the danger of swimming so far out that I was no longer visible from the shore. These physical exertions made me feel at one with nature, making me conscious that I was young, healthy, and free—and glad to be so.

But at home a sense of returning unhappiness frightened

me. Mother was becoming increasingly embittered and was losing her mental equilibrium. Moreover, Father pointed this out to her in the crudest terms possible. The younger children were more than ever left to fend for themselves. It had been a long time since Father had joined in our games, pretending to be a child himself. He had obviously had enough of family life and no longer cared what the rest of us did. In the autumn he began to say that he had to stay late at the factory every night. He appeared in the house only for meals, which he sat through in silence. His employees bore the brunt of his increasing brusqueness, and he now treated me no differently from them. Dismayed by this treatment, I tried desperately to discover what the reason could be.

I was not left in ignorance for very long. My office friend and I were often alone together in the big city, grey room with its rows of tables, its shelves covered with files and ledgers, and a huge charcoal stove, which made the air stiflingly hot. Another clerk came only in the afternoons, a fourth was often away. In the breaks between work we still exchanged more or less frivolous remarks or pursued more serious conversations which we interrupted and then picked up again later in the day. He was twenty-five, very masculine and full of energy, with an olive skin and lively dark brown eyes. He talked easily and at length. Yet there was always something about him which jarred, and I didn't always bother to conceal this. Not that he would attach too much importance to the comments of a little girl. The only thing that surprised him was my independence, so accustomed was he to think of women as naturally servile and submissive. I knew very little about him. I had heard a vague rumour that he had courted a woman before he went into the army and that she had tried to kill herself when he rejected her on his return. My father didn't like him. He tolerated him because he was a good worker, but if ever he found us chatting together he would rebuke me.

Perhaps as a kind of revenge, this man told me what many

people in the village apparently already knew — that my father had a mistress, a young girl who had been a worker in the factory; that the affair had probably started when Mother and I were away in the spring; that papa went to see her nearly every evening; that she, together with her large and poverty-stricken family, was maintained at his expense in a house outside town.

My father! A thousand little incidents were clarified for me. I was forced to believe the terrible revelation. Sick with pain and shame, I wanted the ground to open up and swallow me.

Until then Father had been my model; yet in an instant he was transformed into an object of horror, a man who had brought me up to respect sincerity and loyalty but had deliberately concealed a part of his life from Mother, and from us all. Oh papa, papa! Yesterday I had been so secure in the knowledge of our superiority, and now that was all gone: corrupt as the people around us might be, we had fallen lower than them. Oh, my innocent brother and sisters! And my mother, did she know? I suddenly felt drawn to this unfortunate woman as my heart filled to bursting point with anger and remorse — some of which I started to turn against myself.

Perhaps when she had tried to kill herself Father had already been unfaithful. I had rejected the thought at the time with serene conviction, and I rejected it again now. It would be too horrible. But neither could I accept that her physical and mental illness since then was any justification for his behaviour.

If only I could bring him to his senses, match my courage and determination against his, and save the whole family from ruin!

But now the man who had told me this, who had dealt me this terrible blow, either maliciously or unthinkingly, convinced me that such a response would be useless. At the same time he painted a gloomy picture of the future. In other circumstances I would have found the pity he lavished on me offensive. Now I hardly noticed it. He pressed my hands, stroked my hair, and unconsciously, although I trembled with rage and despair, I submitted to the pleasure of the contact.

I couldn't understand what this powerful force, this presence of which I had just become aware, could be. Was it love? The picture I had drawn of it from books had been so romantic. Could love be a terrible, degrading experience? Was it strong enough to master and humiliate even my father?

I had not thought very much about what life had to offer. I always assumed that it contained an endless supply of goodness and beauty. Now it seemed despoiled, incomprehensible.

How many days did I live in this dreadful state of torment? I no longer know. All I do know is that in the periods of depression which followed my initial frenzy I heard a young, ardent, persistent voice beside me murmuring increasingly open words of admiration. I might be exhausted, in a stupor, but the voice continued, accosting me with eloquent passion. And I began to respond, always with a sense of disbelief, but also with new hope: I became gentle and submissive.

I didn't tell him I loved him; nor did I even think it. All I told myself was that here was a man who cared about me.

Somehow Mother did find out about Father's affair. One evening, for some reason I now forget, some men called to see papa after dinner. One of them was a solicitor, an insignificant, soft-spoken man who had become my father's closest friend. My friend from the office was there too. They were all chatting. Suddenly my mother burst into a violent fit of laughter and asked the solicitor, "Tell me, is it true that you and my husband go walking at night along the river? Tell me what you talk about . . ."

The men exchanged glances, appalled. White now, and trembling, Mother got up, saying she felt ill, and left the room. The rest of us remained behind. There was terrible, suppressed anger on Father's face. Slowly, almost in a whisper, he declared: "That woman is going mad!"

Suddenly I burst out, "And I shall go mad as well, papa!"

As I glared at him in rebellious despair, I was shaken by a terrible convulsion.

"You hold your tongue," he yelled. Enraged, he lunged toward me as though he wanted to tear me limb from limb. But then he restrained himself with a great effort, and shouted, "Leave the room!"

I do not know how I managed to get through that night. The next morning Mother stayed in bed with a temperature, undoubtedly waiting for him to go to see her so that she could beg his forgiveness; but he didn't go. As for me, I was told that at the end of the month my job would come to an end. That was his response to my outburst of the night before.

By the time I reached the office I was in tears. I loved that factory life intensely, I couldn't bear to give it up. I couldn't imagine doing anything that would suit me so well. All this I poured out to my friend, who had come to stand beside me.

"And what about me? What shall I do?" he whispered. Going back to his desk, he hid his face in his hands. His shoulders were trembling nervously. Forgetting my own pain, I went up to him. He caught hold of me, pressing me tightly against him.

"You were beautiful last night, so proud. I wanted to throw myself at your knees and kiss you . . ."

I closed my eyes. Was he telling the truth? With all my heart I wanted to know. My eyes were closed for some minutes. His lips descended on mine. He wouldn't let me go. Instead of arousing my senses, it soothed them. I waited, expecting to be filled with overwhelming pleasure.

A sudden noise made me start away from him. The next day we were alone again, and I went to him for comfort. He told me he loved me, stopping my mouth with little kisses. It disgusted me a little and I shook him off. But I seemed to need his company in the days that followed. When I was with him I forgot my unhappiness, forgot the sense of disbelief I felt whenever I looked my father in the eye. My feelings seemed paralysed: I wanted only to forget.

My friend sensed my ignorance and noticed my frigidity —
that of a girl of fifteen. Using gestures and playful smiles, he
concealed his own sexual excitement. Slowly he caressed my
body, making me stroke and kiss him as if we were playing a
game of forfeits. In my imagination I was beginning to sketch
out a great work of love, and this seemed only the pleasurable
preface.

And so, one morning, I was standing in the doorway
which divided father's office from ours, with a childish smile
on my lips, when he surprised me by an unusually brutal
enbrace. Trembling hands ransacked my clothes, turning my
body over until, still struggling, I was half-lying across a
bench. I felt suffocated and began to moan, my voice rising to
a scream, which he suppressed by covering my mouth and
flinging me away from him. I heard the sound of footsteps running and someone slamming the outer door. I staggered into
the little laboratory behind father's office, hoping I would be
safe there. I tried to pull myself together, but my strength
seemed to have gone. Suddenly I felt suspicious. Rushing out
of the room, I saw him. He seemed bewildered and was breath
ing heavily, his eyes silently pleading with me. I must have conveyed immense horror, for as he came toward me I saw his sudden look of fear and his hands clasped in a gesture of sup-
plication.

FOUR

Did this man own me?

I have only a vague and depressed memory of my indescribable confusion in the days that followed, but I know that
gradually I came to believe that he did.

My life, already shaken by my father's desertion, was now
suddenly turned upside down, tragically altered. What had I
become? What would happen to me? My childhood was certainly at an end.

I had taken such pride in being independent and thinking
for myself that I now suffered agonies; but this same pride prevented me from indulging in tears. I was forced to accept that
I was also responsible for what had happened.

And I desperately tried to explain to myself something
that still astounds me. I had known this man for about two
years, had seen him nearly every day, and had accepted his
friendship and advice at work. My attitude to him had been
one of frank, childish appreciation. I had even been amused
by his occasional clumsiness. Then, one day, he had calmly
shattered my respect for my father . . . Why had I never, even
for an instant, doubted his word? Because I knew nothing
about life. His greater experience had immediately instilled in
me a sense of deference, and on top of that he had offered me
his sympathy and pity. From the moment he had witnessed the
anguish of my sudden sense of loss, he had seemed different, a
new person, endowed with all the qualities I now felt my father
lacked. He seemed so dignified as he disdainfully passed judgement on my father, and so touching when he defended my

mother's rights! There was only one occasion on which I re-
coiled from him: when I asked him if he would support me
with his evidence if ever I decided to confront my father, and
he implored me to keep quiet about it, to say nothing . . . After
that he engulfed me in a wave of loving words, which softened
my feelings towards him again. Not for one second did I ever
question his devotion. I accepted it, arrogantly, my old sense
of superiority still very much alive.

I was also overwhelmed by exhaustion at this time. Perhaps he was aware of that. He would take me in his arms, tell
me he loved me, and I was always prepared to listen . . .

Never for one moment did I imagine that I might be the
victim of a cold-blooded strategy. I was sure that it must be
love that was responsible for what was happening. Yet I felt so
unprepared for this mysterious guest! How true it was that my
excessive and exclusive admiration for my father had left me
ignorant of life! I had never acknowledged that being a woman
might affect my future, and here I was, suddenly become a
woman, just at a time when I could no longer confide in my
father, when the past I had shared with him was becoming
devalued, and when my mother was no longer capable of
advising me or answering my questions.

I was never tempted, not for one instant, to reveal my terrible secret to her. She had already suffered enough, wrapped
up as she was in her own misery.

My father seemed miles away, cut off from my life for
ever. All the same, I felt unendurable torment, hiding the up-
heaval I was going through from him.

Alone and in silence, I allowed myself to succumb to a
sort of wishful thinking, a conscious make-believe. Perhaps it
was an after-effect of the sudden physiological shock I had
received . . . When was it that I first told myself that perhaps I
should return this man's passion, accept from him, for the rest
of my life, the support and security he offered, and separate
myself from everything that had so far made me what I was? I

can't remember clearly any more. I began to believe that perhaps I had loved him for months without being aware of it, that, although I couldn't explain what it was, he possessed some quality which had seduced me, however unimpressive he might seem from the outside.

And then I started to tell myself that although I hadn't foreseen a future life based on love and sacrifice, perhaps it might give me the security, the tranquillity, and the happiness I so desired. I would be his wife . . . Wasn't I his wife already? He wanted me, he was intended for me, and events had been pushing me towards him even when I had believed that my life was developing in some other direction . . . The bridegroom of fairy tales, whom I had always thought such a childish figure, really existed. It was he!

As soon as I began to think like this he realised that he had achieved his objective. Perhaps he wasn't very surprised. But for a brief moment he had been uncertain of the outcome, and now that he was more confident and hopeful, he began to encourage my sentimentality, the romantic, effusive declarations I made to him and expressed in my letters. If ever I demanded explanations or questioned him about what had happened, he stopped me by kissing my hands and hair, solemnly repeating that he would never, as long as he lived, be able to repay me for the gift I had made of myself. Then he would try once more to take possession of my body. But my initiation had been too brutal, and I refused. Like many young girls, I had read novels which stirred up shapeless fantasies, never clarified for me. Although my experience with this man had disgusted me, I could not believe that it encapsulated the whole reality. I imagined that when I was married I would enjoy unutterable raptures which would compensate me for everything I had experienced. At fifteen, my understanding of sexual matters was still too rudimentary for me to suffer very profoundly. And perhaps I was also spurred on by an unexamined pride which sustained my stubborn and desperate cultivation of the wish to sacrifice myself for love.

But Father noticed that I had become withdrawn and agitated. Suddenly he carried out his earlier threat and instructed me not to return to the office.

Such an abrupt separation agitated me even more. I was convinced that I was enduring the most terrible days of my life. Eventually I managed to send a letter to the young man, who urged me to tell my mother that we were in love; and she, sad, disheartened, well on the way to a complete mental breakdown, seemed to grow young again as she drank in the words of her love-struck daughter. Was she picturing herself at twenty, deluding herself that she saw resplendent in me the happiness she had dreamt of but never achieved for herself? Certainly something of her was pushing through me at that moment, for the first time ever: perhaps she was intuitively aware of that. The poor woman had no way of knowing about the drama which had cut short my adolescence. She thought — she too! — that, magically, a new emotion was blossoming within me which would save me from the arid existence to which she had always feared my education would lead me; and she gathered together all her resources in the hope of assuaging my fears, and seeing her own dreams of happiness triumph at last in her daughter's life.

I watched her with tender sadness, yet I was also vaguely fearful for myself. When I recognised that I was as fragile as she, I couldn't help but wonder whether I would be any luckier, and whether I wasn't deceiving myself, as she had done, by putting so much faith in love.

My father treated the whole affair as a triviality, and seemed not to believe in my feelings. But I joined forces with my pathetic hero in order to convince him that the only thing we wanted from life was to be married. We wrote to him, and we argued with him. He erupted in a terrible fit of rage. Even so, he never suspected the truth: how could he have imagined such criminal audacity when he was so confident of the fear he inspired in anyone who came near him? He was simply exasperated by the thought that his favourite daughter, brought up to despise all illusions and to rely on herself alone in life's battles, had fallen victim to a nonsensical infatuation. He certainly was not prepared to take his share of the blame, nor to face the fact that I had been deprived of his love and care at the very time when I most had need of it.

All the same he suffered. Although a complex man, he was also very primitive, incapable of working out at all precisely what was going on around him, and therefore unable to put forward any solutions. All he grasped was that now it was his turn to be isolated and that he had alienated the only person who understood him. From the moment at which social disapproval began to be centered on him to the point at which he realised that he faced imminent catastrophe, his only weapons were his desire to dominate and his determination to be victorious, whatever the cost.

He was amazed by my mother's insistent defence of me. They had avoided all communication since the evening of her outburst, but now she was demanding my right to happiness as if it was one of the terms of a peace treaty. She seemed to be saying: "I may be old, but at least I can still be a grandmother. Even if I can't find peace of heart, I can find peace of mind. Once our daughter is happy and I can look after her children, there will be some beauty in my life . . ."

He refused to speak to me. He realised that he had lost all my sympathy and that all the hopes and dreams he had once built around me were at an end. He told my young man he could not think of marrying me yet; I was only fifteen and a half. We would have to wait a few years. Meanwhile, he could visit us in the evenings and sometimes accompany us on our evening walks.

He asked him about his prospects. Was he intending to find a better job? Would he try to make a career in the civil service? He warned him that I wouldn't have a dowry. For the moment, however, he could keep his job in the factory. I had imagined that my friend would resign and find himself another job immediately, even if it meant moving to another town. In fact nothing happened: he didn't think it at all undignified to remain dependent on his future father-in-law — a man, moreover, of whose conduct he disapproved. On the contrary, he was sure that when we did get married my father was bound to give me some money.

So he came to our house in the evenings like any fiancé. He never encountered Father because Father unfailingly went out as soon as he had eaten dinner. The younger children would sit around the table, reading or playing games, while Mother and I embroidered to pass the time. My young man amused himself by teasing me, systematically contradicting everything I said. Every now and then he stole a kiss, paying no attention to my mother's protests or the children's laughter. That pacified me. He left towards ten, and I went with him into the dark hall, where we embraced. Sometimes his hands gripped me restlessly, reviving in my senses the now distant thrill of terror.

At the beginning there was a lot of talk in the neighbourhood about our relationship: the more malicious gossips interpreted my sudden removal from the factory as the result of a discovery my father had made. The same voices, a year earlier, had whispered that my father's affection for me was more than paternal; they seemed to take pleasure in repellent and monstrous lies. My parents had no knowledge of these rumours, and their ignorance and sense of security made me feel increasingly ashamed.

I felt that the least my fiancé could do was to defy the slanderers. But he seemed to have acquired a new, special dignity in the eyes of his friends, as if he had suddenly gone up in the world. On the one hand they envied him, yet on the other they were pleased that a local boy had humiliated the arrogant outsiders. I could tell that they were sneering at me whenever I passed them in the street, but however disdainful I felt I dared not show it. My fiancé would laugh at the gossip, and that shocked me. He even laughed when they dragged up a story which I had not heard before—that he had seduced the girl who had tried to commit suicide because of him. He neither tried to defend himself nor give any explanation.

As the months passed the gossip died down. By now I had anyway become isolated from local life. My fiancé was jealous and demanded a thousand absurd renunciations: I must never appear at the window; if any man came into the house, including Mother's doctor, I must hurry to my room. I had been so used to freedom that occasionally I rebelled, but then I would remember what had happened, and I considered it so irrevocable that I was only reminded more intensely of my sickening defeat.

Indeed, I wrote and told my girl friends that I was happy. I wanted to deceive myself, and I was able to stimulate my fantasies until they intoxicated me.

I was so determined to love him that I didn't reflect on the unpleasant emotions my fiancé could arouse in me. I discovered a range of unexpected defects in him. I knew he wasn't very well educated, but I had thought him more quick-witted. Most importantly, there was something evasive, something hard to pin down in his character which deeply disappointed my expectations; and often he so offended my love of rationality that I would start up, surprised and indignant . . . But I quickly suppressed all this. I wanted to believe in my happiness, present and future. I wanted love to be a grand and beautiful experience. I was sixteen and wanted a love which would incorporate all the mysterious poetry of life—and there was no one there to look me in the eyes, ask me directly about my feelings, and talk to me about them truthfully and forcefully in words I would have understood.

My face, now paler, framed by my hair, which I had let grow again, lost its vitality, its individuality. Had there really been a time when I could go to the beach whenever I liked, plunge into the sea for hours on end, roam around the countryside, and abandon myself to endless dreams of beauty and future work?

Now I spent my days almost entirely within the silence of my little room. I prepared by trousseau and sometimes paused for long periods in a state of suspended reflection, watching my hands as they rested against the white muslin. My future as a wife was marked out. Father had agreed, more easily than I had expected, to give me away in marriage within a few months. And I seemed prepared for it, even though I could see how narrow my life would become. I had no scruples about leaving my family — my mother, who was increasingly weak, increasingly and frighteningly confused, my brother and sisters, who now had no support or love from anyone.

And what was happening to my fiancé? Was he beginning to respect the child he was taking from her home? Was he convincing himself, egoist that he was, that he could make me happy?

He had decided not to give up his job, calculating on early promotion and the future succession to my father's position. We argued for a long time about the dowry. Finally he resigned himself to accepting that we would only get a monthly allowance. Even so, he wanted it legalised, but Father was so indignant he threatened to break off negotiations. My fiancé took responsibility for nothing except refurbishing his own wardrobe and buying me a wedding ring. Father gave us the money for our furniture. The only contribution my future parents-in-law made was to marvel at my family's lack of generosity.

Although we never spoke about it, the situation became increasingly painful for us all. So why prolong it? We fixed the wedding day for the end of January.

Slightly less than a year had passed since the event which so changed my life, and I had spoken not a word to anyone about it, not even to my fiancé himself. The preparations hurried forward joylessly. The night before the wedding, papa, in one of his now frequent fits of rage, found an excuse to abuse me bitterly . . .

That night my mother came to my bedside. She tried to find words to prepare me for what lay in store for me the next day. I interrupted her hurriedly, hugging her, stroking her grey hair, as my body shook with suffocated sobs. And twenty-four hours later, with my husband, watching from the train as the countryside turned white with snow under the stars, I thought about how my parents had managed to conceal their anguish, so different for each of them that day, making an enormous effort to be cheerful with the guests who had come to the wedding . . . I wondered if now, at home in their lonely rooms, they were weeping.

FIVE

The dining-room windows of our small apartment gave out on to a wide street, beyond which stretched some gardens: behind these, a line of hills and a band of sea. The other rooms looked over a small, forsaken garden, overrun with melancholy box-tree hedges, and a railway track. Every now and then the house shook slightly as the trains came and went and the echo of their whistle reverberated through the rooms. There were lodgers on the floor below, but we hardly ever saw them. When my husband and the servant were out I tried not to make any noise as I moved around.

My new flannel dresses constantly reminded me that I really was a *married woman,* a serious person, whose place in life was irrevocably fixed. The first time I went out along the main street of the town at the side of my husband, my one-time colleague, horribly weighed down by a feathered hat and my body awkward in a fashionable dress, it seemed to me as if an abyss of time and things separated me from the child I had been only a year before.

Confusedly I felt the need to take, as it were, citizenship of the place, to identify myself with the customs and feelings of the people who made up my new family, and to absorb the atmosphere in which my husband had grown up and where my own children would be educated.

Occasionally, when I visited my mother, the difference between the world I had come from and the one I was now joining became extremely clear. It filled me with a sort of unconfessed anger against my past, instinctive, unreflecting, and unjust, directed against my mother, my sisters, my father, and all my past romantic hopes.

Her illness gave my mother a strange sensitivity. She was the only person who noticed how I felt: two or three times in those first days of my married life I could read on her white face, now increasingly devastated by suffering, the painful surprise she felt at my silence. The feelings I brought back from our honeymoon were hazy, or rather already rapidly fading. There had been no emotional satisfaction or sensual arousal. Oh, the expectations of a young girl! I hadn't had sufficient time before I was married to construct a complete world of rapture out of my dreams, but my disappointment was as bitter as if I had. Of our honeymoon, all that remains in my memory is a quarrel we had for no serious reason on the third day, which kept us locked in our hotel room in spiteful silence for the whole afternoon. And why was it that when I introduced my husband to my friends and relations in Milan I was afraid to find amazement, even disapproval, in their eyes?

I didn't want to hear the questions I asked myself, let alone answer them. That was why Mother's anxious solicitude made me so uneasy. I knew very well that she expected me to come back a different woman, more a sister than a daughter, my perceptions deepened by emotions which for her must have been among her few bright memories. She finally forced me to admit to her, and to myself, that for me there was no more *mystery,* that there never had been, that everything had been revealed to me a year before, on that dark, terrible morning which until then I thought I had managed to forget.

I owed my mother-in-law no such confidences. All I wanted was to win her and her family over, and I did not believe that would be difficult. They already seemed to think me different from them, made of finer, more precious metal, and this was a source of intense pride. To the two old people I seemed like a child. My sister-in-law, on the other hand, must have had some sense of the strength concealed behind my fragility, but probably judged me incapable of being a serious enemy. And to all of his family, my husband was without question the ideal husband, worthy of having won me.

I went to see my mother-in-law in the evenings. I would find her crouched beside their great stove, its flame sometimes the only light in the kitchen darkness of the ground floor, where the door was nearly always open on to the garden. When her cheeks were flushed, she looked younger, and her regular features seemed almost beautiful. She smiled hesitantly as she called me by the formal *voi*.

Even my father-in-law couldn't say *tu* to me. He was tall, almost a giant, but hunched, and slow in his movements. It was he who did the shopping each morning. "And is madame happy?" he used to ask his daughter, a silent woman of thirty who was always finding something to complain about. She was an imperious, self-centred character, cold yet moody, and even her mother was afraid of her. In fact locally she had a reputation as a termagent, but I didn't know this at the time. Nor did I know that they weren't a very popular family. Many years before, my father-in-law had been put on trial and imprisoned, not an uncommon thing in the town. His son told me a complicated story of insults and revenge to demonstrate his father's innocence, and had been so agitated by it that he convinced me. Now, in the shadows and reflections of their kitchen, watching the old man's cramped movements, I sometimes imagined that I saw the walls closing in on him until they made a cell, the prison he had lived in for two years . . . He was gentle and careful, with rare flashes of what must once have been an outgoing nature, and he always stirred up in me mixed feelings of pity and fear.

The relations between the members of the family seemed strange to me: in my home everything had been more ordered and disciplined, more clear-cut. On the other hand, what fascinated me about that cruder environment was the sense of tradition, the deference to custom, the tenacious will which inspired these people at times to glorify their bonds of blood, family, and land. In a thousand tiny ways, from their method of preparing food for a particular feast-day to my sister-in-law's dogged defence of her brother against outsiders when only a moment earlier they had been close to blows, I observed a way of life totally foreign to the one which had shaped my character and tastes. It was a life full of contradictions, and often mistaken (I add that judgement almost compulsively) but not without its attractions.

As time went on I was taken over by a sort of lethargy. I seemed to need to do nothing except abandon myself completely to my new surroundings. As a result my body submitted to my husband's wishes although I found him physically more and more repugnant. I put this down to my exhaustion, my tiredness. I never tried to overcome my frigidity, although it astonished and sometimes saddened him. More demonstrative behaviour seemed inconceivable. My only pleasure was to feel desired: but even that disappeared when what I saw disgusted me and when what I heard seemed either brutal or senseless. I closed my eyes, stopped myself thinking, and lay as if in a coma.

Afterward I slept. How old was I? Not yet seventeen ... My sleep was long and peaceful: the sleep of a young girl.

The woman who came to clean the house left every morning at eleven. I prepared lunch and dinner myself, willing to do it though it gave me no pleasure. And without knowing how, the days slipped past. I kept some of the factory accounts — a job I could do at home, which father had given me so that I could pretend at least to myself that I was keeping some independence; but it only needed two or three hours of my time. I subscribed to magazines and read a little, and wrote to my old friends and school teachers. During the first months of our marriage, all the important people in the area came to call on us, and I repaid their visits, both amused and irritated by my new role as a married woman.

I was happier in the evenings, when my husband's friends came to see us. My husband would show off our coffee machine and then invite them to try our wine. The men smoked and drank, and, forgetting me, sometimes lapsed into vulgarity. When the conversation turned to politics I joined in, feeling my shyness drop away a little. By and large the men I argued with were of the same intellectual level as my husband and, confronted by my logic, quickly capitulated.

On the other evenings we went to the house of one of his relations, the leader of the local democratic group. Many of the members of the town's middle class, some with their wives, met there. The trivial chatter and gossip of the women alternated with the men's noisy arguments, and I felt I was being watched with a sort of ill-concealed distrust, as if they were remembering my eccentricity as a young girl. Only one person, a young doctor, recently appointed from Tuscany, who lodged with our relations, made me feel from the first that here was someone like me in his tendency to consider carefully what he said, the correctness of his language, and his outlook on life. He was a well-educated, quick-witted man and must have been curious about me. I felt he noticed the contradiction between my external life and my inner feelings, which, I suspect, sometimes surprised him when he noticed the fleeting shadows they cast over my childlike face.

Although I had hoped to become more involved in local affairs, I was by now cut off from any contact with the workers, peasants, and fishermen. The middle classes in the town seemed even meaner than I had imagined. I never admitted it, but I secretly feared that their narrow-mindedness would infect me. I had already started to envy the local women their inertia. Cooking, religion, and the lazy, rough and ready care of children was their entire life. Even if the men affected agnosticism, they still expected their women to go to church. Perhaps my husband secretly wished that I would too, but if he did he never mentioned it. On the other hand he was deter-

mined not to have children and often told me so. Was it that
he didn't want to share me with anyone? As yet I had not felt
either any surging desire for a child in my life, someone to
possess and care for, someone who might give my world a new
meaning.

"My friends are always telling me how intelligent you are.
They say they envy me my wife..." he reported. I wasn't so
sure about this. I certainly had the impression that they
thought me graceful and perhaps attractive; but when I looked
at myself in the mirror I couldn't see myself in this way. I
thought I looked sleepy, like an old baby. Yet even this failed
to disturb me very much.

Only once during those first months did my old pride
blaze up again. One evening I was tidying a box where my husband kept his papers, our correspondence, and some souve-
nirs. I was astonished to find, next to mine, the letters his first
girl friend had written to him six or eight years before! She was
still unmarried and still living in the town; sometimes I met her
in the street, and how her eyes sparkled with hatred when she
saw me! I read only one of her letters. It was badly spelt and
full of phrases copied from a book of standard love letters. My
husband sat beside the stove, a particularly fatuous smile on
his face. As I went on rummaging, other, shorter notes from
women fell out. "They are... from when I was a soldier, you
know... that's from the daughter of an inn-keeper..." But I
wasn't listening. I was reading a telegram, signed with a
woman's pet name, and looking at the date—it was from last
summer, while we were engaged. I tore these papers to shreds.
He didn't dare protest.

Why didn't I just believe the web of lies he spun me? Why
did I suffer so much? Did I really love him? Or was it rather
that something was crumbling, that an edifice I had carefully
constructed in good faith was collapsing before my eyes?

I burst into tears, and my sense of shock dissolved. I decided to try to forget, to stop tormenting myself. Whatever had

happened in the past, he was my husband now and I was certain that in time he would slowly be influenced by my honesty.

I no longer saw my father. My husband, who found him increasingly demanding and harsh, talked to me about him. So did my sisters and sometimes my mother. He was almost always out of the house and had lost all interest in his children's lives. When he entered the house he brought fear with him; as soon as he closed the door behind him the children were forced to witness the spectacle of Mother's collapse into tears and lamentations. Even my youngest sister had to make an enormous effort to calm her and bring her to her senses. My other sister, now thirteen, a quiet, sensible girl, had almost without being aware of it taken over the running of the house. When my brother came to see me he launched into violent attacks on Father because he had been forced by him to take a physically demanding job at the factory rather than being allowed to go to the city to continue his studies. Everyone seemed to be waiting for a catastrophe.

I had no desire to pass judgement on my father. In fact I sometimes thought that my unhappy fate had contributed to his moral collapse. Hadn't I abandoned him, without attempting even a gesture which might make him stay at home, near the children he had once been so proud of? Had I, at fifteen, had the right to cut myself off so self-righteously from the man to whom I owed everything that I valued?

And some of these criticisms rebounded on my mother. Her weakness, her renunciation of the struggle, exasperated me much more now that I was forced to admit that my own fatalistic resignation to my situation simply demonstrated to me how alike we were. But the poor woman was suffering terribly, not only in her emotional life, but physically as well. She was gradually succumbing to some dreadful organic disease. I saw traces of it in her disjointed conversation, and it somehow made me fear for myself and for my own newly discovered womanhood. Yet, strange as it seems, these feelings prevented me more than ever from being able to comfort the woman who was my mother. Instead I wished that I really was the loving wife she imagined. I thought that only if I had been happy would I have been able to treat her compassionately as she reached out longingly for all the good things in life that she had lost.

What my father was going through I don't know. Nor do I know what he was told by the doctor, who prescribed tranquillisers for mamma and did his utmost to persuade her to change her way of life, to go away and trust in her own resources, in the effects of time, and in her children. Perhaps the doctor begged my father, as my unhappy mother certainly did, to lie to her, to have some pity for her. As far as I understood what was happening, they had now reached a point where she would accept his affection even as charity and even if she had to share it with her rival.

I felt that papa would never change now. He was, at forty-two, at the height of his career and at war against men and things, inspired as never before by a bitter refusal to acknowledge any failure. He certainly avoided thinking about the past, and just as certainly failed to recognise that there had been a time when he might have avoided this disastrous situation. Was he distressed? Was he even alarmed? No word or gesture from him ever gave me any indication. All I know is that by now the open hostility of the whole community, the rejection of him stirred up by the parish priest, the envious local gentry, and the workers he had dismissed so inflamed him that he had become deliberately provocative, and was losing all sense of reality.

Meanwhile the weeks passed. When summer came I hardly noticed. My lethargy seemed to be physical, not just emotional.

One night there was a knock on our door. It was my mother, leaning heavily against my father-in-law, half-dressed, a fixed stare on her face, making inarticulate sounds. Unnoticed by the servants she had left the house and was wandering the streets, for how long no one knew, until she met the old man, who brought her to the house. Perhaps she had been driven by some obsessive idea of looking for Father.

I was thunderstruck. Suddenly I visualised my old home, its door wide open to the street while the children, ignorant of events, slept inside. And confronted by my mother, that embodiment of human misery who had come to me for help in the night, I experienced a total, savage rebellion . . . I trembled, in a fever myself now . . . And I hurled harsh, angry words at the unhappy woman, words almost as mad as her own. Oh, my mother . . . and all for the sake of a man who no longer deserved her anyway . . . !

I can still see myself in my nightclothes, barefoot beside the bed, while she leaned against the wall, watching me and crying submissively. Later on her doctor arrived and made her take a strong sedative. After a time she asked to be taken back to her house and her children. I went back to bed. In the darkness and silence I went over that terrible scene again and again, and I felt my fever mounting and with it a turbulent hatred of life, disgust and endless weariness . . .

The doctor came back. Although I had been unaware of it I had been carrying a new life in my womb. Now I had lost it.

SIX

For many days I lay in bed without moving, repeating softly to myself the same word, again and again: mother. Yet I was uncertain that I could ever have loved the child who had been growing inside my body, and therefore felt incapable of passionate mourning for what I had lost.

But at the same time I was stung by remorse, which depressed me, robbing me once more of my self-esteem and appetite for living. I thought about my mother and the stream of pitiless words which had issued from me on that terrible night . . . What did she really mean to me? Did I really love her?

I didn't dare answer these questions. I was seeing myself in a new light, after the devastation wrought by a sudden hope of maternity, which had vanished as soon as it had come to me. I began to think that I had never made any contribution to my mother's happiness, except perhaps when I first came into the world, when my parents were still in love. She, it is true, had not played a central part in any of my happiest memories either; but was that enough to explain the indifference I had shown for so long towards someone who suffered so much?

I now managed to construct a much clearer picture of her past than any I had built before.

This unhappy woman had lived with her husband for eighteen years. The few pleasures she had experienced as a wife had turned into endless burdens; even as a mother, she had never been fully appreciated by her children. Not once had she been able to express her true feelings — throughout her entire life she had never found anyone who understood her. As a child, her parents had thought her romantic, excitable, and incompetent, even though she was the most intelligent and serious of their numerous offspring. Because they disliked her husband she had cut off all contact with them without complaint. Her religious beliefs were so mixed with an austere mysticism that she never enjoyed church ritual, so even religion hadn't relieved her pain. Although her imagination was lively and fierce and she had fine taste, she had never applied it; nor had she ever been so involved in any work of genius as to give her an interest outside herself. She had never made a close friend or found a confidante in all her life. In addition to all this her health had always been precarious so that her physical strength had been slowly undermined by illness . . .

The poor, poor woman! Beauty, goodness, intelligence, had all been useless to her. Her life had required strength, and she had not possessed it.

Love, sacrifice yourself, and submit! Was that her destiny? Was that every woman's destiny?

It took me about a month to recover. I saw my mother only once, on a day when she was calm. One of her more comprehensible remarks was, "Oh, if only you could have had a child!" It terrified me to realise how much she longed for a grandchild, for renewed maternity!

Then the doctor forbade further visits from her. Every afternoon my brother or youngest sister came to see me for a short time, wide-eyed and almost speechless with sorrow. Mother no longer listened even to them; she fluctuated between hallucinations and threats; the nurse was no longer equal to the task of looking after her. My sister flung herself into my arms and burst into tears, my brother tortured himself with not being older and able to take the unfortunate woman away from my father, who, it seemed, had no pity left for her.

Papa was sullen, impenetrable. He never spoke. And we were all still terrified of him, and paralysed and disheartened by our fear . . .

Finally the doctors said that she needed proper treatment

in a nursing home. They also thought that she should be moved away from contact with her frightened children. Her departure, after so many months of anxiety, was in fact a liberation for them. The sweet, melancholy person they had seen bending over their cots had been transformed into a ghostly presence, by whom they no longer felt loved and who they feared would never love them again. Yet they longed for her to return soon, to blot out the memory of the nightmare through which they had been living.

And I? Had I been able to ask for forgiveness, to tell her how unutterably appalled I was that I had been so inhuman, and make her feel that at last I understood her?

No. I would never be able to communicate with her again. I would never be able to talk to her, I knew it, I knew it; everything was over. Nothing would be left of her, of what she had been, except a memory, a grim warning . . .

The round of days and weeks began again.

Slowly I became physically more active, although my emotional energy seemed to have died. I had no complaints. I imagined that because of the sequence of tragic events which had buffeted my short life I now had a complete picture of the world. It was a strange prison . . . everything was meaningless: joy and pain, effort and rebellion. The only dignity lay in resignation. I didn't even attempt to take care of my sisters, to temper their unhappiness and give my life a sense of purpose. A young governess arrived shortly after Mother went away and did her best to secure their affection for herself. Reluctantly I watched this elegant, flirtatious woman as she set about her delicate task, thinking that perhaps I should try to ensure that she didn't dominate the girls too much, but in fact I left them to draw imperceptibly away from me. Papa sought my company even less than they did. No one ever mentioned the absent woman's name to him.

My husband, with typical lack of curiosity, was satisfied

by my outward calm and my increasing submissiveness. He wrapped his incalculable selfishness in a cloak of tender solicitude. Although I didn't believe his expressions of affection, they served to prevent both quarrels and frank discussion. It seemed as if we were both afraid to confront our real feelings, and therefore by unspoken agreement we maintained reasonably friendly and tolerant relations. But it wasn't really like that. He believed that I still loved him, and for his part I think that he loved me in a possessive, proprietorial sort of way, giving and taking affection from some conventional notion of obligation. He felt proud of my beauty, which had flowered again, my intelligence, and my calm obedience to those of his jealous whims I didn't find too insulting. The only cause for displeasure I gave him was my increasing refusal of what seemed like his sexual perversity. Being more ignorant than brutal, he found this inexplicable, and it tormented him. For my part, I was only interested in defending myself.

And the days, the weeks, went by. A few memories come up now and then from that time, but even so it remains the most confused and indecipherable period of my life: all that is clear is that something, I don't know what, saved me from total bitterness and irredeemable depression, and forced me to live in a mechanical way, accepting my fate without complaint, but also taking a strange pride in my capacity to do so . . . Memories of my childhood were oases to which I could sometimes escape, but whenever I did so I was unfailingly confronted with the image of my tormented mother as I had first seen her in her terrible asylum a few weeks after she left home, and I felt a sudden quiver, like the sensation of someone lost on a glacier who feels vibrations from the rope that ties him to a companion fallen into the abyss. Oh, my mother's voice, already so changed, saying such incoherent things! And the enormous building with its many rooms, resounding with a confused hum of laughter and tears, the echo of a storm of madness walled off from the rest of the world, the vast deserted corridors along which nurses glided, bunches of keys at their waists, and the doorways where I sometimes caught glimpses of people with wide eyes and grinning mouths, like images from an hallucination; and finally the white room, with its iron bars to which Mother was clinging as she called out to the town stretching away outside, beautiful in the sunlight, as a child might call out to a lake or a wood, by name, as if it were human. I came out of that place of suffering trembling inside, unable even to cry or speak, in a state of mental pain which was almost physical, it so flattened and appalled me. I felt a dark, inexpressible longing, a compulsive wish to escape: to escape life, to escape the road which may lead to madness.

I spent a year like this, enveloped in dismal fog. Then . . . then I felt the pulse of a new life inside me, and so started a period of fervent waiting.

At the beginning I was almost petrified with fear. I was tormented by doubts, never openly expressed, about what my child might inherit from my husband and myself . . . And there were other worries too, less profound but still serious, about our material future, about how prepared I was for motherhood . . .

These early feelings soon disappeared. I confronted the future and accepted it with a courage I still find remarkable, given that my deep depression, the worst I have ever experienced, persisted. Gradually I became aware of my maternal feelings. I felt able to devote myself to the child who was developing inside me so mysteriously; I felt able to love it with a love I had not yet given anyone. And I felt an unspoken, vigorous happiness growing within me, nourished from time to time by the first tears of joy I had ever shed. At last I had a reason for living, an obvious duty. My child must not only be born and survive: it must be the healthiest, most beautiful, biggest, best, happiest child. I would make it a gift of my energy, my youth, and my dreams. And I would set myself to work to be the best mother in the world.

When I first told him I was pregnant my husband was angry, but afterward he became very considerate and treated me kindly. I realised that he already felt himself a loving father, completely instinctively, and that he felt no anxiety about the responsibilities which we would have to face.

His mother, for whom our purely civil marriage had been a nightmare, implored me when she first heard the news to make a "Christian" of the child, and I promised her I would, remembering that papa had made the same concession to my mother about us. But I also told her that I would not tolerate either her or her daughter's interference in the upbringing of my child. I did not want to inflict on my child any of the barbaric practices still thriving in the area. I did not want them to procure amulets for the cradle, or swaddling clothes for the infant, or any other dangerous prophylactics. To all this she responded with a boldness much in contrast with her usual timidity: "Well, I've had ten children and nursed all of them!" Of these ten, six had died in infancy, and the survivors could count themselves lucky. She thought that all children had to go through at least five or six illnesses, during any of which God might claim them to be his angels.

The poor old woman! She helped me cut out and tack together shirts and vests, and revelled in the work. In the peace of our little room she seemed calmed by a sense of ease — of which she felt unworthy, like all those who suffer all their lives and therefore believe they are not intended to be happy. And shortly afterward something else was to happen for which she would hold herself responsible.

Coincidentally, both my husband and father-in-law suddenly took to their beds: my father-in-law with long-neglected rheumatism, my husband with a severe attack of angina. The old man's illness didn't seem very serious, but his wife and daughter stayed at his bedside, and I found myself left alone to look after my husband as his illness rapidly grew worse. One night I thought he was having difficulty with his breathing. The doctor adopted desperate remedies: the illness had all the symptoms of diphtheria. He couldn't very well hide this from me, despite my condition, but I felt absolutely certain that I would do nothing to risk the life in my womb, and this kept me calm and confident. I didn't let my husband know how dangerous his illness was, but nursed him through the night, feeling that carrying out my duty in a spirit of goodwill could never result in harm to my child. After a few days the crisis passed. Only then did I tell my husband what a narrow escape he had had. His pleasure was short-lived, however. His father's condition deteriorated: two weeks later he was dead.

Although it was the first time anyone at all close to me had died, I wasn't grief-stricken—perhaps because I was at the limits of my endurance, and perhaps also because all my mental energy was concentrated on the event around which I had now focused my entire life.

The rhetoric of mourning was revealed to me. My husband and sister-in-law, who had never so much as smiled at their father since they were children, who had never thought about him except as a provider of money, proclaimed tremendous anguish—and perhaps genuinely believed that they were suffering terrible pain.

These events caused me to reflect on some of the things I had heard my father say. He had often talked to me about the terrible hypocrisy which reigned in the neighbourhood. In reality, he said, parents, whether of the middle or working class, were exploited and ill-treated by grown-up children, and no one ever complained. In particular, many mothers suffered great cruelty in total silence. Not one wife was honest with her husband about the household accounts; not one man took his wage packet home complete. Few couples were faithful to each other, and my father pointed out to me the mistresses of several men he knew—women living on their own or with their husbands, with unacknowledged sources of income. A short time before, a household had been torn apart by a terrible parricide: the son had surprised his own wife and his father making love. Many girls sold themselves, not because they were starving, but because they loved to dress themselves up. By the age of fourteen no young girl was still completely innocent, but all of them stayed at home, boasting about their integrity, defying the neighbourhood to testify against their honesty. Hypocrisy was thought a virtue. Woe betide anyone who spoke against the sanctity of marriage and the principle of paternal authority! Woe betide anyone who tried publicly to show these people up for what they were!

It was for taking a public stand on all this that my father had been so savagely condemned and had earned the hatred of a handful of people, people utterly inferior to him. His exposure of their hypocrisy had made him a social outcast.

And this was the environment into which my child would be born!

I awaited the birth with intense absorption, warding off each attack of despair, preoccupied with detailed preparations. I was aware that in the supreme moment of giving birth I would acquire a new dignity, and this moved me. The image of my mother was constantly with me: my young mother in those far-off and unknown days, when I was a baby. I felt an overwhelming need for an affection as warm as that with which I was surrounding my eagerly awaited child . . .

SEVEN

When in the uncertain light of a rain-filled April dawn I first placed my lips against my son's small head, I felt that I had, for the first time, experienced heaven in my own life. I was filled with a sense of overflowing goodness. I had become a tiny particle of an infinite universe, ecstatic, unable to think or speak, cut off from my past and future, adrift in a radiant mystery. My eyes were full of tears. I clasped my baby in my arms: he was alive, alive! My body had created him, my spirit lived inside him: he already contained all of me and he could demand anything of me, now and forever. I gave him life for a second time, in that long gentle kiss, promising him that I would give myself to him, in a perfect commitment.

I saw my husband cry with joy, I saw how everyone was smiling, and then I dozed . . . Later, rested and more comfortable in fresh linen, I remember smiling at my sisters when they came to see me, and looking at myself in a mirror one of them brought for me. I saw my rosy cheeks, my radiant eyes and open face: I seemed the very image of maternity. Later, my father came, and the doctor recounted to him the different stages of the birth: the first labour pains at two in the morning, a rapid progress toward the climax, half an hour of suffering, the last contraction, and finally the relief as we heard the first cries of an exceptionally robust and perfectly formed baby. His words reached me like news of a distant event, recollected only dimly by my senses. Yes, my body had been wrapped in coils of fire, my forehead covered with icy perspiration, I had become — was it for an instant or for an eternity? — a poor creature pleading for compassion, all else forgotten, whose hands compulsively gripped imaginary supports in the air above, whose voice had changed to a hoarse death rattle. Yes, at the point at which my son was entering the world I had thought I was about to die, had screamed out rebellion in the name of my lacerated flesh, my guts which were being devoured, my consciousness which was being torn apart... When was all this? Before, before! Before I knew myself a mother, before I looked into the eyes of my little one; after that moment it was as if none of this had ever taken place, because that warm little body in its baby clothes was in the bed beside me, because I felt a delicious relaxation creeping through my limbs, because that day I had given my breast to that little mouth and had heard from it a sound which made me want to both laugh and cry.

My most insistent preoccupation throughout the whole period of pregnancy had been whether or not I would be able to breast-feed my child; even the night before I had said to myself that I would willingly endure a few days more pain if that would ensure that I could feed the child myself. So, when I saw his little mouth sucking avidly, and heard his throat gulping down the liquid which flowed from my breast, and then saw his satisfied face as he lay asleep in my arms, I had a fresh moment of unutterable excitement. For a week I lived in a magnificent dream. I had boundless emotional energy, which warded off exhaustion and allowed me to think that I was beginning to take control of my life. While my son slept in his white cot beside me, and silence and darkness reigned in the room, I let my fantasies roam free, and two distinct plans came together in my mind: the first, which concerned my son, brought together all the thoughts I had had in the months before the birth, and outlined the serious pleasures of my task as nurse, teacher, and companion; the other was my first overwhelming impulse towards giving artistic expression to a torrent of new, distinctive emotions—emotions which I had never before articulated but which were now flooding over me. I began to outline the plan of a book in my mind. I thought I would write it as soon as I was stronger, in my long hours of rest beside the cradle. And sometimes, as I dropped off to sleep, I smiled at the grandeur of my images.

On the seventh or eighth night after he was born, as I turned to the suckling baby murmuring words of love, I saw his childish face form a smile, a long, miraculous smile, full and splendid. It had such a powerful effect on me I thought I would faint.

I did not believe the doctor when he said the next morning that the smile could only have been a muscular contraction, absolutely unconscious, produced by physiological pleasure in that moment of satiety and rest. It was much more soothing to think that there was already a current of sympathy between me and my child, and that in the mystery of the evening, charmed by the sight of my loving face, he had already affirmed his human existence!

The doctor looked at me affectionately; he warned me not to excite myself and above all not to worry, as I had begun to do, if the baby seemed to be losing weight; he assured me once more that my milk was sufficient and that I had nothing to fear.

All that day I warmed myself with the memory of that smile, which seemed only a prologue to the bliss my son would bring me as he grew up.

In the evening my sisters and their governess came to see me. I was chatting quietly to them, sharing my deep contentment, when my sister-in-law joined us. Giving no indication that she had seen my visitors, she kissed her nephew, then stood apart, glowering and silent. The others, after glancing at each other, went on calmly with the conversation, and when they left shortly afterward bowed slightly in the direction of the indomitable shrew. She didn't even wait until the door was closed before rushing towards my bed, furious, hurling insults. She had always resented my sisters because they never went to see her, but I had never seen her show her anger so openly. My husband intervened half-heartedly. I could feel only contempt for them both as I sank back, feverish, against the pillows. On the whispered advice of our maid, who had become anxious, I pulled the baby away from my breast. My sister-in-law was still beside herself with rage. She couldn't stop shouting . . . By the time she left I was exhausted, half-unconscious, unable either to reproach my husband or to explain the state I was in . . . That night the baby wasn't satisfied by his feed and cried. On his morning visit the doctor found me shedding desperate tears over my son, whose mouth was sucking at my breast in vain.

I had no more milk. For the next fifteen days I tried every remedy, every diet, but to no effect. I was obsessed by the wish that I should be the only one to nurse my child, whatever the cost. The energy which had sustained me until then seemed entirely to have vanished; I cried and cried, quietly, like a child, watching my breasts, which would not swell, and finding to my despair that my child was losing weight. I had to resign myself to the thought of seeing his little head drawing food from another breast. This was a new sort of pain, physical as well as emotional, which devoured me and in the process blasted the magnificent dreams which had grown as I watched over the cradle; and I fought it indignantly, as a young man fights when he comes face to face with the monstrous injustice of early death . . .

I had to give in or the child would die. I managed to arrange things so that the wet nurse would stay with us and my son would still sleep by me. But I think that I hated the girl who took my place, with her stolid, classical face and her clumsy, heavy movements. Even she, however, did not have enough milk—now that my son had experienced hunger he had become a glutton. And after a week she in her turn was replaced. The new nurse, a mild-mannered woman with a calm, gentle face, finally soothed my anxieties about the child's health. Sensing my maternal jealousy, the poor woman even resisted the temptation to kiss the child to whom she gave her milk, and did her utmost to follow the rules I had made. Because of her efforts I was able to overcome my distress and resign myself to overseeing the tasks I could not perform myself, while I tried to restore my shaken health. I can still see myself, in a white dress and with a white face, buried in an armchair as I tried to get warm in the May sun and listened distractedly to the doctor. He came to see me every day, and was the only person who brought an element of spiritual companionship into my life. I was now suffering from persistent anaemia: I didn't worry about it, but it affected my nerves, over-stretched as they already were. My child's health had become a total obsession, driving me to excess: I must have been cruelly demanding to the wet nurse, even though I was, in calmer moments, extremely grateful to her. My son grew like a flower between his two mothers. As time went on I loved him more and more extravagantly, and felt that everything that was of value in me was contained in him. My life became completely concentrated in his small body.

I didn't notice that my husband had become utterly indifferent to me, nor did I realise that I had stopped thinking about him. I now tolerated him only out of habit. He was the father of my child; one day my son would have to respect him, and my behaviour towards him was motivated by a stubborn desire to maintain an illusion of his integrity, so that he might seem worthy of me and of his son. I was grateful whenever I saw him touched and happy at some new sign of our child's development, and grateful too when he shared my incessant worries and put up with my nightly irritability and my discontent with everything except the way my son smiled at me.

Towards the end of the fifth month the nurse lost her daughter, and this diminished her flow of milk. It seemed that a Jonah was presiding over the nursing of my infant. A new woman came to the house, a boisterous, shapely brunette, with a very different character from the woman who had just left. I had never encountered anyone more eccentric, unreasonable, and imperturbable. For months, as the baby grew adorably in grace and strength, I waged a continuous battle with myself in order to tolerate this peasant woman. She had a ringing, fatuous laugh, whether she was being obsequious or impertinent, a laugh which offended me all the more whenever I saw it exploding only inches away from my son's little face.

My husband was critical of my attitude, and this made me even more bitter. Didn't he realise that I was irritated by her defects because I wanted her to be a second mother to my child and these mannerisms deformed her? . . . I feared, most of all, that my son would suck in the germs of that coarse, bilious nature along with her milk. And seeing my husband so insistent on defending her, a suspicion entered my mind which offended everything I valued in life.

This suspicion horrified me so much that I shrank from finding out if it was true. In fact, apart from the energy I expended on the child, I was increasingly unable to look around me, to want anything or to do anything: it was as if mental weariness had been superimposed on physical exhaustion. I was dissatisfied with myself, reproached myself with having neglected my best qualities, with having repressed and concealed all there was in me that was deeply and honestly felt. But in fact it wasn't illness but a fundamental deficiency in my life which was making itself felt. The mother and the woman in me couldn't live together. That rosy, breathing infant gave me pleasures and anxieties which were essentially uncomplicated but which seemed constantly at odds with a sense of instability, a strange oscillation between lethargy and excitement, desire and indifference. I couldn't explain where this instability came from, but the result was that I began to see myself as an unbalanced, incomplete person.

EIGHT

I recorded all the major events in the life of my fragile, precious child in a little notebook: by now I lived and breathed for him alone, as if he was sufficient for me. Those notes, together with some hurried observations about the first signs of his intelligence and my differing responses to them, were my first attempts to write.

I can still see my son's naked body as he lay in the bath, propped up by my anxious hands: he was beautiful, with a perfect beauty I contemplated with more timidity than pride. I imagined possible deformities and wondered if I would still have loved him had he suffered from any of them; but I always ended up telling myself that whatever he had been like he would have made life wonderful. I remember his incommunicable look, as radiant as a patch of blue sky, and his deliciously elegant mouth, his little head covered with fine chestnut hair, and his restless, tyrannous hands, always busy. And I see myself, leaning over his cradle for hour upon hour, day and night, often depressed but always conscious of an undertone of grave, almost mystical, joy. I was as necessary to my son as he was to me. Because of my watchful care he was a happy, healthy child; I was the only person who encouraged his development ceaselessly and obstinately. I was the only one who gave myself fully to him, therefore he really belonged to me alone; his father, grandmother, and the others enjoyed the drama, but I was the author of it. Everything he would ever learn would come from me.

The wet-nurse left before he was a year old. The following

spring and summer I began to go out with him in the sun. I held him up as he toddled unsteadily, or picked him up and carried him across the fields or along the seashore, panting sometimes but also smiling at the physical effort. What did we say to each other, my son and I, during this time? I hardly remember. He would call out "Mamma," and, all attention, I would respond. Sometimes I wrote letters to friends or did the factory accounts with him on my knee; or else I read, stretching beside him on the rug as he played with his favourite toys. Sometimes a spark of cunning gleamed in his deep blue eyes, velvety between long lashes: he realised how omnipotent he was and that I would always give in to him. How could I deny anything to someone who looked at me with such adorable slyness?

My mother-in-law no longer complained that I refused to use her magic recipes against the evil eye and similar dangers. She was still in mourning, and whenever she came to see me she looked smaller and more exhausted than ever, but her face lightened as she watched her graceful grandchild. The local people said that her daughter now treated her abominably. She never complained to me, but I noticed that her figure was increasingly hunched and that she had grown more silent than before: I wondered if she was beginning to be dominated by feelings of bitterness.

After the baby was born, my relations with my brother and sisters improved. The governess had left their house for a better job, and no one had come to take her place. Every two months we went together to see our mother. By now she no longer asked to come home with us, and she was less and less responsive to our anxious questions. The doctors were worried because she was putting on weight and was gradually reverting to the language and expressions of a child. The others, realising that she was now completely isolated emotionally, became more specific in their criticisms of Father's behaviour, though they seldom discussed this with me. They were aware that I wasn't very happy, and pitied me. But they seemed to think that I wasn't a very sensitive person, and although I was distressed by this, I felt no incentive to prove to them that this wasn't so, or to try to win them over to my side.

Sometimes I met papa. He now rented the factory and cared only about increasing its profit. He never spared a thought for the situation of the children he had deserted, even though his own circumstances were now more comfortable. He treated my little boy like a playful animal. My husband, whom he had promoted to deputy manager, still annoyed him greatly. He had become entirely estranged from the life of the region, and there was too much venom in his criticisms for me to be able to tell which of them were justified; yet, even so, talking to him, I seemed once more to move into a more expansive world of ideas, and when I went back to our tiny rooms I felt suffocated, as if I was falling into a narrow well. Even my conversations with my friend the doctor failed to bring out, as my father could, the forceful and original aspects of my character.

Although I enjoyed hearing the doctor's sensible and often pessimistic opinions, he perplexed and sometimes disconcerted me. Perhaps it was the strong similarities in our tastes which made us such close friends, despite our different upbringing and education; but all the same, I lacked self-confidence, and he never made me feel secure about my own ideas. Yet how did I seem to him? For I was as careful with him as I was with other people not to act as if I was a woman who felt sorry for herself.

I was finding it increasingly difficult to maintain tolerable relations with my husband. Now even his egotistical affection for me seemed to have cooled. I developed new doubts about his fidelity when he defended an impudent factory girl, wrongly, against my father. Even so, he was still jealous and displayed it in increasingly tyrannical ways.

One day, when we were embroiled in some pointless argument, he stood up in a rage, seized a new dress I was about to put on, and tore it to pieces . . . I felt that it was really me he was attacking. He quickly regained his self-control and tried to make some excuse for his behaviour. I tried to forget it; I didn't want to dwell on the incident . . .

Sometimes I watched him. When he was with me he was always sure of himself, satisfied with his position, yet in front of his superiors or in a crowd he was fearful and indecisive. He seemed to lack all insight, so that he was equally incompetent as a lover and as an adversary. I thought him useless, extraneous to my existence. He wasn't aware of my scrutiny. When I looked down at my son I instantly forgot the chill of terror produced by my instinctive assessment, so revived and calmed was I by his smile.

That winter we started to spend two or three evenings a week again at our relatives' house. The doctor, some married businessmen, the secretary of the local council, the school teacher and his children, and sometimes my brother and a friend of his — a student who was almost always on holiday — regularly gathered there. Sometimes there were over twenty people in their drawing room. We listened to the secretary's repertoire of Neapolitan songs, gossiped, and had rather inconclusive discussions.

My sister-in-law was always there. I noticed with some amazement that she had decided to try to be elegant now that she had put away her mourning clothes, and that she was turning into a flirt. She was openly envious of girls younger and more graceful than herself. Luckily no one took much notice of her — except for the doctor, who had treated her some months before for persistent neuralgia, and would sometimes aim mocking comments at her, smiling enigmatically. She would bend her head without replying, as if confused by him.

It was clear that the doctor was pleased to see me taking part in these festivities. I didn't always like what went on there, but I had so little to amuse me I was glad to go. And I was treated with a respect I found flattering, coming as it did from people who were generally contemptuous of women; I was convinced that it was my air of being a polite and thoughtful little girl, rather than my husband's reputation for jealousy, which checked those men's behaviour and forced them to display their less philistine qualities.

One evening while the secretary was singing, I suddenly realised that the piercing eyes of a man sitting opposite me were fixed on mine in a way I had never experienced before. He was an "outsider," as the locals called anyone not born in the area. He had told us all that he liked to travel and had therefore lived abroad until just three years before. In fact, he could speak several languages and was certainly, apart from the doctor, the most well-educated and intelligent of the people I knew there. He had a small private income and lived with his wife and their beautiful baby son, who was the same age as my own.

Our two families had been friendly for only a few weeks: I found his wife somewhat unpredictable — there was always a slightly sarcastic expression on her white, consumptive face. Her husband was a fair-haired man of thirty, not tall, yet athletically built, and he had the most extraordinary voice — calm but ringing. His behaviour was always correct, yet it was hard to tell what he was thinking and I hadn't felt particularly interested in him. Indeed, no one had yet made up their minds about him. He and his wife had come to our district only because they hoped the climate would be good for her health.

But now the intensity of his gaze made me jump. What on earth could he want? It seemed to me that he smiled ironically, as if he was satisfied at having made me aware of his look; I felt his silent amusement like a slap in the face. But a sort of hypnotic compulsion made me seek out his eyes again; they were no longer smiling, they were dark, imperious, ardent. When I went to bed that night I was in a turmoil, as if an unknown enemy had suddenly declared war without my knowing why or what the outcome would be. For the first time since I was married, a man within my circle had dared to look at me as if my reputation for being proud and severe meant nothing to him. I was indignant, but I was also very surprised.

For several more such evenings I was followed wherever I went by those implacable blue eyes; but no sooner did they lose the commanding expression which had so alarmed me than they grew sensuous, as if he was living in an ecstatic dream. Normally he spoke very little. Whenever he could, he withdrew from the others and stood in a corner, staring at me, unnoticed by anyone else. One evening as he wished me goodnight he held my hand in his for a moment longer than was necessary, but never said a word. I walked home with my husband through the wintry countryside weaving fantastic stories in my mind. At home I found the baby sleeping, watched over by the weary servant, who immediately went home to her hovel. My heart contracted. Once in bed, I anxiously waited for sleep.

Next morning my head felt heavy. I looked down through the dining-room windows to the street and saw him loitering there. He looked at me but didn't acknowledge my presence. A moment later I left the window to go to play with the baby. That evening, before going out, I paused before the mirror as I had never done before.

During those evenings the schoolmaster's three children often whispered together, observing my sister-in-law's pleasure in listening to the doctor. Once my brother pointed her out to me, murmuring with a grin, "Your sister-in-law's secret is coming out into the open . . . The doctor can't be very proud of his conquest!" I wanted to ask him to explain what he meant, but was afraid to. What was he saying? What could there be between my friend and that poor creature? It puzzled me, and then I felt strangely uneasy. I felt more alone than ever, unnoticed by everyone except that man . . .

By now his intentions were quite clear: he liked me and wanted me to know it. So . . .? What did he expect of me? What did he imagine might happen? Sometimes at night we left the house of our relatives and walked along the road together with him and his wife. He looked at me over her slim shoulders with his penetrating gaze, and it was only after a time that I could drag my eyes away. Then I would look at the other two, walking unsuspectingly beside us. "What are you doing?" I would ask myself. "Are you really going to let this continue?"

It is true that all I needed was the energy to make a decision. By now I thought about him all day long, whatever I was doing; everything else came second—even my son could no longer release me from my obsession. Yet I didn't feel passionate or even friendly toward him. My heart didn't beat faster when I thought of him—how could it? I hardly knew him, and besides he only seemed to see me as a flower ready to be plucked from its uncaring owner... All the same, he must have realised too that this charade couldn't go on for very much longer.

New Year's Eve passed. One day when my husband was away I received a letter. In it my admirer pleaded with me to send some confirmation of the hopes he now cherished in his heart, aching with love and pain. I had to smile. I could see that some resolution was near, even though I found his words unconvincing. Why should I reply?

Much as it astonishes me still, I did reply. I don't remember exactly what I said, but I advised him to allow his heart manfully to reclaim its peace and to brush away what was only the shadow of a dream. I asked him, too, to forgive me for having through weakness allowed empty hopes to grow. My letter was sincere, and though it had an edge of irony it still expressed my regret for the sterility of our feelings. Some of my weariness, the bitterness I felt about my resignation to fate must have emerged in it. I reread it before I sent it, and thought that in it I had crystallised my own state of mind—it seemed to have been written for myself alone. As I became aware of this I went through what I imagine a breakdown to be; for the first time I understood how appalling my isolation was. I felt the chill of being twenty and deprived of love, and burst into wild and desolate tears. And when I became calmer, I realised just how extensive was my misery.

I stayed at home for a few days after I had sent my reply. He didn't answer, and I felt both saddened and relieved by this. Without knowing it, he had made me look very closely at my life, had forced me to reveal to him the extent of my despair. I couldn't forget him all the same and gradually began to feel that I was being taken over by a deadening tor-por: it was neither resignation nor was it yet rebellion, but simply the anxiety that some unexpected change in my life would cut me off from this new awareness of my pain . . .

Before very long I found his silence intolerable. A few nights later I went back to the house at which we had first met. As soon as I entered I saw the face I feared. He turned white: his eyes avoided mine; later on I heard him saying in a hoarse voice that he had been ill for the last few days. The next morn-ing, secretly, a second letter came. This one was violent. He told me that his love couldn't be controlled, nor could he con-ceal his passion: he had nothing to forgive me for, but every-thing to ask for, now and forever, and that he held me, and my right to happiness, more important to him than his own, so unworthy was he of me . . .

I couldn't tell if it was a skilful tactic or the truth — whether he was used to manipulation and had had experience of such affairs, or if I was going through such a crisis that any voice which offered me liberation was irresistible.

I no longer know what I replied. I know I let my feelings speak. I'm sure I complained miserably, confident that he would understand, that behind that taciturn appearance I had found a fellow spirit. I told him that the next day I would cele-brate my fourth wedding anniversary . . . and that my life was finished, that only my son was still able to give me any hap-piness . . .

And still I refused to examine my turbulent emotions. Instead I waited to see how things would turn out. My brain was too paralysed to allow me to imagine for myself what the course of events might be.

I knew that his wife hadn't long to live, and knew too that she was an irritating woman, so cold that she could neither give nor accept affection. But I didn't consider that sufficient reason to deceive her; nor did I think that I had any reason to take revenge on my husband. I even deceived myself into thinking that I was sincerely sorry for the two of them. It was mainly the thought of my child that weighed me down. But this too became weaker, and all the issues lost their clarity . . . Perhaps I had come to the false reasoning of many women who reconcile love for their children with marital deceit. Was I really prepared to imagine such a cowardly future, sharing my happiness between the pleasures of motherhood and the embraces of a lover?

I don't think so. I was, however, attempting to persuade myself that at last life was offering me real love and that I should accept it, taking myself and that other part of me, my baby, simply and loyally to the man who deserved us both. I so much wanted to love and be loved, to give myself without reserve and to feel I truly belonged to a man. That way I would learn to live, would be born again!

How many days did I struggle with my feelings? I no longer know, but certainly not many. When I saw him again, at a dance organised by our friends, and he carried me off in a whirl of spinning steps, whispering brief words of love, and I realised that in that whole extravagantly decorated room not one person had reached the heights of a dream such as ours . . . and I felt young, rich blood rushing through my veins and saw, in a flash of lightning visible only to me, that his ardent words were true, that I was a beautiful woman, the only beautiful woman there . . . then I told myself that this man would be able to kindle a fire which might utterly consume me . . . and I thought my destiny was fixed, and with that thought I tasted my first, my only intoxication.

My husband was suddenly called away again for several days. I was frightened when he told me of this. It was a grey, freezing afternoon; he was sitting by our stove, and I went to him and clasped his knees as I used to do once, during our half-forgotten romance. For a moment I forgot that I owed my unhappiness to him. The only thing that concerned me was that when the approaching disaster came he, like me, would be utterly overwhelmed by it. He stroked my hair for the first time in months, and observed how changed was my face. He was touched, and found tender words for me when he saw my surging tears. Was he perhaps still in love with me? I didn't know: all I knew was that I could never have loved him, since the woman in me had only come alive during these past weeks — a woman with a fierce desire for the unknown, ready to throw herself in full recognition of her own worth on the mercy of a man much stronger than she . . .

What could I say to my husband? I let him go. The other man knew I was alone and with great daring simply sent me a note, asking me to expect him the next evening. The die was cast. I realised that I had arranged a lovers' rendezvous.

He came. The situation was new to both of us, and we were both so embarrassed that we almost forgot the shared excitement of the preceding days. For some reason I found him very clumsy as he sat facing me on the other side of the round table, fumbling with words and deprived of his usual air of bravado. I was rigid and mute, not elated at all. Overcome with shyness, I kept one ear trained on the room where my little boy was sleeping.

I can only remember odd bursts of conversation: "Certainly we both have obligations, two-fold obligations, but you can't deny how you feel... Your heart has its demands as well... You needn't belittle your obligations, you needn't make anyone else suffer..."

What else did he say: He didn't find it easy to talk, and I didn't help him.

"No one else need suffer...we will be able to reconcile..."

Our obligations? He became confused. Then he pulled himself together, stopped explaining and took my hands, his eyes brightened as he told me that he loved me and that I certainly loved him, and that we would soon be happy, he called me *tu*. He stood up and pulled me to him, kissing me suddenly on the mouth. When I protested and moved away, he declared yet again that he wanted nothing which I didn't feel myself spontaneously ready to give. It was enough for him, he said, to know that my heart was his, to hear this from me occasionally, and to read in my letters the passionate words which so intoxicated him. He drew me close again, and, leaning against his chest, with his cheek next to mine, I suddenly felt that he was a drowning man and was trying to pull me under with him.

Suddenly, violently, I pushed him away. He grabbed me, started to maul me... I had a flash of memory. He was just like my husband! I felt sickness rising to my throat and burst into hysterical laughter.

He was so astonished that he let me go. I flung open the outer door and ran into the other room.

After a time I heard the street door being carefully closed. Once more I was alone in the house, alone with my child, who was still breathing peacefully. I neither looked at him nor touched him. He was my one pure love. I undressed rapidly and took him in my arms only when I was under the bedclothes, biting the pillow in my pain and wishing I could die...

NINE

Until that day I had been confident of my sound grasp of moral principles, principles so simple and obvious that I could base my life on them, never doubting them, secure against any test. Even if the reason for existence escaped me, even if I had felt my enthusiasm, my rebelliousness, and my pride gradually diminish over the years, even if I constantly betrayed and rejected my own individuality, I had never lost my belief in human will. Up till then I had never been able to understand how people could be defeated or collapse spiritually simply because of their emotions or their sensual needs. I had first experienced great pain in my relationship with my father, because I had discovered human weakness in a man I thought a god, and had felt it more important to admire people than to love them. When I agreed to marry a man who had oppressed and assaulted me when I was young and unprotected, I had believed that I was obeying nature, that my destiny as a woman was forcing me to acknowledge an inability to go through life on my own. But I had not wanted this destiny to be more powerful than me, and had hoped that if I accepted it as a full human being, I could make it my own.

Was I now going to allow my already wretched life to become the plaything of this outsider? How did I know that he wasn't mocking me? Was I finally to admit that I really was an unstable, irresolute woman, at the mercy of everyone around me, an easy prey to the demands of those with whom I came in contact?

My immediate response that night was to wish I could die.

In fact I slept and woke again: I had to pick up my baby and make his breakfast, I had to look after the house. Life here went on so impassively, but in my books and magazines I read about evolution and struggle . . . I flung open the windows to let the sunshine and the sea air into these rooms where the memory still lingered of the few radiant dreams I had had when I still felt boundless hope for myself as a woman and as a mother.

Then my twenty years rebelled . . . Why had I never tasted a moment's happiness? Why couldn't I find love, a love stronger than duty or need? I demanded to know, with all my heart. This man had enslaved me now for many weeks; he had discovered a way to dominate my thoughts . . . Why? Why was I alone, unloved, parched, yet filled with desire . . .?

Him? Was it really him I wanted, that miserable wretch who, the night before, stripped of all poetry and illusion, had appeared such a brutal and ridiculous figure? Suddenly I felt seized with anger against myself, but this quickly fell away, giving place to a deep feeling of shame. I had betrayed my own ideals. What little I had made of myself, the modest yet splendid figure of dedicated motherhood, I had thrown at the feet of a philistine, a stupid egoist, who wanted to trample me down as if I was simply a plant growing in his path. Had I really fallen so low? My insane desire for a new life must have blinded me. The life I wanted was mistaken and degrading . . . I would confront my husband: we were equal now, although I was more despicable than he because I realised how low we had fallen.

A few days later I took the baby to play in my father's garden. I had just returned home — an armful of flowers was still lying on the table — and I was gloomily trying to work out what my future might be, without success, when to my surprise I saw the doctor coming towards our house. He had a strange look on his face. He should have been making his professional rounds at that time.

In a few words he told me why he had come. He had just been at the house of my abortive lover. His wife had found one of my letters in his pocket that morning. She had been suspicious for some time, though her discovery hadn't particularly distressed her. She knew that she hadn't long to live, and besides, it wasn't the first time he had been unfaithful to her or the first time that she had realised how deeply she hated him. All she wanted was revenge. That was why she had called the doctor — she knew he was a friend of mine.

He had managed to make her give up the letter to him and to promise not to talk about it. He handed the letter to me. My face crumpled under the insult and I burst into tears — and all the kind young man could do was nervously to repeat my name . . .

We clasped hands, and this silent pact of friendship seemed to give us both some comfort.

What did he imagine had happened? How could I explain?

He told me what he thought we should do to ward off disaster. For his part he promised to help all he could: he would spare no efforts on my behalf.

"But don't have him here again. Promise?"

I didn't reply. He stood up, and only then, as I took his hand again, did the lump in my throat dissolve; I managed to stammer out that I thought I hadn't done anything which would make him lose his respect for me, and then broke off with a sob.

"I believe you," he said, watching me sadly.

I brooded on my humiliation for two days. When my husband found out he would interpret the incident in the crudest way possible, and this thought drove me to inarticulate revolt. I felt an increasing urge to tell him myself about my failed attempt to find a new life, so that he would finally understand me and send me away from his house, in full recognition that I didn't belong to him, that I could give myself to another man, and that perhaps one day I really would. But I was in such emotional chaos that I found all determination ebbing away, and with it went my sense of my own identity. Despairingly I felt that I must give up all my preconceptions about myself and who I was.

The other woman either couldn't or wouldn't keep the incident a secret; she unburdened herself to a friend, and the shameful, incredible piece of gossip spread until it reached the ears of a ringleader of the local clerical party, a man nicknamed "the little lawyer."

On hearing the first rumours the doctor came to see me again. He told me that we must act as if everything was a slanderous lie.

I found him increasingly agitated; he was watching over me. What was behind his concern? I couldn't look for a reason then — when the outlook was so bleak . . . But I hadn't forgotten the suspicions I had had about his relationship with my sister-in-law. He was as isolated as I in those hostile surroundings, and he, too, had capitulated and humiliated himself. Perhaps he recognised another victim in me. I felt that no one had ever been as close to me as was this gentle, depressed young man.

He returned that evening and asked if he could speak to my husband alone. I put the baby to bed, listening, as if in a daydream, to the continual murmur of their voices in the next room. Then they called me in; the doctor had told my husband that the "little lawyer" for his own amusement had been spreading rumours about the evenings we spent at our relatives' house, in particular the recent dance. I and another woman were the main targets of his gossip; she was alleged to have several lovers, I only one — platonic as yet, since all they could find to talk about were glances from the window and an exchange of letters . . .

The doctor was his usual calm, good-natured self, eager to reassure me; he had advised the other woman's husband and now mine that they should demand an explanation from the scandalmonger. This was the only way to stop his insolence once and for all and show him that his talk didn't frighten anyone.

My husband turned pale, but he kept his self-control. And at first when we were alone again he managed to restrict himself to criticising my flightiness and complaining about my new love of socialising; according to him it was only a way of my showing off how elegant and charming I was. If you wanted peace in a small town like ours you must never go beyond your own front door.

But he had his doubts about the doctor's story, and gradually his words took on an acrimonious and bullying edge. He was one of those people who are so whipped up by the sound of their own voice that when the final storm comes they end up in a paroxysm. I knew that nothing would stop him now. He was well on the way to a full-scale inquisition; I could feel his suspicions growing and intertwining in his mind. Unable to gain control of himself in any other way, he demanded that I deny all the insults he had hurled at me, and that at the same time I should tell him I loved only him. His contorted face turned purple. His eyes were nearly popping out of his head. He terrified me. I felt suddenly that I was a tiny, defenceless creature at the mercy of a blind, bestial power. I became speechless, rigid with horror.

Then, equally suddenly, his passion sparked off a similar rage in me. I made my decision. Why should I lie? I had made an appeal to that other man. Perhaps I had even loved him! I had also rejected him, just as I had rejected my husband, and I hated the two of them . . . Let him drive me away! Let him kill me! I could feel his implacable vanity mounting, and I sprang to my feet in an outburst of my own. He asked me no questions about my story, instead he threatened me, making more and more accusations. He didn't believe me; he told me I must have given myself to the other man, and that I had to admit it to him . . .

I remember nothing more. I can still see myself thrown to

the ground, kicked away like a piece of dirt, and I can still hear his stream of revolting insults, liquid, boiling like molten lead. As I lay with my face against the marble floor I wondered if he would kill me. With a strange tranquillity I began to wonder whether, if I died, my soul would ever in any way be reunited with those of my mother and my son.

I also have a confused sense of my despairing anger when, after a horrific night in which my face was alternately spat upon and kissed and my body became no more than a poor inanimate shell, I realised that I was being asked to simulate suicide... "I must kill you myself; but I don't want to go to prison: they'll have to believe that you did it..."

For days and weeks I endured silent and useless anger, recurrent despair, appalling physical agony, and then fear of madness... Everything is enveloped in mist: I can no longer distinguish the sequence of suffering, delirium, and stupor. My father was told about the situation and attempted, together with the doctor, to persuade this despicable lunatic to forgive me and to accept that it had only been a momentary aberration. My mother-in-law and sister-in-law were worried by the whiff of scandal. Anything rather than public disgrace! And, all together, they surrounded me like characters out of a nightmare: they believed me a slut, but they wanted to keep me alive because they were afraid of what might happen if I died.

Every night he tortured me; every day he felt remorse and promised to try to calm down, to forget. Perhaps he was frightened when he saw what he was doing.

Meanwhile life outside had to go on as if nothing had happened. I had to go out with my husband, and sometimes our baby came too, like a radiant little flower trapped between two parents who hated each other.

My reputation had already become such a public matter that the members of the two political groups in the town had to take sides over me. Even if the democrats privately despised me, they still had to sing my praises in public. I was snubbed by the clerical faction, dominated as they were by the lawyer and the parish priest, who insisted that I was a fallen woman. And I was still worried about what attitude the man who had caused this odious dispute might adopt. His wife was now so ill that her parents had taken her away, but more than one person had noticed his walks beneath my window. It was within his power to take up the position of declared lover. And when the doctor had indicated that he might do this, I became afraid.

One day my sisters dragged me to see our mother. Almost four years had now passed since she had been moved to her dismal asylum. She had completely lost her memory and didn't even recognise us. There was only the occasional spark of life in her eyes. She examined our dress material, our ribbons, and our hats as if she was a child; her monosyllabic speech, spoken in an unrecognisable hoarse voice, was all that distinguished her behaviour from that of a one-year-old. She had put on even more weight since our last visit, and her tiny, delicate features were by now almost submerged in her fleshy cheeks and chin. Yet sometimes they looked tormented, as though they still lived and wanted to remind us of the subtle and sensitive person she had once been. They seemed to ask us to remember.

As I kissed her grey hair I thought I heard a warning voice say, "You will never kiss her face again."

Going back along the road in the carriage that warning rang obsessively in my head. Outside everything was fresh and green; my sisters chatted to each other, and after the grim sight my mother had presented they seemed a picture of sweet innocence.

At home my child was waiting for me. He was two years old and he loved me, oh! he loved me with all the strength of his little heart. He was intelligent, strong, and handsome, and when I looked into his eyes I could see some of my mother's mildness there. He wanted to tell me about his day. Since his father was in a bad temper, we left him alone; when I put my son to bed, I rested my hand against his warm cheek until I could tell from his breathing that he was asleep. Then I went back into the dining room.

That day my husband had met the man he assumed to be my lover, and imagined that the man had looked at him sarcastically. His rival had been with two friends. They must know all about it. What were they all thinking? What did they know? For God's sake, I must tell him.

I was lying on the sofa, unable to move. To tell the truth I couldn't really hear what he was saying very clearly. My life seemed to be unfolding before me, narrated in a few scenes, and I seemed to be watching this drama from another shore, through another person's eyes. The episodes were brief, unpleasant to look at. When my son knew about all this, what would he think? I was certain that if he had been able to understand what was happening and talk to me that evening, he would have begged me to take him in my arms and go away into the night with him, facing poverty if necessary, hunger and death if need be.

"You're not saying anything. Why aren't you talking? What are you hiding from me? Are you going to drag us through the mud again? Tell me, tell me!"

And once again I found myself on the floor. I felt him kicking me, twice, three times. I heard him repeat his obscene insults, followed by fresh threats.

As I lay stretched on the tiles, feeling a sort of comatose relief even though my eyes were open, he left the room, slamming the door after a parting insult.

Had he woken the baby?

No. When I could finally move I dragged myself through the dark rooms to the child's bedside. "Oh, my son, my son. Your mother will never see you again . . . She has to—she can't live, she's too tired, and she doesn't want you to suffer . . . Although you have her blood in your veins, you will be stronger, you will win through . . . perhaps one day someone will tell you that your mother loved you as she never loved anyone else; that she wasn't wicked and that her dream was that you would grow up to be happy and good . . ."

I went back to the dining room. In the cupboard there was a phial of laudanum, almost full. I swallowed about two-thirds, until my throat no longer tried to vomit up the bitter liquid. Then I lay down on the couch. In a short time I felt drowsy and my body began to relax . . .

When my husband came back an hour later, he first thought that I was pretending to be asleep; he started once more to abuse me, though less violently than before. I could hear his voice in the distance. He must have suddenly seen the phial on the table. He bent over me, realising what had happened. Taking hold of the glass with the rest of the poison in it, he threw it into the street. Dimly I welcomed the thought that nothing could save me now.

Then two women came. My mother-in-law stoked the fire and heated some water, and my sister-in-law chanted spells over me . . . afterwards my husband came and cried at my feet. I watched everything as if through a veil, feeling no pain; I was almost prepared to believe that I was dead already and that my spirit was watching over the last convulsions of my mortal remains.

A woman shook me and gave me some water, but I couldn't swallow it. She produced a piece of paper. "At least write down that you did it, so that your poor dog of a husband won't be in trouble too!"

Who knows if the smile of pity which flickered in my mind sketched itself on my parched lips? She put the pen between my fingers, but I couldn't keep hold of it. At that moment the doctor arrived. I managed to make a gesture of refusal as he held out a glass; surely he at least, who knew the truth, would leave me alone.

But his firm, inflexible hand took hold of my head, and insistently forced me back to life.

PART II

TEN

To wish my life goodbye had been a simple decision, even though I had taken it in a moment of great confusion. My action seemed a response to a distant command, rather than an impulsive, immediate need. I had to end my life; the woman I had been until then had to die, trapped as she was in a situation from which there was no way out except the abrupt closure of death.

How long had this crisis been building up inside me? Surely since the day the turbulent man I later married disrupted my life so brutally, leaving me vulnerable to corrosive influences which gradually wore me down, physically and mentally. But I had not been aware of the psychological crisis he had initiated until the last moment; all I knew was that I was tired and frightened . . . my final defeat was unexpected, yet seemed entirely logical. I felt no rebellion; I wasn't even surprised. A cycle was being concluded, order was being restored — that was all.

From another shore . . . it was as if at the moment of trying to kill myself I was born again, able to see myself and the world through completely new eyes. I relived my childhood; for several weeks I was like a baby. Like a child I took delight in just *being*.

The sunlight, the tree tops I could see from my chair, my son's beauty, all gave me enormous pleasure. I was moved by everything that shone, that flowered, that appealed to my senses, everything in tune with the process of living. My intellect registered nothing. I knew that I had tried to kill myself, I knew that everything was changing around me and that eventually I would have to carry on once more. I watched sun and shadows rapidly following upon each other, feeling neither fear nor hope, neither revulsion nor doubt. At most I was vaguely optimistic, as if, however fearfully and half-consciously, I was abandoning myself to the future. I could still taste the bitter poison in my mouth, and my head felt remarkably weak — the slightest sound reverberated there, cutting me off from any clear perception of what was going on around me.

Yet, surprisingly, I hadn't suffered any serious physical damage; I was confined to bed for only a few weeks. Everyone, including my father, was kept in ignorance of the episode. The world outside followed its normal course, and after a time I even went back to my housework. At no point did I neglect any task to do with my son. Sometimes I looked in the mirror and observed that my drawn face had been changed by illness, and was even more graceful than before.

I can't remember any exchanges between myself and my husband during those first days. He must have been distressed by my calmness in the face of death, must have found it hard to explain; indeed, he seemed crushed by it. But what was it that he felt exactly? Was it remorse? Fear? Humiliation? Jealousy? Whatever his feelings, for him everything was merged into a single experience of pain, acute pain, mainly in the form of physical suffering which swung him from extremes of depression to high excitement. Perhaps too the doctor had pointed out to him that there was a danger that I might go mad. Once he had seen what chaos I would have left behind had I died, he must finally have recognised that I was the centre of our home, that I had created it, had indelibly left my mark on it. It seemed that he was beginning to think . . . But what did he think about? Did he realise how negligible his contribution to our relationship had been? Did he recognise that over the past four years all my dreams had been shattered? Was he aware that I might, as someone still growing up, have special needs? And did he regret his own foolishness in ignoring all the signs I had given of my deep unhappiness? Perhaps he had become more aware of my good qualities just at the moment he felt enraged with me for what he believed was my crime. He was still utterly convinced that he was in the right, but I had at least shown him that I could be resolute, even dramatic, and this seemed, inexplicably, to attract him once more.

I could tell that my body was now more sharply and painfully desirable to him than before, and this terrified me. Perhaps he didn't connect my invincible dislike of the sexual act with the way he had violated me when I was a young girl, but he must at least have reproached himself for his want of delicacy and lack of consideration for my immaturity. It must by now have become clear to him that he hadn't been able to arouse me as a woman or to communicate to me the exhilaration and the pleasures of healthy lovemaking.

He also felt completely isolated in his distress, convinced that no one could know how profound it was. His mother sympathised with him only for a simpler sort of pain; the doctor's attitude, while indulgent, was tinged with contempt. Sometimes he broke down in tears and confessed to me just how miserable he was.

He had stopped beating me. He went down on his knees before me, pleading my forgiveness for his lack of generosity, for having driven me to such a desperate act. "Stay alive, I beg you! For our son's sake!" Coming from a man usually so devoid of tender feeling, his appeal was heartrending. Seeing him in tears, I started weeping too, like a child, out of sympathy. I was so aware of my own failures that I started to think of him as a companion in misfortune — like me, the plaything and victim of blind destiny. I told myself without much conviction that we needed each other and must depend on each other if we were to re-establish our lives, even if only for the sake of our child.

Then a strange thing happened. One morning my husband began to question me again about the incident which had caused the two of us so much misery. Patiently and in minute detail I repeated once more the story I had told him so many times, and as I did so I realised that he was managing to keep calm and think about it. After each of my replies there was a long pause. Finally he took a deep breath and I realised that he was beaming with ill-concealed pride and pleasure. It became obvious that in all the inquisitions he had inflicted on me before, he had never taken in a word I was saying: he had never before been able to listen through to the end or to control his outbursts of insane jealousy . . . And now the whole episode was reduced in his mind to an insignificant encounter which could be forgotten. I could see that he was beginning to feel more important than the other man, that he was enjoying the other's humiliation, and that he felt grateful to me for having stayed true to him. I had made him feel more sure of me, more confident that I was bound to him and him alone, that I was his love, his woman.

June arrived resplendent, turning the fields golden. The sea must have appeared one massive glitter, a dazzling dream; I didn't see it that year, though, because I never left the house except in the evenings, when my husband sometimes took me for a short walk along the deserted railway track. Despite everything, he was still jealous of me: I could move round the house in the mornings because our maid was there, but I wasn't allowed into any room that looked on to the street. After lunch, for fear I should have a visitor, I was locked into the warm, cluttered bedroom, which looked out on to our wilderness of a garden. And there I stayed with my baby boy until six o'clock, when my husband came home.

My son slept for two or three hours. I sat sewing by the half-open window, sometimes finding pleasure in the play of sunlight on my thin hands as I drew the coloured thread through the linen. My imprisonment did not disturb me in any way. On the contrary, I took an almost sensuous pleasure in the negation of my rebellion through this harem-like captivity. I also told myself that I was still resting, simply gathering strength. I felt resigned and calm and increasingly sorry for my gaoler. Love? I had allowed him to hope that I might love him eventually, and, just as easily, he had let himself be convinced of this. When he held me in his arms I went rigid, but since I knew that sexually I could never be completely his, I wanted to compensate him in other ways. In any case, I was now certain that it was somehow intended that I should experience the pain of love rather than its joys...

My husband was placated by my tranquil docility. His references to the past now took the form of questioning me about the ways in which I had felt deprived. He openly accepted his responsibility for my feelings. I found it painful to answer him. I wanted to protect him, but sometimes I felt an irresistible need for relief. Even so, I found that our conversations demanded more of me than of him. My confidences were those of someone stumbling to find direction as they slowly regain their vitality and independence. They were made up of painful, impoverished, and fragmentary reminiscences of a time still cloudy in my mind, of a life I felt I had lost. As I talked, my face gradually lost its expression of gentle submission and became a frozen mask with lifeless eyes fixed on an indeterminate point — perhaps in the past, perhaps in the future. And I had to make a huge effort to pull myself back from that momentary retreat, about which even I understood little. Instead I tried to concentrate on guiding him back to happier thoughts. He, for his part, became absorbed in his own reflections, frowning sadly, like a child, attempting to understand something of great importance which only bewildered him and made him realise just how impotent and cut off he was.

We found some relief in our son, who helped us believe in our declaration of friendship. If anything gave me any happiness in those days it was he. I felt secure when he was there — at least he was happy, at least he gave me real pleasure. Though I never talked about it, I constantly remembered that in that night of total despair I had tried to imagine this child, created by my own body, alone in the world, not even knowing his own mother. I constantly reminded myself as well that I had never swerved in my devoted commitment to him. I now lived only for him, and because of him would live long enough to become a really splendid person, a mother in the best sense of the word. Perhaps this was just my fantasy. Yet I felt confident and serene whenever I bent over his cot to watch him sleeping, and realised how much I revelled in those exquisite features which already bore the stamp of such a definite personality. As I looked at him I asked him silently for his forgiveness and felt no shame as I did so. Perhaps this conviction that I had loved him unceasingly and that he had been uppermost in my mind even in my most insane moments made me feel worthy of his unconscious blessing; or I might have been reaffirming our biological bond, but I was certain that since his body had come from mine we must be animated by the same feelings and that since he was created by me, his life was bound to reflect mine. We had to struggle together to make a better life.

For the first time I realised what a healthy influence my child had on me. My feelings for him were deeper and simpler than before: they had lost their morbid and infantile aspects. I repeated his name to myself as if it was a talisman for the present and a symbol of the future: in the brief syllables of his name were contained for me all promise of hope and change.

For a time conditions at home remained unpleasant and monotonous. My sisters, not realising what was happening, had left on a short visit to our uncle in Turin. I was still locked up, with the excuse that I was being protected from inquisitive or malicious neighbours. Luckily my husband's mother and sister stayed away from me. Sometimes the doctor came to see me for a few minutes in the morning, but we didn't talk as much as we used to, and he was worried about my health.

Occasionally I referred, with a hint of a smile, to my continuing seclusion, and he would bow his head and frown. Then, with a visible effort, he shrugged the problem off, urging me not to be crushed by it and to ask for a holiday or to wait for better days. He would play with the child, and seemed relieved that even without fresh air and exercise he was still active and healthy. Each time he came he seemed more affectionate yet more reserved, as if he had grown to respect me and therefore felt warmer towards me. I was grateful for his visits. When he was there he at least brought a subdued echo of that world I thought I had finished with. He made me feel a part of it despite myself, and although those people had hurt me terribly, I still felt comforted to know that they were there.

It was from him that I found out that the repercussions of my escapade were not yet finished. Most people, in fact, had not believed the allegations; the majority thought it must have been merely a brief flirtation, ended almost before it began, but the opposition party had made an issue of it. My honour was in their hands, and it had to be vindicated.

According to convention this was my husband's responsibility. But the other man had started to act as if his honour was being directly challenged too, and was trying to force a quarrel so that he could demonstrate his superior gallantry — and, doubtless, to give the impression that he had his own reasons for defending me . . .

I was already so aware of local corruption and hypocrisy that I would not have been so upset by this caricature of morality were it not for what it revealed about my husband. For he too thought that there should be a duel — not for my sake but for his, because of the injury to his pride. But the prospect terrified him.

The doctor did everything he could to find a way out. After sundry negotiations the lawyer was persuaded to give my husband's supporters an elaborate and ingratiating document in which I was described as "completely respectable." My husband accepted it, and the two groups, having turned my reputation into a public matter, now seemed satisfied.

But I wasn't satisfied. My pleasure in martyrdom, my enjoyment of suffering had long since vanished. I could no longer suppress my frustrated determination to bring the truth of the matter out into the open. Much as I longed for peace, much as I wanted to forget, everything came to the surface again: I experienced once more the humiliation, the ignominy I had been through; I remembered the compromises and the lies, the lust, the intellectual cowardice, the irony and monstrosity of my situation . . . This agreement between the parties was the climax of a long day of horror, noonday resplendent over a devastated battlefield. Once I heard about it I could deceive myself no longer. I had been totally humiliated, utterly deprived. I couldn't even allow myself the luxury of making excuses for my oppressor. From now on I was condemned to carry my burden alone. And I began to see in my son another victim, bound as he was to two shackled prisoners. Would nobody ever save him, take him away to a place where he might learn real human freedom?

ELEVEN

Once the hateful agreement was concluded, my husband relaxed, and his obsession with our past relationship disappeared. He still restricted my movements by keeping me indoors, locking me in our room every afternoon, numbering my sheets of writing paper, and refusing me all visitors except the family, the doctor, and the maid. He did all of this while pretending that I was really completely free, and had I not been utterly depressed I would have laughed at the ingenuity of some of his subterfuges. But I was careful not to worry him, at times even anticipating his demands—although unlike previous times this came less from pity than from my determination to win some peace of mind for my child and myself.

Once more he became the obtuse, unthinking, unworried man I remembered from the past. Indeed, he was so determined to have an easy, uncomplicated life that he was even prepared to count himself lucky for what had happened, since it had delivered me defeated and resigned into his hands.

Without indignation, I watched him going back to his old ways: I felt that from that moment on I would be unable to do anything for him or for myself, and I no longer expected anything of him.

Yet my isolation seemed interminable; no one ever spoke to me; I had given up all hope and trust. When salvation came, it was in the form of a book.

It was the first book I had looked at for months. Father had sent it to me. He rarely saw me now. I thought he was bitter because I had never confided in him about my situation

and had refused to take refuge in his house, as he had invited
me to do, when my husband was treating me so badly. This
was a new book, written by a young sociologist, which was
making him a reputation throughout Europe. In it he described his travels in newly formed nations, and eloquently and
vivaciously invited sceptical and detached readers to think seriously about the problems arising from the contrasts between
different civilisations. He had a rare quality of intuition and a
brilliant capacity for synthesis, which made this forthright
though rather hasty work extraordinarily suggestive. I was also
impressed by his humanity, which shone through on every
page.

Had I been given instead a poem celebrating sensuality or
a discourse on mysticism at this point, the course of my life
might have been different. Or I might have rejected them, and
fallen back into incurable depression.

At the time it didn't seem like a revolution: I did not feel
particularly inspired, nor did I burst into tears as I read. His
argument ran parallel to thoughts I had been developing since
I was a child. Yet it was precisely because this book didn't hurl
me to the brink of some unknown that it seemed so providential. Subtly and urgently it was leading me back, without
my being altogether aware of it, to areas of my mind which
thronged with ideas I had never fully explored, reminding me
once more of riches neglected for too long. I now spent my
hours of imprisonment reading, and as I sat and thought
about what I had read while my child played, my fascination
slowly grew. I started to recall discussions from the past, from
childhood, and then added my own perceptions and my own
ideas to those of the author, unconsciously participating in the
construction of an intellectual world. Gradually my new
absorption in this work drove all my recent fantasies, all my
despair, into the background. And I began to make a virtue of
my isolation, feeling that at least it protected me from the
petty realities which reminded me how irredeemably wretched
life was.

When my husband's good sense finally overcame his jealousy and he took me out again for public walks, I felt unutterable loathing for the way people looked at me. I was terrified, too, that we would bump into the other man and that my husband's reaction would be to treat me with the same primitive brutality as before. Sometimes I saw that figure I knew so well in the distance, on his own or with friends, and I turned away — as did my husband, who watched him as anxiously as I. I felt a terrible coward. Why couldn't I regard his existence as completely irrelevant to me? I didn't exactly hate him, but I trembled at the thought of him, as if he was dead but had nevertheless once brought me and those near to me close to death.

I felt just as terrified when I was with my sisters. They were flourishing, but I was tormented by the thought that they might find out about me — that even years later people would repeat the story and they would come to hear it. My oldest sister was seventeen. For some months now she had been going out with a young engineer who came from a neighbouring town. He was inclined to be moody, but was one of those born to struggle. He was clever as well, with his head stuffed full of new ideas. My sister had been uncertain about starting a relationship with him; I had advised her to think hard and long before deciding definitely against seeing him. After a time she realised that she did love him and told Father so, adding that she intended to wait until he was established before marrying him. Father did not seem too happy about this, but since the marriage plans were to be delayed he made no objection.

So the two young people wrote to each other, went for walks together, and began to get to know each other better. His initial passion for her developed into real affection and a desire to protect her, and her liking for him into devotion and gratitude. Their recognition that each respected the other made them extremely confident of their future happiness. Their love affair was like a breath of fresh air in that gloomy house. The young man's influence began to predominate and had a really healthy effect on the others, and I too became more cheerful as I watched them. I supported the lovers whole-heartedly: their warmth for each other reminded me of my own early, unrealised hopes.

Towards the end of that summer my husband decided to take us on holiday. He wanted to relax and enjoy himself, and hoped the trip would restore my energy and do our son's health some good. We went to Venice, but although its beauty can soothe and relax the most despairing visitor, it held no charms for us and we spent a gloomy week there. Because of the child we couldn't explore the churches and museums as systematically as I would have liked. Yet even had we been able to, I would not have found my husband pleasant company. He knew nothing about art and had no natural appreciation either, so he often managed to spoil my spontaneous enjoyment. We were both thankful to leave. But even when we arrived in the Tyrol, where we had decided to spend the rest of our holiday, I couldn't shake off my depression.

Our hotel was in a marvellous setting: a narrow valley covered with fir and pine trees, surrounded by snowcapped peaks, where the air was always full of the sound of rushing waterfalls. This austere landscape with its distinctive country smells and the clarity of the sounds which echoed through the valley brought my childhood flooding back; these images had been buried in my memory for so long! If only I could stay with them now, alone with my son in these woods! I would bring him up surrounded by nature, ensuring that if ever in his future life he was overwhelmed by childhood memories it would never be an experience as painful as mine at that moment! His life would have some unity—he would feel an honoured guest in an hospitable world.

He was so happy trotting bravely down the grassy paths, calling to the cows, whose silver bells hung round their necks. Everyone in the hotel adored him, kissing him as if he were an exquisite flower whose fragrance they wanted to absorb. They appreciated his rarity, coming as he did from a part of Italy which these taciturn and melancholy Northerners would not even have been able to point to on the map.

My husband had never been to the mountains before and was overwhelmed with delight, coming out with amazed exclamations and naïve statements about what he saw. With his usual self-confidence he was thoroughly pleased with the refinement he had shown in choosing this way to spend our savings. And he desperately wanted my gratitude. Whenever he noticed me looking unhappy he felt angry and let down. What sort of woman was I? Would nothing satisfy me? Then, immediately repentant, he tried to persuade me to make plans for when we returned home. Perhaps writing would take me out of myself? Surely I must feel inspired by this magnificent landscape.

I listened wearily. He seemed like a stranger, talking about my health and giving me advice without knowing the first thing about me. Not that I myself knew what I needed at that moment. I was simply aware of my withdrawal into increasing isolation. It might be my duty to share my feelings with my husband, to be like an open book to him, but I knew full well that the bedrock of my feelings was unreachable. He wouldn't have been able to help me plumb the depths of what was going on inside me, even had he wanted to. I was constantly trembling internally . . . How can I convey or explain what those weeks were like? Sometimes, on waking, we have the distinct impression that we have spent a night densely packed with dreams and elaborate fantasies. In the fleeting moments between sleeping and waking we seem to have lived a deep inner life. But we cannot reconstruct our visions and we cannot re-create our night time thoughts. Only later do we realise that we have had an intimate forewarning of our future and that this is why apparently new actions never really surprise us.

The last afternoon we spent in the mountains remains

impressed in my mind's eye in an unusual way. Normally I absorb only the mood communicated to me by the places I visit: my feelings give shape to a scene, and that is what I commit to memory — the character of the place itself serves only as a framework for my feelings at the time. I can still see myself on the wide road which we were to take next morning for the interminable journey down to the railway line where it meets the Benaco River. Although the day was grey and damp, every sound could be heard with extraordinary clarity. Everything looked larger than it really was, awe-inspiring, monumental. As we walked slowly beneath the great ashen sky I felt that we were nothing but two minute, transitory points protected by the Earth herself, our stern but loving mother. For the first time in my life I held my arms out to this Earth like a reverent daughter. Time and space seemed to melt, carrying me away in their stream. I was Humanity in transit, without an objective, but at least possessing an ideal. I might be enslaved by laws, but I had the rebellious determination to break through them, to create another, better life . . .

That very day I had finished a second reading of the book which had so gripped me weeks before and which had been my wise and constant companion during my stay in the mountains. At this moment of revelation two strong feelings were fused inside me — one stimulated by the ideas I had developed while reading the book, the other provoked by the landscape I was about to leave. They produced a mystical fervour only experienced by great religious believers or great lovers — by those, that is, who worship a life above and beyond themselves. *I,* with all my misery, disappeared; all I could see was the beauty in humanity's effort to create something new within the grandeur of Nature.

My soul drank in the experience and jealousy preserved it. Though the revelation might not have been enormous, it acted on me like the sun's warmth on seeds germinating beneath the soil. They feel the warmth, and both fear and desire the full splendour of its rays.

When we arrived home the doctor told me that the other man's wife had died, and that he had left his son with her parents and gone to America—still in search of new adventures. Although he had no particular plans, he was determined never to return. That was the last I heard of him. The doctor left and I burst into tears. At last I was free. Life surely must be easier from now on. I would be able to move freely again and, more important, so would my child; my husband would feel more secure, I would be able to reclaim some of my independence. Now that this man was no longer there to remind me of the past I could calm down, secure once more in my own strength of purpose . . .

Why, then, did I weep? I wept because although a source of injury was being removed, a strip of healthy flesh was being torn away too—and because my faith in love was not yet dead. I wept as I offered my last farewell to the fantasy that had momentarily deceived me, because I still hoped I might find a powerful radiant love. Away he went, disappearing like a hurricane, this man with whom I had once exchanged promises of future happiness.

He would never return. Did he know that I would never forget him? That our brief meeting had transformed me? I am sure that he did not. I am sure that if someone, years later, was to mention my name to him, all he would feel would be passing irritation.

The taste of death was no longer with me, but my despair increased as I morbidly began to revel in the emptiness of my isolation, the desolation of my gloomy days. This obstinate unhappiness worried my husband, despite his own tranquillity and his desire for a quiet life. He began to insist that I must study, that I must write, a memoir of my own transgression if need be. His own behaviour filled him with such conceit that he suggested I might even celebrate his goodness in verse.

One day he brought home a packet of writing paper for me. Just looking at it made me blush for shame. How far could his insensitivity go? Nevertheless, a few days later, on a warm afternoon when my son was with my sisters, I found myself poised, pen in hand, over the first blank sheet. Oh, if only I could tell someone about my pain and misery! Even myself! Perhaps if I could tell myself about it in some new way it might have the power to shed some light on what had happened and on what would become of me.

So I wrote. Perhaps for an hour or two . . . I really don't remember how long. The words poured out, weighty and solemn. I tried to sketch a portrait of my state of mind. I examined my pain, I asked myself whether to suffer in such a way could ever be productive. I felt strange stirrings in my mind, like intimations of growth to come. I had never before felt that I had such resolute powers of expression, such an acute gift of analysis. What should I expect of myself? Should I join in the collective endeavours of the human race, the only thing that gave life any dignity? Should I use my resources in this way to gain some peace of mind? Or should I resign myself to a life without happiness, losing everything that might make my son respect and love me?

I stopped writing, ran to the bedroom, and fell to my knees on the very spot where so many nights before I had whispered to my son that I must kill myself. For some reason I called out my mother's name and started to weep. I had a sudden paralysing wish to pray, to call on the same supernatural power my mother must have asked for help when she was in despair. It was the first time that I had ever claimed to believe in divine intercession, and I clasped my hands together, hoping for a sign. Into my appeal I put all the desperation of someone who sees the long road they must travel, but feels too weak and exhausted to go on . . . I consciously forced myself to be humble. Perhaps I was afraid, in that moment of fervent idealism, that a new, different, even crueler disappointment lay in store. I begged my poor mad mother to intercede for me. I felt I must renounce all pride. Remembering her terrible defeat, I told myself how ridiculous rebellion was in someone as dogged by misfortune as she had been. The least of her wishes had been that her children should have some security; and if God had appeared to me then what would I have asked of him? That He should save my child from suffering and guide him to act always for the best . . . What if, like hers, my voice wasn't heard? What if this terrible cycle was destined to continue for ever?

As I knelt there I was interrupted by my husband. He would sometimes come home in the afternoon to make sure that I wasn't abusing my limited freedom. I leapt up, ashamed of exposing my momentary weakness to him. And then I realised that I was still a poor, sick woman, and had just been giving way to an attack of nerves.

Anxiously he asked me what was wrong. With a movement of my hand I tried to reassure him, but the tears began to flow again, copious, liberating. I was grateful for them. Eventually I calmed down, and suddenly I felt able to accept my stringent commitment to walk alone, to struggle alone, to bring to the surface everything that was strong, beautiful, and uncorrupted in me. Afterwards, I blushed with shame at my long, sterile path of suffering. I realised then that my self-neglect had bordered on self-hatred. And finally I savoured life again, relishing its taste as I had done when I was a young girl.

TWELVE

A strangely intense period followed. I lived now only for my reading, for my own thoughts, and for my son. To all else I was completely indifferent. The introspective routine I now established freed me from anxiety and from any need for subterfuge, giving me a sense of deep repose.

Some strong instinct made me put aside emotional problems and kept me away from the romantic novels I had enjoyed so much as a girl. Now, social questions preoccupied me. They seemed to carry less risk to my imagination. Until then I had carried around with me an indescribable mish-mash of humanitarian principles, which I had never felt the need to justify. Even as a child, listening to my father's autocratic opinions, I had nourished a secret sympathy for the poor. To my pleasure and surprise I had even been able to muster a few rhetorical phrases on the subject. My father's smile had been indulgent as he listened. The education he had given me had been a strange amalgam, completely incoherent. I had never read any of the classics and as far as I was concerned the past barely existed. It stretched back no further than my grandparents, who were mentioned to me occasionally. The history I learnt at school seemed to have no connection with my own experiences — I never imagined that people in the past might have been like me — it was more like a tapestry, a web of fairy tales, hanging before my imagination. With this background all I could hope to do was to examine immediate reality, treating everything as an object of scrutiny. This meant that I thought about the people I met with exceptional intensity, and, without noticing, I developed a kind of commitment to humanity as a whole which was totally untheoretical. Nothing in my family background had encouraged me to recognise the meaning of social inequality, yet some of the things I noticed in passing, at school or in the street, were enough to give me a confused desire to make amends for my own privileges.

When we lived in the city in my early childhood I had acquired that sense of solidarity which seems an inevitable result of urban living. But when catapulted into a backward, rural environment I had become more and more dominated by my father's ideas and quickly lost that sense. I began to think, like him, that society was divided into two groups: one small, composed of superior intellects, the other much larger, made up of an invincibly ignorant and well-nigh insensitive mass of people whose job it was to serve the others. But this view had been short-lived — one of the first incidents which undermined it occurred when I was thirteen.

The owner of the factory run by my father, an aristocrat and millionaire, came to lunch with us. He flicked through one of the magazines to which my father subscribed and commented that it was good but "very expensive." My parents immediately rose in my estimation as I compared them to this rich man who owned two pairs of horses but couldn't afford such magazines... I must have been encouraged to chatter too freely because at one point, talking about my work, I referred to "our factory." Mother told me to be quiet, but the count remarked, "Oh, leave her alone. My coachman does the same. He talks about "my horses." His remark made me very angry, but he had shattered my confident picture of the social order.

And then, when I married, my intellectual development stagnated altogether.

Now, at last, I was discovering how important it was to have a wider perspective. My own problems seemed less obscure when I looked at them in the light of these larger issues. I began to feel the resonance of other people's lives and dreams. Thanks to my books I no longer felt alone. I felt that instead I was someone who could listen, sympathise, and contribute to a collective struggle. I began to feel that all human pain was caused by ignorance and doubt, and that if they were to be overcome some people would be called upon to suffer more intensely than the rest.

When I was small, my father had talked to me about Christ. He explained that Christ had been the best of men, that he had taught sincerity and love and had accepted martyrdom for the sake of his beliefs. I remembered this, and clung to Christ's name as the embodiment of perfection. It was not that I worshipped him, but I was reassured to know that there was an example of the *best,* that a human being could, if he so wanted, raise himself so that he represented divinity—that man could aspire to the eternal. I found Christian mythology childish in comparison. If Christ was God he was nothing. If he was man he was superb — not a diminished God, but man at his greatest and most powerful. Jesus of Nazareth, lover of children, never bitter, serene in his judgements and his prophesies, brought light to my life. He was an ideal figure; one who, if ever I turned away from goodness and truth, would be infinitely saddened.

After years of confusion I now remembered his compassion again, and once more turned to him for inspiration. For a time I toyed with the idea that I might create a philosophy unifying the teachings of Galileo, originating as they did in the study of nature, with new, powerful theories resulting from scientific experiment. I wanted to combine the concepts of freedom and determination with love and justice. This ambition helped me in some way to orient my thoughts, made me believe that some sort of harmony might be possible.

At the same time many things around me began to take on new meaning. I realised with an increasing sense of shock that I had never asked myself whether I might have any responsibility for the horrifying things I saw around me. Had I ever seriously considered the condition of the hundreds of workers my father employed? Had I ever thought seriously about the thousands of fishermen and their families who lived in hovels crowded together, not a stone's throw from my own house? And what did I think about the middle classes—the clergy, teachers, local administrators—and the aristocracy, people I knew who lived close by? Had I ever felt more than the most superficial curiosity about them? In my attempts to avoid both arrogance and servility I had drifted between these social groups, feeling isolated from all of them. Yet I had never wanted to think of myself as a detached and privileged observer of life. Increasingly I began to think that my neglect of the living world around me was a far more serious fault than my ignorance of the world of science and philosophy.

What was I to do? I could neither merge with the working people nor return to the milieu which had proved so disastrous for me. My habits of seclusion had by now become so natural that they couldn't be broken without disturbing our household routine yet again. All I could do was to sit in my room and listen to the noises from the street below.

That winter the young man my sister was now engaged to became involved in a struggle which finally turned my father against him: he was organising the workers in the factory into a trades union. Thanks to him, socialism was beginning to be a serious force in our town. My father told the girls not to have him in the house again. This upset my sister enormously. Although my husband opposed me, I invited the young man to visit our house, and my sister was overjoyed when she arrived one day and found him there! The only thing I could do for my brother, now sixteen, and the two girls, was to guarantee this sort of support: although they were my own flesh and blood I was so heavily engaged in efforts to restore my own strength that I had little energy left to look after them.

The young man spoke to me in some detail about the

movement which was beginning to call on workers, throughout the world, to rise up and oppose the class which exploited them — the class to which I belonged. His own family were workers, but he had travelled and studied abroad and when he returned to his home town two years earlier to supervise the construction of the railway line he had felt an overwhelming need to try and do something for the underprivileged people with whom he worked.

My sister accepted everything he said *a priori*; ideas lived and breathed in this young man, and she couldn't distinguish them from him. I argued with him, growing passionate. But because I wanted to be honest, and yet felt inexperienced at his style of argument, I grew hesitant, lost my nerve. So I tried, after he left, to find intellectual freedom at the writing desk, confiding my new thoughts to the same notebook in which I had recorded my private suffering. When first I yielded to this impulse it made me happy, but later it embarrassed me. I worried that I might be the victim of foolish pretensions, that I might be *acting a part* as I had done as a child in front of the mirror, mimicking the gestures of a fascinating lady. But I went on all the same, and with increasing energy.

I was thinking! However could I have gone so long without it? Everything I looked at now — people and things, books and landscapes — triggered off an endless series of speculations. Some of my thoughts surprised me, others were so naïve they made me laugh, and yet others seemed so intrinsically interesting that I had to admire them!

I seemed to possess an internal language eloquent enough to move millions. The variety of my thoughts was infinite. Did I really possess such a wealth of ideas? I told myself I was no one special, that everyone had an equally rich store, and that only circumstances prevented these resources from being tapped. But I didn't really believe it; how could I, when I was surrounded by so much indifference and ignorance . . .

The doctor might have helped my studies by giving me

the benefit of his scientific knowledge, but he seemed no longer interested even in his own intellectual development. He was so preoccupied with the daily demands of his work, and so sceptical, that he could no longer believe that anything would ever change conditions of life formed over centuries, or that inherited poverty could ever be relieved. He lent me some books—biology text books, medical handbooks, and pamphlets on natural history. When I showed him my summaries and the notes I had taken he smiled at me, sympathetically but also mockingly.

In a melancholy way he still interested me. I still wondered from time to time if he was, or ever had been, in an intimate relationship with my sister-in-law, though I found it humiliating even to think about it. All the same, how did he manage as a bachelor? My father's affair had made me curious about people's sexual needs, but the conclusions I drew were somewhat cynical. Here was a young man who claimed to respect me so much and to respect high ideals, who led an exemplary life according to convention, yet he too had a secret life he would probably never openly acknowledge.

Was there anyone who dared to tell the truth and live their lives accordingly? I felt sorry for this so-called life. Everyone was so anxious to preserve it, even when it was gloomy and petty, that everyone capitulated: my husband, the doctor, my father, socialists as well as clergy, whore and virgin alike. Each resignedly contributed their own lie. Individual revolt was sterile or destructive; collective rebellion weaker—ludicrous even —once one had seen how frighteningly large was the monster to be defeated.

I also began to wonder whether a sizeable portion of social evils might not be the responsibility of women. After all, how could a man who had had a good mother be a bully, betray the women he claimed to love, tyrannise his children? But a good mother must not be simply a victim of self-sacrifice, as mine had been: she must be *a woman*, a human individual. But how could she possibly become an individual if her parents handed her over, ignorant, weak, and immature, to a man unable to accept her as an equal, a man who treated her like a piece of property, giving her children and then abandoning her to perform his social duty, leaving her at home to idle away her time — just as she had done as a child?

After I had read a book on the women's movement in England and Scandinavia, thoughts like these kept coming insistently into my head. I felt irresistibly drawn to these exasperated women who protested in the name of all their sex, often at the cost of suppressing their deepest needs for love, beauty, and motherhood. Almost without my noticing it my eyes lingered a little longer each day over the word *emancipation*. I remembered it from childhood, having heard my father use it once or twice very seriously; since then I had heard it used derisively by all kinds of men and women. I began to compare these brave rebels with the great mass of unthinking, resigned women, shaped by centuries of conditioning, to whose ranks I myself, my sisters, my mother, and all the women I knew belonged. And I was filled with an almost religious awe. I felt I was standing on the threshold of *my own* truth, that I was about to unravel the secret of my long, miserable, and sterile anguish . . .

These moments were intensely solemn. I will never recapture them exactly, but they still live within me — revelations of a higher human destiny, distant but nonetheless attainable through the efforts of those who might be weak and immature now, but still have that dignity which befits the future inheritors of the earth.

THIRTEEN

One day I read a newspaper report of an incident which had taken place in the provincial capital. It prompted me to write a short article and send it to a paper in Rome. They published it. It was in this article that I first wrote the word *feminism,* and when I saw the austere-sounding word in print it suddenly seemed to take on its full significance. I realised I had discovered a new ideal.

By now I had covered many sheets of paper with my jottings. I experimented with different forms—descriptions of landscapes, quick character sketches, my own thoughts about life, in literally hundreds of notes, to which I tried to give proper shape. I began to love these magical pages as something *better than myself,* as if they took my image, refined it, and then returned it to me enriched. It was these writings that finally convinced me I could live both intensely and usefully. By now I wanted to stay alive not merely for my son's sake, but for myself—for everyone.

I began once more to see my isolation as a blessing. The memory of my bitter calvary was constantly with me. I became fascinated by the thought of the countless others who had climbed their own, without even the consolation of a public crucifixion and the hope of posthumous justice—men and women alike, massed together, yet every one of them so helpless and alone. Was this what it meant to be human? How dare people define humanity in a neat formula? And as for woman, a slave until now, she was completely *unknown,* and all the presumptuous psychologising of novelists and moralists only demonstrated the inconsistent foundations of their arbitrary constructions. Man could not know himself fully without his other half; isolated in life with his pleasures and pains, he stupidly renounced woman's spontaneous, open affection, which alone would make him appreciate how splendid the world really was. Weak or strong, he would always be imperfect. In different ways both sexes were to be pitied.

No book could have diverted me from my new convictions; indeed, none that I read now made a very deep impression on me. I discovered that my critical faculties, after long paralysis, had deepend. Yet at the same time I felt an aching nostalgia for everything my education had denied me. Poetry, music, and the visual arts were almost unknown to me. Yet I longed for their enchantment. I wished that my thoughts could take wing and merge with sound and light. When I was writing, my inability to give lyrical expression to my bleak inner world often gave me acute pain. Everything I failed to express seemed to fall back forever into the unknown abyss from which it had momentarily emerged.

We now employed an old woman to do the housework I had once performed single-handed. A tall, stooping woman with a bony, ugly face, at first I disliked her, but she quickly won me over with her extraordinary intelligence and tact. Her history was no different from many of her class: worn out by childbearing, then deserted by her husband, an emigrant, and finally a slave to her children. She talked about herself timidly, revealing to me a stoic commitment to life. My interest flattered her. From the beginning she had been amazed by my girlish figure, my long plaits, and my rosy face, so similar to my son's. And my solitary existence, together with the subjects I discussed with my husband at meal times (whenever he felt like listening), filled her with cautious reverence — a mixture of admiration, pride, and unrealisable hopes for herself and her children.

I began to treat her as a discreet and reserved friend.

After all, she was the only one I had. I tried to educate her, and she made such touching efforts to understand! If she could not understand, her shoulders would slump. "Oh, if only I was thirty years younger madam. Who knows what you could have done with me then!"

This woman, together with my mother-in-law and the laundry-woman who sometimes came, represented for me the most extreme degree of women's submission not simply to poverty but also to male egoism. Their grey heads were permanently shaken by a tiny tremor, as if they were constantly remembering past suffering; their tired eyes often dared not hold my gaze. As I watched them I often felt like hugging them: not for their sake alone, nor from a passing sense of pity, but because, without their knowing it, they inspired in me passionate plans for the future.

I also thought a great deal about my mother in her terrible asylum. I was convinced that if she had been involved in activities outside the family when she was young, she would not have been so crushed by misfortune. I was twenty-two, and I now believed it possible to accept a life without love. More, my conviction that I would never fall in love again even gave me a sense of security.

I had no real insight into how much was lacking in my life. Had I been aware of it there would have been an abrupt end to my naïve enthusiasms. Had I seriously looked at my daily life I would have been appalled! But I had travelled so far beyond the bounds of any normal life and was so convinced that I was achieving something exceptional that the contrast between what I was thinking and what I was doing made no impact on me, beyond an occasional twinge of pain.

In the middle of that summer I embarked on a piece of work I had been thinking about for some time — a study of social conditions in the region in which I lived. I completed it in a few days, weaving it from my own observations and my new vehement emotions.

I showed it to the doctor, and from the way he talked to me about it I felt that he was finally convinced of my new abilities. I also knew instinctively that he had seen in this absorbing activity of mine a new obstacle to the feelings he cherished for me . . . Was I pleased or sorry? I no longer knew. But I realised that by beginning to live my life differently, I was isolating myself more than ever.

But what did it matter? By now my withdrawal from the world was total. For all my youth and beauty, the crisis I had been through had made me think of myself as immune to sensual desire. The direction in which my intellectual development took me was not in the least affected by intimacy with my husband, to which I depressedly resigned myself. Moreover, whenever in my reading or daydreams I encountered women, historical or contemporary, who had chosen celibacy, I saluted their splendid iciness, feeling myself to be one of them, their sister.

I sent away my article, having incorporated the doctor's careful corrections, and one morning I received a copy of the magazine in which it had been published. My son immediately seized it from me. Although he couldn't read I had taught him to recognise my name at the end of my articles, and when he found it he smiled at me with the knowing, happy smile he always had when he looked at my name in print. That smile was my reward, his mark of approval for my daily efforts. He seemed to be saying, "I can tell you are working for me, mamma. I can tell that you are growing, learning, living, becoming strong and active. And I can see that you are preparing a good life for me . . ."

That morning I responded with a smile as wise and joyful as his own. I felt as if on a high plateau, holding my son's hand in mine as I looked over an endless, beautiful landscape I was about to cross, strong and certain. Nothing lay behind me, nothing to either side of me. I felt absolutely at peace, rested, and I forgot all other preoccupations as I faced that as yet undefined but compelling image of the future.

Some weeks later my husband returned from work very preoccupied. That same day I had received a letter from a well-
known woman novelist telling me that she was starting a
woman's journal in collaboration with a new publishing house.
She asked me if I would work with them, offering me a small
salary. I had hoped my news would cheer him up. Instead, he
told me to hold my tongue. He had just heard that the house of
my sister's fiancé, the engineer, had been searched. A wave of
reaction was sweeping across Italy. My husband took the copy
of the magazine with my article in it and all the letters I had
received in response to it, and threw them on the fire. For good
measure he added a heap of newspapers and journals, and
then started rummaging through my private papers.

I remember that day as one of the most bitter, yet most
significant, of my life. As I watched the petty behaviour of the
man I was bound to for life I realised what enormous conflicts
I was living with and felt more than ever alone. His actions, so
grotesque that they inspired a certain awe, left me quivering
with anger.

Once this panic had passed I was able to write and publish
again. Other people began to write to me and send me their
work — I was not as isolated as I had thought. An Italian professor who had lived in Switzerland wrote regularly, and put
me in touch with a Venetian woman who, through our correspondence, became a friend. Though I had never seen them,
these different people began to live in my imagination. I didn't
even try to picture some of them — there was a scientist from
Genoa, for example, who had dedicated his life to teaching
seamen, and I came to admire and love him without knowing
anything more about him. There were others, though, particularly the young men who wrote about poetry in the magazines
to which I contributed, who communicated an instant vision of
timid, silly faces. But it was the women whom I felt the most
inquisitive about: I wanted them all to be beautiful. The ones
who sent me their portraits were certainly very pretty . . .

Were these truly my sisters? Who can tell? A few early

disappointments put me on my guard. Gradually I gained some insight into the position of intellectual women in Italy and their attitude to feminist ideas. To my amazement I discovered that they virtually ignored them. It has to be said that in doing so they followed the example of some of the most famous women writers of the time, who, paradoxically enough, openly opposed the movement for women's emancipation. As I read through the range of female literary production in Italy I concluded that most of it was mere rhetoric, without logic, conviction, or ideas of any kind. And most of the women active in politics were in fact foreigners.

The younger women, in spite of their university degrees, seemed almost contemptuous of the struggle for equal rights. My new Venetian friend, brilliant though she was, came into this category. Older women occasionally gave me a glimpse of how difficult and exhausting their lives had been; they persistently tried to persuade me not to become too involved in the struggle, to moderate my enthusiasm and concentrate on becoming an artist if I really wasn't satisfied by my home and my child. There was no doubting their sincerity, but their letters bewildered me.

My son, young psychologist that he always was, watched the interplay of anxiety and calm in my expression. When he saw that I was worried he kept quiet, and whenever he observed bad feelings between his father and me he would grimace... As far as he was concerned I represented everything that was best in the world. I was the wisest and kindest person he knew. Even my rare fits of temper, which shamed me and which I attributed to my permanent physical tension, never seemed to make him resentful; he must have told himself over and over again that *mamma was right,* and nearly always he asked my forgiveness. No punishment seemed harsher than the sight of my pain... My poor son, my poor, adored child! Yet I believe that he experienced real happiness during those first years and that the long times we spent together allowed him to store up resources of energy which few children enjoy. At times I thought we were in the grip of some strange power which could see into the future, and was preparing all possible defences for him . . .

Two years of our lives had passed . . . I can only recall them in fragments. How can I describe that extraordinary time? I went out, holding my son's hand, along deserted roads hedged with hawthorn, fragrant in spring, dusty in summer; in the distance a double range of hills — foothills in front, the Appennines behind: small towns perched on top of the hills, with their crown of battlements, and small brown houses grouped around bell-towers evoked the Middle Ages. Sometimes the landscape and sea were dazzling, sometimes ashen; there were days when all was still and strangely silent, others when every blade of grass, every drop of water, seemed to affirm its presence with a whisper and the air was peopled with sounds so vivid that they seemed to touch the skin.

I had known that landscape for years. I had never, even as a child, stopped to examine what I saw before me, I never attempted to discover the secret of a harmony which could move me to tears, could stimulate intense excitement, could relax me, or could make me tense with frustration. I simply identified myself totally with it, allowing myself to be absorbed in its enigmatic yet overwhelming fascination. I had become, over the years, passionately aware of its moods. They gave me clear, unambiguous signs of the shifts and developments of a continuing life cycle, and I used them as symbols of my own suffering, my own happiness, my desire for love or for death. Perhaps there was still time!

By now I had reached the conclusion that my past had been determined by an omniscient, if pitiless will and that my painful experiences had been a necessary preparation for the future.

Yet what was this future to be? I had no clear view of it. And without clear direction my development was bound to be chaotic. What did I want to be? Not a journalist: I was beginning to realise the uselessness of that squandering of half-baked ideas. An artist? I didn't even dare consider that option, so burdened was I by the thought of how much I lacked culture and imagination and how blind I was to beauty.

A book, *the book*... Surely I didn't want to write that? But sometimes I felt such urgent longing when I thought about the book which should be written: a book created out of love and pain, compassionate, yet inspired by an implacable logic, heart-rending, yet optimistic. Such a book would show the world for the first time what it was to be a modern woman, instilling in the feelings of her unhappy brother, man, regret for the past, and an intense desire for change... It would translate into print all the ideas which had so chaotically troubled my mind for the past two years—and it would bear the marks of real suffering. Would no one ever write it? Had no other woman suffered what I had suffered? Had no one drawn the same lessons from their lives? Surely it was possible for a woman to take the core of her experience and create a masterpiece from it—the equivalent of a life?

FOURTEEN

One afternoon my husband arrived home unexpectedly early. He looked extremely distressed: his face had the ugly expression it always took on when his temper was up. It turned out he had just left the office in a fury, threatening never to return.

I suddenly remembered how Father had been the day he left his job in Milan — so calm, obviously pleased at the prospect of a future which, though uncertain, would give him some independence.

I now felt a similar tranquillity, bordering on euphoria. But my husband found it hard to control his anger. It wasn't that he was upset at having insulted his father-in-law — the man to whom, after all, he owed everything. No, he was angry with himself because he had ruined his chances of taking Father's place.

Reconciliation was out of the question. Father had no reason to forgive my husband's outburst. For several months now his feelings towards his children had changed from indifference to virulent resentment, and my husband's behaviour had given him a convenient outlet. My father now spent all his free time with his mistress, and it is possible that she influenced him against us. Or perhaps he suspected that we all felt cheated of his money because he spent it so lavishly on her family. Whatever the reason, I didn't have the heart to condemn him for his behaviour. I was convinced that the knowledge that he had lost our affection must have hurt him terribly and that sometimes he must long nostalgically for the past, for the intellectual excitement and the warmth of our shared love.

I still saw him sometimes when I visited his garden. Someone had told him about the articles I had written, and he would talk to me about them as we walked among the flowerbeds. I remembered my childhood, and how stimulating I had found the impromptu lessons he had given me in the garden of our old home. He watched me now, flintily, through narrowed eyes, and silently seemed to be asking me to admit that he was still superior to anyone else I knew. And I would be anxious, indefinably afraid . . . What had happened to him seemed a mysterious, inscrutable warning to me.

When he realised that my father was not going to reinstate him, whatever apology was offered, my husband was overcome with despair. He had never imagined that such a disaster might occur.

I found myself at a turning point.

I wasn't in the least worried about earning a living. All work seemed honourable to me, and I had thought since childhood that where there was a will there was a way to survive. But my husband found it very difficult to come to terms with the idea of leaving the region. He wasn't young any more, had no qualifications and hardly any money. In spite of his high opinion of himself, he was very frightened.

Yet I felt that I had to escape from these surroundings. I had already reproached myself for my acquiescence in my father's exploitation of the workers — an exploitation justified by my husband. At least that would be at an end. At least I would regain some dignity. I felt more relaxed about my son as well. I could take him to another place, where he would forget this ill-fated town where he was constantly witnessing behaviour which contradicted everything I tried to teach him.

One day I hinted to the doctor how happy I was at the thought of leaving. He looked at me, silently; and confronted by that silence I felt sudden regret.

He looked tired, worn out. There was a typhus epidemic in the town, and all day, every day, his exhausted figure trudged to and fro from one poverty-stricken house to the next. In tones tinged with melancholy he tried to give hope to the sick and comfort those who were dying or who were afraid they might die. He rarely came to see me.

Some weeks passed without our making any decision. It humiliated my husband even to think that he might have to look for employment elsewhere. All that we had to live on was my allowance from papa: when he dismissed my husband he also put an end to my work on the factory accounts, so we no longer had even that income. I began to think of other ways of earning some money.

One morning I suddenly had an idea. My son had collected the post and, with his unerring knowledge of my likes and dislikes, had selected one package to give me before the rest. It was a magazine from Milan, and, in fact, I did rather like it. The editor was a man with a long experience of political struggle, who had generously given many young writers their first opportunity. He used to send affectionate letters to me, trying to persuade me to make my reputation by writing something more substantial than the short articles he was always pleased to publish. I decided to write to him and tell him what had happened.

His reply came within a few days. He said that there was nothing he could do for me in Milan, but that a publisher in Rome was just starting a new women's journal and he had written to him. Sure enough, I received a letter shortly afterwards from the same woman novelist who had written to me before. She was sorry I hadn't responded to her first letter, because she could then have offered me an editorial position, which had since been filled. Nevertheless she could offer me work as a sub-editor. I would need to be in Rome but I wouldn't have to work in the office. With her letter she sent me the first numbers of *Mulier,* her magazine.

Though the journal looked attractive, it had such a frivolous tone that at first I was taken aback. I read the editorial, full of fine-sounding passages: "Let women speak for themselves at last. Men have either praised or condemned us. Some men, claiming to be great intellectuals and serious thinkers, bear us an unconscious grudge. Because women neither seek out nor appreciate their work, they think us backward. Other men claim that they understand women because they have had so many love affairs. They have made use of many women, but they have never taken the trouble to know one in depth. All they know is how to extract the maximum pleasure for themselves by exploiting the sensual needs of women. That's all. In fact *woman* as a concept is a product of male fantasy. When we look at reality we see that only *women* exist, and that they all differ enormously!"

The article was unsigned, but I knew that it had been written by the famous novelist herself. She had never in her life created an original female character, but perhaps now she would be able to portray some of the new women who were coming into the public eye. Her editorial concluded: "We do not promise anything new or different. Do not expect too much of us. If you want an ideal woman you will not find her in our magazine any more than you will find her in life. What we hope to do is to take this ideal woman, bring her out of the realms of fantasy, and confront this dream with the reality of ordinary women."

Reading through the magazine, I was forced to admit that it contained little trace of any "ideal." There were articles on art, illustrated interviews with actresses, photographs of duchesses in evening dress, sports reports, accounts of charity balls, and a medical column. The only place where there was any discussion of feminism was in the foreign news.

I felt most unenthusiastic when I told my husband about the offer. He took the magazine, looked carefully through it, then paused for a long time. He liked its tone: it seemed suitably moderate. But it also seemed very fashionable, and that disturbed him. If we were to come into contact with high society we might be intimidated. I pointed out that I would work at home and would therefore be isolated from the rest of the staff. He relaxed. If I was to take up the offer we had to make a quick decision and he had to work out what he would do in Rome. It didn't take him long to think up a scheme: he went to the local landlords and persuaded most of them to let him organise the sale of their produce in Rome and elsewhere nearby. He only needed a few thousand lire as initial capital. His mother, reluctantly, gave it to him.

The day before we decided to leave, the doctor took to his bed. No one was particularly worried. We all knew that he was exhausted and hoped that this enforced rest would do him good. I was unhappy only because it meant that he wasn't there to advise me when I needed him. Apart from my sisters, he was the only person I would miss when we left.

A week later he was dead.

He had been attacked by typho-meningitis, suddenly and violently, and by then he was so weak that he had no resistance. It was as if during all those weeks he had been carrying the seeds of death around with him. Within the space of a night his mental capacities disintegrated: his body, however, struggled for life for a few days longer... Nobody could believe what was happening.

His death agony lasted a day and a night. As soon as we realised that his illness was incurable we sent for his mother, a woman of seventy. She came immediately. Even to look at she was a strange combination: her silver hair gave her an air of authority, yet her smile was still that of an innocent child. She had already lost one son, who had died at the age of twenty during his military service. Her husband was recovering from a stroke, and as a result she had taken charge of the complicated finances of their scattered family. She was someone who believed utterly in unflinching self-sacrifice. She was also sure that she would be rewarded for her commitment in the life hereafter. She took no advice and accepted no criticism from anyone outside her family. I was deeply impressed by her behaviour during that last night of my dear friend's life. With one hand she wiped the sweat from his ashen forehead, with the other she pressed the image of a saint to his lips, lips already so rigid that we could barely squeeze the drops of medicine through them. Her movements, so calm and tranquil, almost persuaded me to expect a miracle.

But as the priest arrived to give extreme unction the death rattle began. I wanted to stay, out of respect for his poor mother. But after a few minutes I left; I could not stomach my friend's subjection to a ritual he had consistently repudiated when he was alive. I found my husband, the doctors, and some friends in the next room. Through the walls we could hear the subdued chorus of women's voices accompanying the priest's monotonous chant. I felt outraged. I asked my husband to take me away, home, anywhere. Nothing was left in that house of the friend I had so valued.

At dawn they came to tell us he was dead. My husband immediately got up and left the house. I wanted to cry, but I could not. I felt too overwhelmed by the monstrosity and solemnity of the mystery of death. It took more than an hour before I felt any sense of loss. As I became aware of it, beginning to feel sorry for myself and for all those others who would never hear his firm, kind voice again, I wept desolate tears.

He had been close to me for six years—since my wedding day. The two of us had always felt lonely, cut off from the rest of our circle. At one time I had felt that he was reaching out to me. Could I have loved him? If we understood each other so well why had we never come together? Why had nothing forced us into each other's arms? Was it simply that we had never spoken those crucial words, or moved sufficiently towards each other? Or was it destiny?

He was gone, and I would never know. I was left behind, more isolated than ever—going who knows where? Towards some kind of purity, I hoped, towards freedom, freedom both from love and from hatred.

The last few days I spent in that town are shrouded in mist. I can only remember a few, particular details...

I can remember my son bursting into tears when I told him that he had to say goodbye to the room where he had been born. I can still feel the lump that rose in my throat when I went to say goodbye to my father, hoping that he would be kind to me, and instead was offered only bitter complaints, cut short when he abruptly turned his back on me... I remember another painful scene: my sister-in-law flaring up at my sisters when they came to see me at her house on the day we left. My mother-in-law moaned and sobbed as we said goodbye...

I paid a final visit to my mother. I tried, unsuccessfully, to make her remember me. I was tormented by her unseeing eyes, her rough, laughing voice!

The sea, the countryside, and the streets of our town had always looked their best in late September, so gentle and sleepy... Eleven years had passed since I had first seen them. Now I was leaving, bound for the unknown. Those eleven years had been painful. My character had been moulded by tears; tears of rebellion, tears of submission, tears of gratitude... Without pausing for another look I left them behind. Secretly, I was afraid that among the shadows I might glimpse a mocking smile, that I might hear a whispered warning that I should not congratulate myself too soon on my escape.

FIFTEEN

The clouds, swathed in sunlight, constantly changed as they floated through the glorious sky. They seemed to pull the landscape behind them as they moved: the piazzas with their fountains, the stone-built houses crammed against church domes, the river, the pine trees on the hillside, the deserted countryside beyond, and the distant mountains. Everything was drenched in the sun's wonderful light, ever-changing yet eternal.

I had seen that sky before, when I was a child on holiday. Then, as now, the sight had uplifted me. Perhaps I really was still the same person, beginning my youth again. I wanted Rome to be mine. I thought that if I desired it enough Rome would give me everything I asked for. One day, the pulse of the city would beat with mine, I would possess everything she had to offer, in one glance... For the time being I took my pleasure from the long, flaming sunsets over the river and Monte Mario, where I lived. After a long day's work in my study, I would go with my son on to my balcony to watch it.

It is as difficult for me to describe my first months in Rome as it is to describe my early childhood. they were too fragmented: I remember only a succession of impressions, of glittering images; an echo of sounds from a world which offered me endless stimulation... All I can say is that the city both moved me to ecstasy and gave me peace.

I decided that I would postpone my exploration of historic monuments until later, beautiful and majestic though they were. Instead I plunged happily into the new suburbs. I found there the same bustle of activity that I remembered from the city of my childhood. But I found too that around every corner I encountered ancient, legendary images, which silenced me and led me to meditation, distracting me from the throbbing confusion of everyday life. I would also find, often when I least expected it, some memorial marking an event that I knew from recent history and culture. Sometimes I felt that the people who had created that history and culture still lived there, and that if I wanted to I could talk to them. Sometimes this feeling was so intense that if I was alone or with my son, and if I was relaxed enough, I wept. The future receded into the distance, the present seemed more enigmatic than ever, and I appeared almost to lose contact with myself.

I also became vaguely aware that there was something else in that city, something it was important for me to know. Encircling its marble monuments to past glory and modern mediocrity there were belts of extreme poverty, people living cramped together; though society tried to ignore them, it was they who held the key to the future.

How did I come to know about these people so quickly? Perhaps it was through you, my new mother, who offered such kindness to me and to everyone else you met. I first met you in your house on the Gianicolo, with its walls covered with portraits of present and past friends, people famous and unknown. When I first saw your plump stooping figure I was reminded of my mother, and you, for your part, immediately called me daughter. You took my child on your knee and looked at us both for a long time, questioningly, as if trying to work out why it was that my son still clung so closely to me. What conclusion did you come to? I didn't talk to you about myself, but I felt that you understood. When you did speak you told me about your work over the years and how much you had achieved by your persistent determination to see justice done. I felt that we became very close.

Most days were dominated by my daily work routine. Two

or three times a week I went to the *Mulier* offices in the Piazza di Spagna, but usually, as we had agreed, I worked at home. Sometimes I wrote a book review, but my main job was to summarise and translate articles from foreign journals.

The editor, though pleased to meet me, had been surprised by my youth. She couldn't understand how someone who looked like a "little Madonna" could write so seriously. An attractive woman in her forties, she divided her time between writing novels, looking after her family, and organising her salon. She had made her reputation some fifteen years earlier and at present was at a critical point in her career. New writers were coming to the fore, and she feared she might be forgotten. Perhaps for this reason she had agreed to work on the magazine; perhaps she hoped it would keep her in the public eye. Her novels were memorable for a few truly superb pages of observation and description, but she didn't think her work out sufficiently clearly, and, as a result, she always wrote too much. Recently she had come into contact with a few new ideas, but she didn't hold them with very much conviction, and didn't really mind if the magazine was turned into a blatant commercial speculation. It wasn't long before I realised that she was not much more than a figurehead for the magazine, and that the business was really run by the publisher, a bouncy little man with a red face. He symbolised for me a whole nexus of interests which the new women's movement threatened. This petty bourgeois, with his impoverished appearance and threadbare suits, could always be found in his dusty poke-hole next to the editor's office. I thought him truly representative of the speculators who grew fat on feminine vanity and foolishness. He was the one who juxtaposed so cleverly the voice of commercial interest with the photographs of fashionable women, the rhetoric of female emancipationists with the moderate advice of the older generation.

The model for the magazine had come from France — almost, I thought, like the latest fashion in hats. A combination of the editor's good taste and the publisher's astuteness gave it some coherence despite the variability of its content. It also found its way into many different homes. Any serious educated woman would be interested in it only briefly, but for a lady of leisure it brought news of what she might feel to be a more meaningful life than her own. Sometimes it even managed to convey that alien and disquieting sense that somewhere a new world was being built.

But very little of the content bore much resemblance to the original manifesto, which had been dictated in a moment of enthusiasm. I often felt humiliated by what I was doing there, and only threw myself into the work — which I found difficult enough, as I was so inexperienced — because I was afraid to face my husband's sarcasm. He still hadn't forgiven me for forcing him to come to Rome. He started on his own project only reluctantly; having been accustomed for so long to a routine job in a subordinate position, he felt uncomfortable with freedom and responsibility. Unable to settle down to a daily routine, he watched me resentfully. I could tell that he was waiting for the slightest sign of independence from me, anything which might justify him reasserting his authority.

But my job did have its advantages. I could take foreign periodicals home with me from the office. And, even more important, for the first time I began to meet and to make friends with many different kinds of women. A woman doctor, for example, who wrote the medical column (into which the publisher inserted advertisements for beauty parlours and cosmetics); a Norwegian woman, tall and blonde, who drew cartoon fairy-tales for children and illustrated the short stories we printed; a young lady who was allowed by her family only to use her aristocratic name and the "distinction" it gave her in order to write a society column. Then there was the editor's salon. Once I had agreed that I wouldn't strike up close friendships there, my husband sometimes let me go. And in fact I usually sat quietly in a corner studying the extraordinary collection of people she had brought together, and thinking that here was a picture of real life more accurate than any I could find in a book.

Not long after I started work I went to visit the printers who produced the magazine. The publisher showed me round, a sarcastic smile on his pudgy lips. One of the compositors was setting a page I had written. He asked me to add a few words for the sake of the layout. Amid the clatter of the great machines, I saw, before the ink had time to dry on the page, my words translated into characters. My eyes filled with tears and my heart beat hard . . .

The days I had spent so proudly and confidently working alongside my father's employees seemed to have returned at last. My long seclusion with my child in that sultry bedroom, where I had constructed so many painful fantasies, seemed a distant dream.

I loved that Roman autumn. I walked through the city, savouring the mystery and the charm of everything I saw, and giving it all symbolic value in my mind. Sometimes I passed strange figures who stared at me solemnly for a moment, as if they were ghosts. I imagined that they were scientists, perhaps, or foreigners who had discovered that the Italian sun could illumine inner truths; or else they were utopians, creating a perfect life for the future. I realised how intensely romantic I was, but I didn't feel in the least embarrassed by this. I found solace in Rome; in some way, because it was so infused with the past, it helped me to believe that in the future anything might be possible, perhaps even happiness for all mankind.

I remember one particular afternoon that November. I am sitting in my small study, shielding my eyes from the sun with my hand. A pale man is seated in front of me. He has large, burning dark eyes, set in a thin face. His expression is remarkably beautiful in its combination of serenity and torment. His mouth and chin convey confidence and determination, his eyes and forehead sovereign peace. My son lies stretched on the carpet. Every so often this man stops talking and, reaching forward, runs his delicate white hand through my son's curls. I can feel my husband's presence at my shoulder. He is abstractedly flicking through the pages of a book, trying to find something to do.

The man who is talking to me had been introduced to me some days before by the woman I thought of as my new mother. I had read his books, written under a pseudonym, and had discussed his ideas with others many times. According to rumour, he was a senior civil servant who had resigned his post so that he could express his views more frankly. People said that he was living in extreme poverty, writing a new book which would finally synthesise his philosophy. I had been completely won over by his frank, friendly smile when we first met. It had given me the courage to invite him home in spite of my husband's usual reservations.

He now tells me so many things! He speaks with a Southern accent, which adds sweetness to his warmth and seriousness. He talks without emphasis, as if rehearsing a speech, about women, law, and the weight of tradition, and he articulates thoughts similar to my own, although he puts them more simply. Unlike me, he is contemptuous of science and modern theories of social reform. With some irony he says that I should be grateful that I didn't receive a formal education. Current research, he says, besides being full of illusions, is totally on the wrong track.

Suddenly he rises to his feet, as if confronted by some marvellous vision offered to him alone. Afterwards he talks no more of error, madness, or sacrifice. Instead he embraces my child, and tells me about his reckless childhood, giving me his hand as if sealing a pact. Then he is gone, taking his vision and his secret with him . . .

My husband says nothing. After a moment's pause he, too, leaves the room. I feel completely withdrawn, and, sensing this, my child turns his attention to his picture book. I think about my father. Many years ago he gave me such mental nourishment, and sometimes, as I listened to him, I shivered with excitement. This has been the first time that I have encountered anyone else with similar originality, someone who might be able to interpret the world and to teach me something. Up till now I had believed that the time for men of vision was past. Perhaps I was wrong.

For an instant I feel dizzy. Then calm returns. I feel able to accept any revelation. Before returning to my poor journalistic labours I go to my balcony and watch the dazzling disc of the sun above the cypress trees of Monte Mario. Two incandescent clouds pass before it, saturating the horizon so that it glows red. This sunset will always be indelibly fixed in my memory.

SIXTEEN

At Christmas, the bushes in the gardens of Trinità dei Monti were covered with scarlet berries, and in the Piazza Navona cribs were put up. My child loved all of this. Then, when February came, we met young foreigners, tall, blonde, and radiant women, carrying great clouds of petals home along the streets. Sometimes we too bought branches of flowers and took them home with us. They added life and colour to the pictures I had put on the walls — Sybils from the Sistine Chapel; Guidarello, tragic and at peace on his stone pillow; a tracing of the sleeping Fury given to me by my Norwegian friend; portraits of Leopardi, George Sand with her black curls, Emerson, and Ibsen. Their presence comforted me in my daily routine, helping me to work and hope. All the same I found my work difficult. So many ideas and images came to me as I walked through the gardens of the Villa Borghese or along the deserted embankment of the Tiber that I often felt too confused to concentrate.

The things I thought about bore little relation to my job, which I tended to do mechanically. I noticed this gap, but it didn't worry me: I had decided that my dream of becoming a writer was much too ambitious. Instead I worked on the issues I was interested in, making a note of relevant news items and any statistics I came across. Sometimes this was enough to satisfy me; all the same, when I saw pouring into the office the mediocre books other women were writing, it was hard for me to restrain my anger. I thought them mere parodies of male literary fashion, written by women even more vain and stupid than the society dolls whose "modern-style" apartments we featured in our magazine. Didn't they know that the literary world was already overcrowded? When would these "intellectual" women realise that they could only justify a place in it by producing books which had a strong character of their own?

Rather hesitantly I said as much to our editor. Usually I was too afraid of her to tell her what I was thinking. She smiled, narrowing her short-sighted eyes, and then sighed. A cloud seemed to shadow her face. I felt ashamed. I was so insignificant compared to her. Did she think her "Perugino," as she called me, had become bold enough to criticise her work, too?

Yet I knew that she wasn't completely satisfied with the novels she produced. I also knew that she wasn't really satisfied with herself or with her personal life. Her husband, a distinguished lawyer, was an intelligent, discriminating man. Everyone thought him a model husband and father, but I doubted that he was really the best companion for her. He had never stood in the way of any of her ambitions, and they respected each other, but although everyone thought that they were happy together I suspected that they only stayed together for the sake of their two daughters.

I had met her eldest daughter, and I felt that she sensed how things actually were between her parents. Although she was only eighteen, she was a determined young woman, her beauty masking a determination to make her life correspond more closely to her ideals. I saw in her a representative of the future. She gave me hope that my insights would be transmitted to the next generation, become a part of the future. I had never felt this before. Yet if this really were to happen, if I were to convey my newly acquired knowledge, I would have to channel my turbulent emotions into something other than internal conflict. And would I ever be able to do this?

I felt confronted by this question particularly acutely whenever I visited my new "mother" in her house on the Gianicolo. She seemed to be asking it of me too. I sat at her feet and listened to the story of her remarkable life. If the editor's daughter stood for a future life where women would be more aware and more self-respecting than I was, this older woman, whose face glowed with vitality even though her hair was grey, embodied a strand of female genius which had always existed but had only been communicated by exceptional individuals, since women had always needed so much strength to overcome the restrictions of law and convention.

When she was young she had been a dedicated Republican. Later she had become active in movements for social reform — by temperament she was more inclined to direct action than to argument. Thirty years before, she had left Lombardy and come to Rome, living openly with a famous sculptor until he died. Throughout her time in Rome she worked unstintingly for improvements in the conditions of the poor — with amazing results. She had campaigned tenaciously for even partial improvements, like reforms in the structure of private charities and the introduction of public-assistance schemes. She had knocked persistently on the doors of the rich, even if the sums of money she extracted were tiny. This was all in startling contrast with her conviction that the oppressive weight of ruling-class institutions would ultimately need to be overthrown by violence. I wondered if she ever passed on her uncompromising philosophy to the young workers she taught at the People's College she had founded. She impressed me because she combined a theoretical rejection of the outworn system under which we lived with a generosity which allowed her to work at a practical level for the amelioration of present conditions. She realised, more than anyone, the terrible beauty of the epoch through which we were living, with its fragmented attempts at social reform, its eager anticipation of revolutionary scientific discoveries, and its search for new and superhuman ideals.

When I went to her house I met people of a kind I had

never met before—just as I did at my editor's salon. But here they were even more diverse. Her lover had formed friendships in the art world, and she had lived among ordinary people, so that her acquaintances were made up of poets and pimps, prostitutes and courtesans, statesmen and vagabonds. I sometimes thought the whole world must be crowded into her rooms. From some of her visitors I heard about peoples I had never heard of, who lived in societies far away, whose basic ideas about life and how the universe was ordered were completely incomprehensible to us. And it alarmed me. Was our civilisation confined to such a small part of the planet? Hadn't Rome been the centre of inspiration, the cradle of culture of all advanced nations? Why did it never occur to the pilgrims who came there, who shared so many aspirations, that from Rome they could draw a spiritual message which might eventually bring them together into one collective mission?

At that time I swung between complete optimism and total despair. My new friend took me to the district of San Lorenzo one day. It made my blood run cold. I wanted simply to destroy it, all of it. When had I ever felt like this before? Outside fierce sunlight scorched the street. In the distance the Tiburtine hills rose up like a haven of peace. But no sun penetrated the tenements we entered. Dark stairwells flecked with damp rose up before us. At every floor we came to badly-lit corridors where half-dressed women gathered to watch us, their filthy blouses barely covering their breasts. They stared at us, hostile, and they terrified me because they had experienced depths of horror of which I knew nothing. In raucous voices they told us about sickness, births, lock-outs, accidents. They asked for nothing; they accepted everything. A fair-haired little girl came down the stairs, her cheeks still rosy, her smile still innocent. Then she disappeared. Foul smells emanated from open doorways; the entire building echoed with shrill voices, shouting, complaining...

Back in the street I suddenly glimpsed once more that peaceful countryside on the horizon. I wanted desperately to escape to its meadows and streams. I wanted to forget the fact that there were human beings — beings like me, like my son, like the saintly woman who had taken me there — who lived in rags in rooms with hardly any ventilation, chilled to the bone, ignorant of the reasons for their pitiless confinement to such hovels.

My duty lay here. I was convinced that I should throw myself into the thick of life and confront this monstrous reality. I wanted to drag there everyone who enjoyed sunlight, beautiful objects, be they simple or ornate, necessities of life or mere luxuries. I wanted to show this place to all those who admired Rome's palaces, who lingered beside her fountains, who gathered at the theatre in the evenings, who crowded together to watch a prince walk by or witness the unveiling of a useless statue. And if, after seeing it, they were still able to ignore such misery I would gladly give the signal to destroy them all!

There was one person I exempted from all this. He fascinated me so much that he made me forget any thought of right or wrong. This was the man who had visited me, the man I thought inspired with the great secrets of life — the "prophet," as our editor nicknamed him. My husband agreed to let him visit me alone at home, the single exception to his rule. Perhaps the "prophet's" reputation for celibacy reassured him. But in fact he rarely came to see me, and when he did he seldom stayed long. We lived in the same district though, and sometimes met in the street and would walk along together for a time. My son always spontaneously took his hand. It is hard to explain what we had in common with this enigmatic, solitary man. He seemed to have an unconscious need to talk occasionally and give someone else an insight into his lonely world; and I was able to listen. I couldn't always make out exactly what it was he was saying, but all the same I was convinced that his work would contain something of value for mankind.

At our first meeting I was worried that he might be a mystic or simply a crank: I had always been afraid of psychical research, although I attributed this fear to intellectual coward-ice. But as this anxiety receded, I discovered to my surprise that I was prepared to accept that his revelation had some-thing to offer me, that I could believe in for mystical reasons.

He talked about the riddle of existence and the way men looked to the supernatural in order to explain their origins and their fate. I was so entranced that I began to feel ashamed of my own easy resolution of my religious crisis during my terrible depression. I had to admit that my capacities for spiritual suf-fering were vastly inferior to his. His suffering might be sterile, but at least he possessed the ultimate nobility of someone who wants to transcend his limitations.

So he made me feel humble. Yet I also felt like a mother and a daughter to him. I was attracted by his austere way of life and by his extraordinary self-discipline — even when this inhibited his wish to confide in me. I also liked to watch his frail body, which he carried with so much pride. It never occurred to me to wonder whether he knew that I felt all this. I never tried to express the warmth of my feelings at all openly, and even my husband felt no need to comment on our rela-tionship.

In all our conversations he never once referred to his way of life. I thought perhaps this was because he wanted people to ignore his poverty and his stoic self-denial. He seemed to accept everything that came his way — a child's smile, a woman's devotion, the sun's warmth — with gratitude, but as if it was only an insignificant part of himself which acknowl-edged them, a part which had no real influence on his thoughts or his intentions. I thought: once he must have suffered enor-mous pain, this caution and self-analysis must have become a refuge. I wondered if he had reached the conclusion that all the things that make us unhappy in our lives — material and emotional deprivation, lack of food and creature comforts, friendship, and care — are ultimately insignificant. Perhaps he had decided that only people who could learn to live without all these things, who could live alone, nourishing themselves in isolation, would become really strong . . .

What I couldn't decide was whether he wanted everyone else to be like him. It was hard to believe that he did, but if not, why did he always counsel me to have patience?

I had met him originally through the radical old lady, and knew that she was particularly fond of him, so one day I asked her about him. Had she ever taken him to see the monstrous poverty she had shown me?

Yes, she had, and he had seen similar places elsewhere — in London and New York.

"But you see, my dear, he simply tells himself that any attempt at social change not founded on his new theory is childish and useless. He is in search of an absolute, and there is nothing more wasteful, more dangerous even, than that. He has come up against the fact that everything changes, that everyone must die, and that the old proofs of immortality don't work any more; so what he is trying to do is to produce a new one which modern man will accept. But men have believed in their immortal souls for centuries without it leading them to improve their social conditions."

She added, sadly: "It would comfort me as much as anyone to think that after I die I shall be reunited with all those who have loved me. I hoped for years that I would die before my lover. But it was not to be . . . Yet now that I am alone and old I am grateful for the memory of our happiness. It helps me carry on . . . And it reminds me that I have had my share. The most important lesson to learn, my dear, is how to live our lives while trying to ensure that *everyone* is happy, that *everyone's* needs are fulfilled. And we don't achieve that by looking beyond the grave."

I sat and thought about him, remembering how often I had experienced him as totally cut off from the world, irredeemably lost in his own thoughts. He had no followers, either. There were plenty of young poets who pleaded in their poetry for a future of mystical happiness. They found the time to hang around the offices of the major reviews, but they never went to ask the "prophet" what his secret message was.

My friend sighed: "Yes, he really is *unique*. It gives me a certain aesthetic pleasure just to meet him sometimes. But I feel ashamed of myself as well because basically I pity him... Have you fallen under his spell? Well, women are never completely insensitive to the charms of mysticism... I admit that I'm an example of it myself. Yes, I do half believe in this 'mystery,' as it's called, and I always, as they say, keep a window open to it. But I can't spend all day at the window when there is so much to do in the house!"

She smiled at me in gentle mockery. I knew her smile hid real affection and that she was telling me, as delicately as she could, that she had realised what my feelings were. I wished I could unburden myself to her, but I felt my anguish slowly mounting. After all, what was she saying? That as far as she was concerned life was love. But if love was the most important thing in life then I had never been alive...

At the end of February there was an influenza epidemic, and my son fell ill. At first his symptoms weren't severe, then suddenly his condition became critical. He had never been ill before, and I was completely distraught. I remember one night particularly clearly. He had several violent fits, started to have hallucinations, and went into spasms of rage which distorted his face so much he was barely recognisable. The change was terrifying. Only a short time before he had been a smiling five-year-old. We began to be afraid that he had meningitis. The word danced in my brain until it drove out everything else. I, too, had been ill for several days and was wearing only a dressing gown as I waited for our doctor. The night air made me shiver. I repeatedly went to my son, who sometimes pushed me away and sometimes looked at me emptily. He had no idea who I was. I would throw myself into an armchair in despair, then get up and start all over again. For an hour, perhaps two, I became completely obsessed by the thought that he might die. I had started to weep when I first saw his convulsions, but my tears dried as I began to work out whether I would be able to find some way of killing myself immediately or whether everyone would be watching me and I would have to resort to subterfuge. If my son were to die I would have nothing left to go on living for. Hadn't he been the only reason for my staying alive on that terrible night so long ago . . .

The crisis passed, but for forty hours he lay silent, giving no sign of intelligence or will; his lips were set in a bitter obstinate fold, his eyes, when they were open, seemed to beseech us to explain what was happening to him and conveyed enormous distress at not understanding our answers. Although I can no longer visualise his contorted face I can still feel the dreadful suffering that look conveyed. I was in a fever myself, and horrible images were crowding in on me, merging with each other, preventing me from understanding properly what was going on. But I remember the heavenly moment when he at last came round. His lips formed a sketchy smile, lighting up his white face as in a thin voice, quite new to me yet somehow just as I remembered it, he answered the doctor when she asked him his name . . . At that moment it symbolised life itself to me.

Afterwards the illness took its normal course. He was a very docile patient, eager to do anything that might help him recover. When his fever abated, relieving him of a lot of discomfort, he asked me, "Mamma, what was wrong with me the other night? Everything went red, and I couldn't see you anywhere . . ." He stretched up his hand to stroke my face. Suddenly the room was flooded with dramatic colours as beyond the balcony the March sky filled with golden clouds. Then darkness fell, and the long night hours began. I stayed alone to watch him until dawn.

During my vigil I kept my gaze fixed on the hazy outline

of his lovely head against the pillow. But sometimes I became aware of my husband's troubled presence. When our child's illness was at its peak I had seen how deeply upset he was, but I was too wrapped up in the drama of my own feelings to feel the slightest sympathy for him. We were like two strangers brought together by a sad accident. Sitting stiffly on either side of the little bed we made not the slightest move, not a single gesture, towards each other . . .

Once my beloved child was out of danger and I was confident that he would live, I was able to have a calmer attitude towards him. Indeed, I felt nearly as detached as I had when I thought he might die. I was still convinced that he embodied the best of myself, firm, innocent, and uncorrupted. Having triumphed over death he needed his present rest, but he would grow stronger. But there was another me, too, a watchful me: she was still being buffeted by the storms of memory and anxiety; painful experiences had weakened her and made her insecure. What was to become of her? She lived more intensely than ever, staring hopelessly into the darkness around her, openly afraid, perhaps for the first time, for herself and for her life ahead.

I had to ask why I had instantly wanted to die when I realised my son was in danger. Had I no life of my own? Had I no obligations to myself, obligations as important as my duty to bring him up and as pleasurable as the task of helping him?

It was nearly three years since I had attempted suicide. My recovery had been long and slow, but during that time I had tried to convince myself and, through my writing and my example, other people too that life had more important goals than individual happiness. I had tried to accept that sacrifices had to be made, and that these could even be easily made once I recognised the links that bound me to the rest of society. I had enjoyed this idea: it seemed to combine self-denial with pleasure in its glorification both of action and contemplation. I felt it could offer me the strength to suppress my emotional and sensual needs without falling into the illusions of religious faith.

Now I was forced to accept that this great idea of mine was itself only an illusion, simple self-deception. I might preach the necessity of living, but my ideals had ebbed away as if I had been bewitched at the sound of my sick child's plaintive cry. Confronted by this undeniable fact, all my fantasies of self-perfection crumbled away. Whatever I would like to think, only one thing lived in me: the bond of maternity. And it was still as powerful and commanding as it had been three years before.

SEVENTEEN

My son was convalescent for many weeks. At the beginning of April, just as new leaves were appearing on the trees, I took him to Nemi for a few days, and there he finally recovered his strength. This chance to be alone with him by the turquoise lake gave me extraordinary pleasure. I thought that his eyes had become deeper and more thoughtful since his illness, that his smile was now even more tender and radiant. He was growing up and beginning to remember things. My own crisis had left me keenly aware of how single-hearted my dedication to him was; but it had also left me in doubt as to whether this would be enough to sustain me in the future.

I returned to work when we went back to Rome: my colleagues had been very kind and considerate to me during his illness, and both the publisher and editor had accepted my prolonged absence.

Even in bad weather I liked to walk the short distance between home and office. When I arrived, flushed with exercise after being pummelled by the winds, I felt that I was just like any ordinary working woman. As soon as I had reached my desk I sat down immediately to cut the pages of the magazines and books which had arrived that day, beginning my daily excursion into the land of culture. I always found unexplored regions, changes in familiar landscapes, sudden, unexpected views. As I leafed through the pages I would take note of which articles I wanted to read closely, which needed intensive study, and which I needed only to skim. And each day I felt a strong desire to take all my treasures home with me so as to be alone with them. But the publisher would always pop out of his cubby-hole to interrupt me, glancing through the magazines himself as he pointed out the items which interested him —usually boring interviews and literary gossip. Woe betide me if I ignored the struggle Catholic novelists were waging against the Index, or the latest statements from the Vatican, or the Queen Mother's receptions for intellectuals.

Petty squabbles continually broke out among the staff as we tried to push responsibility for these areas on to each other. If the editor was in a good temper she would take the most tedious for herself, and with her powers of description she always had the work done in no time. And she always sided with the publisher. "All you need is a little style, and you can get away with anything, Perugino," she used to say. "You can write a celebration of the ostrich who gives us feathers for our hats, or of Saint Anthony, who protects our marriages—but only if you have style." She dismissed all our disputes with comments such as these.

Nobody could deny that she had "style." Our Norwegian art editor brought a set of cartoons of the editor in her stylish poses to the office one day. I thought them excellent. Then one day I went to see her studio in Parioli and she pushed another sheaf of papers into my hand. The odd look she gave me—half innocent, half knowing—seemed typically Northern to me. When I looked down I was astonished to find myself there, on paper, drawn in different moods, some flattering, some shocking, some deeply offensive.

It was as if, standing unaware in front of a mirror, I had suddenly been shown to myself for the first time when I least expected it. Her sketches made me think for the first time about irony, that fruit of bitter disappointment. It is a quality I have never possessed, and think that I never shall—since my hopes all lie so far in the future that I stand no risk of disillusionment.

She was passionately attached to my child, and, even after

his recovery, often visited us. On one occasion she brought these sketches with her to show my husband. He burst into embarrassed laughter. I felt angry with her. Surely she ought to have realised how things stood between us.

To win my confidence she told me about her own history. When she was sixteen her parents had married her to the local pastor. "So boring, my dear, so boring." I began to understand the meaning of this habitual exclamation, which she often used inappropriately. I watched her mobile mouth as she talked, her constant smile, which expressed every emotion from joy to grief, and noticed in contrast the implacable serenity of her blue eyes as she described five years' imprisonment in the home of her pious gaoler. Since then I have learnt to appreciate the depth of feeling and directness of North European literature, but it was she who gave me my first insight into that culture.

"He loved me, you know. We were both servants of God, and companions in that servitude. God was everywhere, all the time, whatever we were doing, in every corner of the house. Oh, it was so boring, so boring!"

One day she told him frankly that she wanted to "go far away from God." There was a quarrel. He loved God first, then her. She told him to choose . . .

"Your Italian God is so much more relaxing," she said to me. "You can serve him without exhausting yourself, because basically you never know whether he's aware of our existence. When you need him, you call on him; afterward, good-bye, and off you go about your business."

She had come alone to Italy, a country she had wanted to see since childhood. First she had worked as a teacher, then as an illustrator on fashion magazines. Lately she had been so encouraged by her success with her own work that she had concentrated entirely on that.

"I was, it is true, visited by a certain lady, sometimes . . . Lady Hunger," she told me courageously, "and, you know, she is very ugly!"

She brought a wave of happiness into our home each time she came. I laughed with her as I hadn't laughed since I was a child. She restored me to life. Even my husband had to drop his habitual scowl as he listened to her. He objected at first to her uninhibited manner and her unconscious provocations — as an artist she was well aware of her own charms and how attractive she could be; but her cheerful, womanly vitality must have disarmed him just as did the elegance and originality of her long, flowing dresses. He made no objections to our growing friendship; he was even prepared to go with us to the theatre if he had an evening free from his work. Sometimes he even risked a joke, and she, appreciating its novelty, would make a mocking rejoinder, provoking his uncontrollable excitement. Once she picked up her pencil and drew a hideous caricature of him. When she showed it to him her laughter carried a ring of contempt. He tormented me for several days after that experience, until she returned and soothed his feelings once more.

She prepared an exhibition of pen and ink drawings for a party the editor gave to celebrate the first year of the magazine's life, and centred it around studies of my son made during his convalescence. He was at the party too, admired by everyone. I wore a dress my friend had made — a white tunic which accentuated my remarkable resemblance to women in mediaeval paintings. The editor was holding court, moving between her guests. It was my first opportunity to see the glamorous women our columnist described so admiringly in her monotonous chronicle of receptions, garden parties, and foxhunts. I thought them a collection of exceptionally well-cared for hot-house plants: some fragile, some robust, some downright unhealthy.

There were two women writers there: a poetess, whose rather precious verses celebrated decadent sensuality in a manner anyone with taste must find repugnant, and a Catholic novelist, whose speciality was the analysis of passionate adultery, usually ending in repentance and the affirmation of the indissolubility of marriage. Their husbands, both Roman princelings, were politically opposed: one was radical, the other a supporter of the Pope. I noticed the women exchanging polite smiles while their husbands bandied frigid compliments.

My Norwegian friend was wearing a daringly yellow dress: her head above it looked like an ear of corn. She was so tall that she towered above everyone else in the room, and when she bent to talk to the society women she looked like a member of another species encountering a group of fragile dolls. There was an old actress there, close on seventy but still a formidable presence. I was watching her as she talked to my friend, when a professor, the husband of our educational correspondent, came to join me. "Are we in the kingdom of *Mulier* or of *Foemina?*" he asked me pedantically. I couldn't match his Latin; all I could do was to point to those two women: "Wherever we are, these at least are real women," I responded.

I had met the actress before, at that house on the Gianicolo. She had been friends with the woman I so admired for nearly fifty years, and their conversations were full of passing references to the heroes of the national liberation struggle. As a young woman the actress had been a protege of Gustavo Modena. Like him she had been an ardent Republican. She had lived to see other, younger actresses come forward, whose success was based on their own nervous responses and their appeal to the audience rather than on a desire to communicate deep emotional truths. As far as she was concerned the theatre was a sacred mission.

She made all the people thronging around her look trivial. I realised how rare and how isolated were women who were really true to themselves. The gallant professor, playing on words, had said to me, "Woman, lady, mistress." When, I wondered, would woman ever be her own mistress? She certainly wasn't now.

A little later my Norwegian friend came over to me,

bringing with her a tall, scholarly-looking young man. He was a physiologist, and when she introduced him I realised that I had already heard about his work. He was very friendly towards me, and I suspected that this was because of his relationship to her. They only exchanged commonplaces, but I had a strong feeling that there was already an intimate understanding between them.

I looked across to my husband. He was glowering in a corner, looking completely out of place. The only times I had seen him look cheerful that evening were when my friend had ignored everyone else and gone to talk to him. Thinking it would give him something to do, I took our child over to him. He hissed in response: "You only want to be rid of him so that you can be in the limelight!"

I was overwhelmed with pain and indignation. I told my hostess I felt ill, and we left. Neither on our way home nor when we arrived there did I speak to him. I no longer interpreted his reaction simply as jealousy. It seemed more like resentment or deep humiliation. Every time he saw me assert my own independence he responded as if to a challenge. I had never stopped to consider if this situation might have its own irony . . . I hadn't dared! It drove me to distraction just to think that others might see it, because deep inside me I could hear someone accusing me of hypocrisy as well as cowardice . . .

I found little relief from my deep dissatisfaction in my fragmented, exhausting job. Instead I began to try and work out why it was that in Italy there was no central organisation which might channel feminist aspirations and feminist activities. There was as yet no widespread political solidarity between women. Only the Church, which had always demanded that women sacrifice themselves, was now encouraging some unified action among them — as long as this was under its careful supervision. Nobody seemed to realise that this new form of religious control was potentially dangerous. Indeed, as my friend the old radical rightly pointed out, the freethinkers in Parliament sent their daughters to convent schools as unthinkingly as their followers in the countryside sent their wives to confession.

"Feminism!" she exclaimed, "organisations of working women, protective legislation, legal emancipation, divorce, the vote in local and parliamentary elections... All this will certainly be a massive task, but it will only scratch the surface: we have to change men's consciousness and create one for women!" Then she would take me to see one of her new projects, born of a nervous energy which always seemed at odds with her plump, sluggish body. "Action! That is the best propaganda!"

One of the places she took me was a centre for prostitutes, an annex of a hospital for veneral diseases, where she was an inspector. It was a simple, white-washed room, in which the patients received some elementary education and were given books and lectures designed to encourage them to believe that, despite their dreadful situation now, they could change and begin their lives once more. I cannot describe the women I met there now. I would have to see them again and learn more from them than I did on that one occasion. It was a long time ago, but I promised them then that I would go back, and one day I will. All I can say is that when I returned home after my visit I clasped my son to me in terror, wondering how I could best protect him from that terrible contagion, so that he would be healthy and free to give himself to the women he loved when at last he decided to marry.

There is an unnatural monster who stands at the threshold of the two parts of a woman's life—between virginity and motherhood. This is the prostitute. She owes her life to the animal desires of male egoism, and her creation is a crucial aspect of the sex war. When a woman who is still a virgin, lost in innocent dreams, first encounters her husband, she often finds him lacking in love and sexual feeling. When she has gained some experience she often discovers that a brutal initiation preceded their marital love. And that first woman still intrudes between them — she takes her revenge; even the memory of her tarnishes their affection.

I asked myself who would give my son his first knowledge of the sacrament of love. Would I ever be able to explain to him how he should treat women?

The world we lived in was so full of cynicism and cowardice! When I went to a debate on prostitution in Parliament I heard it flippantly "abolished" in five minutes by a minister who affirmed that Italian legislation on this issue was the best in the world. Meanwhile, on the sparsely occupied benches, the honourable gentlemen dealt with their correspondence or chatted to each other. A member of the clerical party moaned on lugubriously about the need for this "safety valve for marriage," only to be interrupted by a member of the opposition, who declared with a flourish of polemic that marriage was a fetish demanding human sacrifice. Meanwhile two Undersecretaries kept their binoculars trained on the women in the public gallery. Then the house moved on to consider the budget . . .

I could not believe that educated people could attach so little importance to the social aspects of sexual relations. It seemed all the more strange because it wasn't as if men had no interest in women — on the contrary, women seemed to be their major preoccupation. In their poetry and their novels men continued to construct their eternal duos and triangles, with endless emotional complications and sensual perversions. All the same, not one of them had ever been able to create an original female character.

As I was pursuing this train of thought I came across an article a young poet had written in praise of the image of women in Italian poetry. It so provoked me that I wrote an open letter in response, which was very successful, was widely reported in the newspapers, and delighted the publisher because it gave *Mulier* some publicity. In it I argued that nearly every Italian poet up to now had glorified an "ideal" woman: that Beatrice was a cypher and Laura a hieroglyph. The women the poets praised were all unattainable: they never mentioned the women they lived with, who bore their children! They idolised one set of women in verse, while the prosaic reality of their lives was that even if they married them they turned the women they lived with into domestic servants. Why? Shouldn't poets above all want their lives to be examples of frankness, honesty, coherence, and dignity?

There was another, typically Italian, contradiction that I pointed out: men had an almost mystical feeling for their mothers but treated any other woman with an almost total lack of respect.

My article was opposed by people who claimed that I was only playing around with paradoxes, but I could tell from the letters I received from young people that I had really struck a chord.

One evening, after all this, I went to the theatre. As I came out, I met the old actress. I was crying. I had never cried at a play before or, indeed, in response to any other work of art. There on the stage I had seen a poor doll made of flesh and blood come to terms with her own inconsistencies, decide that she must leave her husband and children, for whom she was only a toy, an ornament, if she was to become a real human being. The play had been written by a Norwegian playwright twenty years ago, but the public, admiring as they were of most of the play, had booed the final scene. Nobody, but nobody, had the honesty to confront its simple, obvious message!

"If I were twenty years younger," growled the actress, her voice resonant with emotion, "I would have made them confront it!"

I became all the more convinced after this that it was up to women to defend themselves. No one but women knew their own psychology; therefore only they could make it clear. People might despise our particular combination of love, maternal feeling, and compassion, but, after all, human dignity was contained there too.

Then summer came. Two months of burning heat. Everyone was away from Rome — my women friends, the "prophet," our editor, who had gone to the mountains hoping that in the fresh air she might find a plot for a new novel. My work load in the office increased. I still made time for a walk to the Villa Borghese each day, so that my son could spend an hour with his new friends. I would sit on my bench and read, and when I paused I found real pleasure in watching the beautiful symmetry of the tall pine trees.

How my husband spent these days I don't know. In fact I have no distinct recollection of him at all — only a distasteful impression of his raucous voice as he seized every excuse to complain and insult me, and a distant memory of his forehead, now furrowed into a permanent frown, his prominent cheekbones, the bad-tempered set of his jaw. We must have spent the nights together — we usually did — but I remember nothing of them. In fact, I could almost believe that he no longer pestered me were it not that I know that he could never leave me alone, however tired or ill I was.

And I was ill. I had become increasingly aware since my son's birth of symptoms which seemed to indicate that I was suffering from some deep organic disease. Sometimes I worried that it might have a mysterious, sexual basis . . . I had been talking to our medical correspondent one day, and she remarked in passing that there were many women who didn't realise that a slow-working, inexplicable illness in them could have been passed on to them by their husbands. I was too alarmed by this to ask her what she meant, and even when I had to stay in bed for a week because I was in such pain, I couldn't bring myself to consult her. Yet when I left my sickbed, at the end of the summer, I felt as weak as a corpse in every limb.

I had also begun to receive sad letters from my sisters.

Father was now completely exasperated because the workers had built up an organisation powerful enough to threaten strike action. His irritation must have been increased by his realisation that everyone at home opposed him. My brother had begun to attend local Socialist meetings, and was as enthusiastic as my sisters about what my sister's fiancé, the engineer, had to say. He certainly had strange powers of persuasion, that young man! So strong was his influence over my brother and sisters that their fear of Father had almost disappeared.

My eldest sister's wedding had now been postponed for two years. I remembered the pride and pleasure I had seen in her misty eyes when she told me how much she believed in her future happiness. Was she happy? I was sure she was . . . even if the growing antagonism between her fiancé and her father could bring her to tears. She would be twenty-one that winter, and was determined to leave her parental home for her husband's house as soon as possible. But she was worried about our sister, who would have to rely on our brother for affection and support to compensate for all she had lost.

And then, very quickly, the situation in the factory became intolerable. Father issued a challenge to the workers. He made it clear that he would rather give up the factory to which he had devoted so much energy for so many years than accept any interference in management decisions from those beneath him.

And he carried out his threat. At the beginning of autumn he put an end to his contract with the owner, leaving him with only one month's notice in which to find a new managing director. My sister wrote to tell me this news in great distress, afraid that Father would make her leave the town before she married.

I said to my husband, with a rather bitter smile, "They should ask you to go there now . . . Would you accept?"

I saw him pause, briefly. Then wearily he said "No," and we dropped the subject.

The next morning a telegram from my sister-in-law brought the news that the factory's owner, during negotiations with the workers, had proposed my husband as the new managing director.

I can still recall my laughter when I heard the contents of that yellow envelope. Go away, back there, see my husband in my father's place... That would really be ironic!

He said nothing. I could tell that he was really disturbed. I was watching him, and thought I saw his face aspiring to a new dignity, as if the mere fact of being considered a candidate for an important job had convinced him of a hitherto unexpected worth. And suddenly I felt my amusement ebbing away.

I remembered that the previous evening he had said "No." Suddenly I felt extreme discomfort. I stared at him anxiously, questioningly, as he seemed to avoid my eyes, to try and look indifferent. This made me even more anxious.

That evening brought a letter from my sister-in-law, giving details of the news she had sent in her telegram, and proclaiming that our return "home" was a certainty. One of the things she wrote was: "Do you remember? I warned you this might happen last Easter..." So he had been expecting this news for all this time!

Two days later he was offered the job. The conditions of employment were good: there was a guaranteed salary, within a short time we would be well off, and in the long term we would be rich. Had I had any pride left I should have rejoiced that this man for whom I felt only pity had suddenly become so enormously important to everyone else... I should have felt pleased too that I could tell myself he still owed his good luck to me and my father—for it was Father who had put his name forward and had bequeathed to him a guaranteed income of several thousand lire. But why was Father doing this? Perhaps it was only that he wanted to establish some link with his successor, so as not to be cut off completely from what he saw as his own creation.

I felt like an insurgent city confronted by force of arms. I wanted life and liberty. Closing my eyes and ears to everyone else's arguments, to everyone else's needs and demands, I concentrated on a single image. It was this: the way to the future was being brutally closed to me. Instead I was being taken back into a desert. And my son was being taken there with me, despite my desire to save him from the terrible environment into which he had been born... Once there, the two of us would stand, perhaps for years, with shackled hands and silenced mouths, confronting a community of poverty-stricken labourers who could only hate us...

EIGHTEEN

Once his contract had been signed my husband went into a deep depression. I began to wonder if his decision had been made so quickly only to pre-empt any possible rebellion from me. He didn't want to witness our friends' surprise and disappointment or my unhappiness as we prepared to leave, so with a show of generosity he told me that although he would leave almost immediately, the child, the maid, and myself could stay behind for a few weeks until my father had vacated the house (which went with the job) and had moved to Milan. My husband would then return to Rome and take us back with him.

But as soon as he had suggested this he grew silent and irritable. He stayed at home all day, sitting at his desk, working away on one of his many schemes. Over the next days he went out on his own to wander round the city as if he had suddenly fallen in love with it and with the excitement of the life he was so determined to leave. Our Norwegian friend came to see us as soon as she was back from her holiday. We had a desultory conversation, which constantly returned to the same question: "Why are you going?" She was very gloomy, and told me how lonely she would be and how upsetting it was to think of my being so far away. My husband simply stared at her, hypnotised.

The night before he was due to leave I woke to find him tossing and talking in his sleep, but I couldn't make out what he was saying. I turned the light on. Although he was feverish, he refused all my offers and help and hid his head under the bedclothes with a despairing gesture. When he seemed calmer I switched off the light and went back to bed. A few minutes later he became delirious again. And then, as if in a dream, I heard him call out my Norwegian friend's name . . .

Poor man! He was struggling with all the confusions of love — that formidable enemy he had never acknowledged. How long had he been feeling like this? Perhaps he had only recently recognised the truth, perhaps only since his decision to leave. Perhaps he still could not accept his feelings, and saw them as weakness or sickness.

It seemed a terrible punishment.

My friend had probably been the first to guess the truth. She told me in confidence, shortly after her return and no doubt hoping I would pass it on to my husband, that she was in love with the young physiologist she had introduced to me at the *Mulier* party. There were problems — his parents did not yet accept the relationship, and her lover felt that it would be selfish to secure his own happiness at the cost of their grief.

In spite of myself, I couldn't stop watching my husband. He noticed this, and was distinctly annoyed — he wanted to preserve his position of superiority. But my pride was hurt. I had lived with this man for ten years and had never persuaded him really to love me. Now he had been thrown into complete disarray by the mocking laugh of a total stranger! I became obsessed with curiosity — I wanted to know exactly how he loved her, to find out whether he was once again at the mercy of his sexual needs or whether this woman had some other qualities that I didn't possess . . . And again, I was forced to wonder if I would *ever* be loved.

When he finally went away, my friend was very relieved. She and I spent some glorious days together. We took my son for walks, visited country villas, and roamed through the countryside, completely absorbed in each other, and at times overwhelmingly happy. Wherever we went she took her sketch-book, and filled it with drawings of everything she saw —

mothers, governesses, children. We spent hours in her studio in Parioli. By now I knew it intimately—always spotlessly clean, high white walls, the furniture simple, made of white-wood, light curtains framing the two large windows from which we could see the Tiber Valley stretching toward Soratte. Her small, dark bedroom behind the studio was furnished only with a bed and a chair. In an attic across the corridor lived a widow with four children: she did the housework and made my friend's midday meal. My friend cooked the evening meal.

I had not intended to so do, but I started to pour my heart out to her, trying to express in careful precise words the ideals which seemed to me the only things worth living for. Yet whenever I talked about the future I just became desperately un-happy. She would take my hand, trying to give me courage.

Her future was uncertain too. She wanted to give herself totally to the man she loved, regardless of social convention, to go somewhere with him where they could be happy together. But she was forced to accept that this was impossible; so she was still living on her own and had no idea how long the situation would last.

I received a somewhat childish letter from my husband. He wrote that he felt completely lost back there and that per-haps it was the wrong place for us. He was desperate to re-turn... I summoned up all my strength and sympathy and replied, telling him that if we were ever to live satisfactory lives we must face the truth about our relationship. I wanted him to confess that he was in love with someone else, and to accept that we must each go our own way. I told him that marriage was bondage even for him.

I was trembling as I wrote: my whole future seemed to depend on his response.

He replied immediately, with the insolence I had grown so used to over the years. He denied everything, and blamed all our difficulties on me. I read his letter calmly, thinking that at least I had begun to face reality. I was still convinced that something could be done, even if I didn't yet know what it was. A voice inside me sang incessantly, "You are free, you are free."

It was also becoming clear what my role would be in the new house he was preparing for us to live in. Although he had once pleaded with me to learn how to live for myself, he now increasingly wanted me merely as a means to his own sensual satisfaction and the oblivion he found in that. I realised that if I continued to live with him for that reason alone I would begin to despise myself . . . I found it utterly unacceptable.

I was preoccupied with these thoughts for two or three days. There was by now almost nothing for me to do on the magazine. The publisher was looking for someone to replace me. He seemed sorry that I was leaving. "It's so hard to find an impartial reader of women's books," he said. The editor was polite, but her mind was already on other things. She said she hoped that I would still work for them from my new home, and then asked me abstractedly if I had ever thought of writing fiction.

Then my Norwegian friend was suddenly taken ill with rheumatic fever. I went to see her every day. So did her lover, and when I first saw him there I was struck by the security of their love for each other.

He had decided that the small, dark bedroom was too stuffy and, although the thought of change upset her, persuaded her to let him move her bed into the studio.

My main preoccupation, however, was still what would happen when my husband returned. I had made up my mind to ask for a friendly separation. If I continued to work and to receive my father's monthly allowance I would just be able to support myself. My child could stay with me during school terms and spend his holidays with his father.

I still had hopes that he would agree to this. I felt he was in the throes of one of those psychological crises when we are often able to accept decisions which go against everything we have previously stood for. I was convinced that his views must have changed.

I didn't want to do anything to prejudice my plan. All I needed was someone to advise me. My old radical friend was still on holiday in Lombardy; at this decisive moment I had no woman friend to confide in. Increasingly, insistently, one person pushed his way into my mind — the "prophet." Didn't he claim to have insight into the truth? Surely he would be able to advise me?

It was some weeks since I had seen him. I wrote to him, saying that I had a serious problem I needed to discuss with him, and inviting him to come and see me.

I was getting my son ready for bed the following evening when he arrived. He talked to my son, who listened trustingly to him before he went off to sleep. I began to speak, shaking with emotion. He listened impassively, leaning forward encouragingly from time to time. Perhaps he had already guessed what it was I wanted to talk to him about.

Gradually I became calmer. His questions were precise and to the point. They helped me disentangle the story which it so embarrassed me to tell, and gave my thoughts direction. I didn't say much about the past or about my early sexual initiation. Instead I told him about my parents and my marriage. I said that although I had been aware for some time that I was unhappy in my marriage. I had thought it my duty to stay with my husband because I thought he loved me and that I could help him. Recently, however, I had discovered that he could love other women, and this had made me hope that at last I might be free. I had never before articulated my desire for independence in a way which corresponded so closely with my secret thoughts. Every word I spoke seemed to make my feelings clearer. I was astonished and pleased to find myself at last able to express my thoughts so lucidly.

He watched me calmly and then he started to talk. He said that it would be pointless to pass judgement on my decision or to try to make me change my mind. Yet he wondered whether I was prepared for the consequences of my plan. Our emotional problems, he added, were often created by pride. He was certain that everything in this life, these problems included, was in the last analysis completely immaterial. Some day I would realise how little was required for us to learn to live righteously. He was pleased, however, that I valued honesty and human reason so highly.

He stood up and began to walk round the room, touching books and photographs. I was standing too, leaning against the table in the middle of the room. He came close to me — he was hardly any taller than I. Quietly he started to speak to me again. When he was younger he had experienced enormous unhappiness. Before then, a firm believer in law and progress, he had measured people's behaviour against an inflexible, absolutist code, and had been quick to condemn . . . Then he had suffered a terrible blow. Both his parents had died within a short time of each other. This had made him realise how insignificant is human life. For the first time he had wanted to know what lay beyond its confines. In the years that followed, he withdrew from all contact with other people, and gradually he had felt a light, yes, a light, beginning to shine in him. He felt that this light would give him the power to explain to others the enigma of our existence, our immortality. Soon he would pass on his message to the rest of mankind, and we would then all experience great peace, and would understand how best to use our capacities during our time on earth. At this moment he couldn't explain any more to me . . . but in the future . . . whatever my final decision, to stay in Rome or to leave, I should still hope, keep trust in his promise.

Every so often, as I listened to what he said, I could hear the trams screeching in the street below. They sounded like the howl of the wind at night on the shore of a stormy sea, while his presence inside seemed to envelope me in a frigidity which numbed by thoughts and distanced me from my determination to give my life a new shape. I felt completely lost amid images of icy whiteness.

When he left, I went to my study. The lamp's glow seemed to be keeping watch over the whole city. I felt a joy the like of which I had never known before. I wasn't interested in trying to find out what it meant. Nor was I really interested in this man's secret. All I was aware of was that I, who had begun to hate love because I thought it meant only self-sacrifice, who had rebelled against life because it burdened me, had at last allowed myself the pleasure of speaking to someone else and of feeling understood by them.

For three days I secretly celebrated this unspoken pleasure. Each evening the "prophet" visited me. He asked me to make a fair copy of his new book, which was about to be published. Some pages were completely illegible because of deletions and additions, and I had to ask him to explain them to me. And explain them he did, with dogmatic self-assurance which swept away all objections. The book was fiercely polemical. I had to agree with its general argument, but though it was intended as an introduction to the author's main ideas, yet it still didn't reveal very much about the elaborate theory he had constructed. His style worried me too — it was so complicated and contorted that it was often illogical. And some of the phrases he dictated to me as we worked disturbed me because of their total obscurity. I began to remember my first impression of him as an emissary of a Mystery which perhaps he didn't really understand himself. Yet even now I didn't have the strength to reach any firm conclusions about his ideas. Indeed in some ways I was less capable than ever of thinking clearly about him, and I still withheld from him any thoughts I did have about his work.

Instead I watched him. He was pale and emaciated, like a living ghost, with a short, black beard and moustache hiding pallid lips which on rare occasions stretched into an enigmatic smile. As I watched his gestures, I began to think of him as a delicate, precocious child who knows in advance what it is that life will deny him . . . and I trembled. Weak and pathetic as he was, I still admired him. He possessed an indefinable power over me. I thought he represented the incessant and awe-inspiring struggle of man against the gods. Then the word *madness* suddenly flashed through my mind, and I was left beset by enormous conflicts.

Yet he was confident that I really believed in him. A distinct gleam came into his eyes whenever he became aware of my intense concentration on what he was saying. Clearly, he had never before encountered such fervent devotion from anyone so young . . .

The only person I talked to about him was my Norwegian friend, who was still ill. I began to spend many hours at her bedside. She had developed complications — the disease had affected her heart. One of her lover's teachers was now her doctor, and he warned me that her condition was serious. Although he was doing all he could to save her life, he doubted that she would survive. Her lover smiled at her with great tenderness, but when he looked at me I could see his distress. She had no idea how ill she was. The only visitors she wanted were him and me and the widow from across the corridor. She was making plans for her convalescence. "This is so boring," she repeated, "so boring!"

Suddenly her illness reached a terrible crisis; she was in even more intense pain and was suddenly afraid that she would die. She underwent dreadful convulsions, spasmodically clutching my hand for support. I stayed with her for two nights, tormented by my impotence. At times she seemed on the brink of death. Hurriedly I wrote to my husband to let him know that I would have to stay a few days longer in Rome.

That night her palpitations were not quite so violent, and she seemed out of danger. Her lover went home to rest. I didn't feel tired, so decided to stay. My friend's smile when I told her I would remain compensated me for being away from the peace of my own rooms, where my child was quietly sleeping. I began to feel a surge of hope for her.

At sunrise I left the patient in the care of the widow and set off for home. I had only gone a short way down the deserted white streets when I bumped into my husband walking towards me with is head down. He was very startled to see me, and looked almost ashamed, but said nothing. I felt only pity and contempt for him.

I told him that she was much better. He began to apologise for arriving so unexpectedly, but I cut him short. All I could feel was that his presence was an insult to my suffering friend.

Even when we arrived home we didn't speak. I rested for a while and then went back to her studio. That afternoon my husband arrived and asked if he could see her. As I watched them I realised that my friend, who had once attracted him so strongly that he had almost refused the job he so passionately coveted, had now lost her sensual fascination for him, poor, withered creature that she was.

She told him that I had behaved like a saint. "Go home, now, go on. I'm all right. I'll rest now. You'll come to see me tomorrow, won't you?"

I had to do as she wished. But there was a heavy silence between me and my husband. After supper, when the child was in bed, we started to talk. Where I was passionate, he was cautious. He tried to justify the things he had said in his letter. I felt I mustn't let slip this chance to expose his lies. Perhaps I was reacting to the strain of the past few days, but I spoke to him as I had never spoken before. I treated him rather as if he were my son, grown up and become a man. He offered no word of defence, and in the end seemed to acknowledge by his silence the truth of what I was saying—even when I told him that I thought we should free ourselves from a relationship which was so oppressive to both of us.

"Is that what you really think?" he asked doubtfully.

"Don't you think we might get on better in the future?" I was amazed. His response gave me hope that I might convince him.

At that moment the doorbell rang. It was the "prophet." I hadn't seen him for several days. And in spite of the fact that I had told my husband about his visits and had explained that I was doing some work for him, when he saw him arrive so late in the evening he reacted with more anger than I had ever seen him show before. Making a brief effort to control his temper he joined in the conversation until my friend finally decided to go, squeezing my hand as he did so to give me courage.

The battle was lost. My husband launched into a brutally sarcastic interrogation. I let him continue, hoping that this time, as on other occasions, his rage would eventually burn itself out. But this submissive attitude only made things worse. The sound of his own voice hurling accusations at me, loosing a stream of obscene insults against my friend, seemed to aggravate his mood. In a final spate of fury he caught hold of me and forced me to my knees, beating me like an animal as I fought back in desperate anger. Our son woke up and called to me, terrified. I managed to drag myself away from my husband and rushed to his bedside. He ran his hands over my hot, tearstained face, whispering in a trembling voice, "Mamma, I don't want to, I don't want to go back there with papa. Stay here with me. Come into my bed. Don't cry . . ."

Why not . . . ? Why not obey this plaintive little voice? The days were long past when I could accept each humiliation without a murmur, when I could ignore those who offered me a different kind of freedom . . . My son was on my side, and wanted to stay with me. He was convinced of my goodness and purity. When he saw how unjustly I was treated he was revolted too.

I made my husband sleep on the couch in the dining room and took my son to bed with me. Once more I lay awake waiting for dawn.

The next morning our maid asked me what had happened. I didn't know how much she had heard. She went on looking at me with intense sadness. Then she took my hands and kissed the red marks on my wrists. Had she had her own experience of being punished like that? I had often noticed in her eyes the cowering expression of a maltreated animal.

There was another scene over lunch. I can't remember how it went, but I do remember my son clinging to me at one point as my husband tried to tear him away, ordering him to come to him and leave me alone with my madness . . . When I asked him once more for a separation he simply laughed. I could certainly stay and earn my own living if I wanted to, but his son would go with him, wherever he went.

Our child was totally bewildered. Oh, my child . . . I would die if he was taken from me. He was my flesh, my life, my hope for the future. Even at such a time, to hold him in my arms comforted me . . .

I became aware of an overpowering urge to attempt suicide once more, but I summoned up all my strength and rejected it. I was not prepared to die. I *had* to live. But in order to live, I was forced to submit to this brutality.

My husband realised that once again he was the victor. He became calmer, less spiteful. Perhaps he had thought things over during the night and had decided on his strategy. Perhaps the emotional fog which had enveloped him for the past months had finally evaporated. Perhaps he had decided to put himself first now, to demand only his own material comfort. Or perhaps he had simply calculated that the threat of separation from my child would be enough to reduce me to total submission. More tranquil now, he tried to laugh off what had happened, as if it was only a momentary weakness. I think he even asked me to forgive him. At any rate, we decided that I would stay in Rome for a few more days until my friend was better.

NINETEEN

Three days after my husband's second departure I was walking with my son when we met the "prophet." He came toward us through the crowd, completely absorbed in his own thoughts. When he saw us, his face came alive with a sudden beaming smile. I was amazed that he was so pleased to see us.

He took my son's hand and began to question him with that mixture of affection and seriousness which children love so much, and which so few adults offer them. I suddenly remembered what had happened after our last meeting and felt so outraged that I could hardly speak. Eventually he asked me directly how things had been. I told him that my husband was incurably jealous and that this meant he would no longer be able to visit me at home. He had suspected as much, but to hear it confirmed by me made him very angry. Then I told him that rather than be deprived of my child I had given up my plans to leave my husband, and that I was going to return to my old, false, miserable existence. He looked at me pityingly, but said nothing. Though I didn't acknowledge it to myself at the time, I was disappointed in him. I thought even if he despised me he might have given me some compassionate word or gesture of support.

That evening, after supper, I was sitting at my desk and my son was playing in his favourite place by the stove, when suddenly I found myself with my head in my hands as tears flooded down my face and my body was shaken by violent sobs. My son turned towards me, shocked. Even I was frightened by this collapse. Never before had I wept so uncontrollably when I was alone with him. Then he came to me and clung to my knees. He stroked my face, begging me with all the endearments he knew to stop crying—but to no effect. As a last resort he seized my pen from the desk and thrust it between my limp fingers, saying, "Mamma, mamma, don't cry; write, mamma, write . . . I'll be good; don't cry . . ."

His moist eyes, watching me so intently, were filled with intense sadness. He loved me so much that he was even prepared to share my pain. And I, his mother, who had made so many plans for his future happiness, his future achievements, could do nothing but gratefully accept what he was offering me.

Write? My son, young though he was, realised that I must plunge myself into my work and my fantasies as never before. His only concern was my safety; he somehow had a sense of the complexity of my needs even though they must have been incomprehensible to him. His love was neither jealous nor possessive. Here, at least, was one person who didn't insist that my life should be completely dominated by him.

But could I take the pen he held out to me? What could I write? Despair had cast its shadow even over my dreams. They now seemed inconsistent, utopian, absurd, full of ironic paradox.

My thoughts ran on to my friend the "prophet." He hadn't been able to help me. What did I mean to him? He seemed to treat everyone, myself included, as a passer-by treats a child they find crying, frightened by some minor mishap; he would bend over them for a moment, then move on. Yet he could so easily remove the cause of their distress. Or could he? The child might think so, and I had been prepared to think so too.

I began to wonder whether his life, far from being one of purification and self-perfection, wasn't instead cold and cruel . . . What Message was likely to come from that? He thought he would eventually have his secret to tell the rest of the world . . . But while he was ritually preparing his Message, my life was in ruins, my friend going through agony; and I might even have killed myself! Wasn't there something despicable about his detachment?

I went to bed, but couldn't sleep. As I lay there, staring into the darkness, my thoughts became more lucid. For the first time since renouncing my hopes of separation I asked myself, What were my expectations? The answers came crowding in, each contradicting the other, frightening me. I despised myself for being so weak . . . I was a coward . . . My suffering was pointless: it brought me no comfort and helped neither myself nor my son . . . I longed for happiness just as much as he did . . . I began to imagine his anguish when he discovered that he had been the price of his own mother's humiliation . . .

A new question came to me: "What if *he* had asked you to leave your son and follow him, to look after him and give his life some coherence?"

Him! Had he become such a part of me? Had he been more than a guide, an example, a source of comfort?

Then came another devastating question: "Were you in love with him? Could you have given up everything for him?"

I remembered him as I had seen him earlier that day, so pleased to meet me in the anonymity of the crowded city. Had no one ever loved him? Had he never known how comforting it could be to be held safe in the arms of a woman who understood him, and could protect him from the darkness of the mystery he found so frightening?

He had called me his sister . . . But a sister could do nothing. There must have been other women, but none had shown him how to be happy . . . So he preached renunciation and tried to convince us all that there is no happiness in this world . . .

Slowly, the answers came. Yes, if he had asked me a few days before, when *I believed in him,* I would have followed him. Yes, *for his sake* I would perhaps have been able to live without my son. I realised that this dramatic change in me was very recent. Only a few months before, when I was afraid my son was dying, there was no one else for whom I would have felt that life might still be worth living.

All the same, what I felt for this man wasn't love; it couldn't be love because I wanted nothing from him for myself. Indeed, I felt that if he had made any sacrifices for me, this would have diminished him in my estimation. If he had kissed me, it would have given me no pleasure.

But if he had wanted me to kneel in adoration of his mysterious inspiration . . . to serve him with all my intelligence, my writing ability, my life . . . then, yes, I would have done that . . . and in doing so I would not have felt that I was depriving my son of anything.

Abruptly, in the space of a week, my Norwegian friend's illness again became much worse. This time her lover said nothing to me: he simply looked at me as if appealing for comfort, and I understood — my dear friend was doomed, doomed . . . she might die any day, at any moment. So why did we continue the ceaseless struggle, the medicines, the treatment we hoped would not just relieve her pain but stem the disease? The answer is because even when medical science tells us that death is certain, as long as the patient's body still pulses with life it is impossible to believe in death. We always believe in miracles, in unexpected interventions. We go on hoping right to the end.

For hours we sat on either side of her bed, hoping: the severe young man, eyes staring intensely through his spectacles, and I, more careworn even than the patient whose will to live still dominated her tired, ashen face.

For her we seemed to merge into one loyal, protective presence. At her worst moments her eyes clouded over with pain and her face flushed while her hands caught hold of our fingers like vices. In moments of respite she tried to force us to tell her whether she was dying, to prepare herself. But in a way she didn't, couldn't believe that she would die. She still occasionally made plans, talked about a country far away, white with snow — such a long time since she had seen the snow! We would all go together to the fjords! We would go soon, when summer came! When the young man stood up after listening to her heart beating like an enormous piston in her thin white chest, I saw his alarm, saw him holding himself rigid to hide his dismay.

Was it long after this that she died . . . ? I don't know. Her suffering seemed interminable, but it must in fact have been quite brief.

One morning when I was with her my maid brought me a postcard from my husband. It was addressed to our son, and contained insulting references to me. His recent letters to me had been cold and sarcastic, with biting asides about the "prophet"; he was no longer interested in our dying friend.

She saw me blench. "Is it from your husband?" she asked . . . And tossing her hair back quickly in a gesture reminiscent of the old days, she murmured, "Don't go back there, at any price . . ." I kissed her affectionately, but didn't reply. "But what if they take your child away?" she whispered, staring at me as if hoping to pass on to me some of her own determination.

The doctor told me that if I was to stay on my feet for another night I must go home and rest for a few hours, then perhaps walk in the sun a little with my child.

I went home and held my son close to me for a long time. I didn't rest. I couldn't. I took him out with me to catch the tram to St Peter's. I thought I would go to the Gianicolo to see my old radical friend. The square in front of the cathedral was almost deserted, the colonnade with its flamboyant statues seemed to shimmer in the brightness and silence of the day. We set out on foot towards the Borgo Santo Spirito, walking alongside the hospital wall. On the other side of the street

children and women in rags interrupted their games and their
gossip to watch us pass, asking us for alms. Their sheets were
hanging over the walls to air, giving out a musty smell. We followed the barred windows of the hospital as we climbed up to
St Onofrio, passing more sheets spread in the sunshine, more
children at play. A group of convent girls, accompanied by
nuns, walked towards us down the street. At the top of the
Gianicolo we stopped to catch our breath. The legendary Gari-
baldi, profiled against the sky, calmly contemplated the great
dome to his left.

The sun's glare, reflected off the compact mass of houses,
towers, and trees stretching before me, was so intense it was
almost unbearable. In the background the purple mountains
stood sharp against the sky, and on their slopes the white
splashes of the villages of the *Castelli* added their dazzle.
Between the mountains and Rome stretched the endless
countryside.

Rome! Perhaps each day on top of that hill someone
found new inspiration as they contemplated that marvellous
mass of buildings, each from a different epoch, each with their
own splendour, their own significance. Perhaps, too, each day
someone had a vision of a future Rome, free of squalor and
violence, where men lived harmoniously, no longer hostile and
uncomprehending, no longer estranged . . .

My son chattered away, happy to have me to himself,
pointing out the birds in the trees, stretching his hand towards
the horizon in imitation of a gesture of mine he had seen many
times. "Look mamma, look, isn't that a pretty cloud? There,
above the pine trees! And look there, over there, where's that?"

The old revolutionary was at home, but she had other
visions, including the editor of *Mulier* with her eldest daughter
and her fiancé, a young archaeologist. The young couple radi-
ated happiness and self-confidence. Her mother told me she
would be able to help her husband when he wrote up his
research, and she wouldn't do it just out of love but out of pas-

sion for the subject: the young man had a real sense of poetry which made the ancient tombs and fragments of pottery he worked with spring to life . . .

The two were listening, smiling into each other's eyes. I had never before witnessed two people offer themselves to each other quite like that, preparing to merge themselves into one. For a moment I felt involved in their love, soothed by it. Then I remembered the young scientist as he bent over his dying love, and immediately became anxious to return to them.

A woman was waiting for me at the door to my house: "Two hours ago, signora . . ."

She was dead. While her lover was giving her some medicine she had slumped forward on his chest, her mouth half-open, saying, "Thank you."

"Thank you!" She could not have realised how profoundly moved we would be by her dying words. I had no regrets at having left her to die in the arms of her lover.

When I arrived at her studio she had already been laid out. But that body was no longer her. Some neighbours and colleagues had come to help; there was a constant stream of visitors. Unable to stay in the room with them, I took refuge in her back bedroom. Shortly afterwards I was joined by her lover, and forgetting my own distress I gave him my hand. To me he could express his misery freely because he knew of my own: we were the only people who had really loved her.

We stayed up together for two nights, watching over her, talking about her and what she had meant to us. Her lovely face was now like ivory beneath her faded golden hair. As the hours passed, it became transformed into a rigid mask . . . Her life was ended, ended . . . I thought about *him,* the man who claimed to understand the mystery of death. If he did, why didn't he come to reveal it to me? Why, above all, knowing that my friend was going to die, hadn't he come to give her the benefit of his knowledge? That would have been a real test!

When we watch someone's life come to an end we know

we have to give up all hope of defying the unknown . . . We realise that human beings are unequal to the task. Our destiny is to live on earth without ever being able to explain to ourselves why it is that we exist! Yet, if in life we pause to look at death, we gain a deep awareness of our own worth: we understand that if we are determined to transcend our own ignorance we may gain some dignity, and if we decide to create a new life here on earth we are acting heroically . . . Contemplating death, we may hear a confused appeal, coming perhaps from someone in the future encouraging us to go on; for everything obscure to us now may have become clear to them. Perhaps this call comes from those who are living in a new epoch, the epoch of the liberated spirit.

The hours we spent by the corpse of our beloved friend did not turn *us* into prophets; but neither did they drain our strength or rob us of the sense that our own lives must continue. Those hours allowed us not only to take over her responsibilities, but to absorb some of her qualities as well, her energy, her ideals, her love; and this enriched us. After our vigil we felt a closeness to the dead woman which strengthened our ties with the living.

The thought that I had done everything I could to relieve her terrible suffering gave me some feeling of tranquillity. She had at least ended her brief, disturbed life surrounded by love; she died confident that we understood her and that she would live on in our memories.

It shocked me to think that, had my suicide attempt been successful, I would have been much less fortunate than she . . . Who would have offered me real affection before I finally closed my eyes on a wasted, arid life? In *my* final moments there would only have been my son at my bedside, uncomprehending . . . alone . . . alone.

I said as much on the morning of the funeral to my old friend, who had come to pay her respects to the body, now bedecked with flowers. We were by the window, standing apart from the long file of mourners. Serenely we gazed at the blurred outline of her body, wrapped in a white sheet, at the walls covered with the vivid paintings she had produced with such inexhaustible talent and, through the window, at the countryside near Soratte. At last she was sleeping peacefully . . .

I could hear the old woman's voice, soft but urgent, asking me repeatedly, "Why are you going away? You must know by now that resignation is not a virtue."

I murmured my son's name and she fell silent, but pressed her hand lightly against my forehead several times.

"Don't go back there!"

It was exactly what my friend had said to me just before she died.

Among the crowd of people at the funeral following the flower-laden hearse, I caught a fleeting glimpse of the "prophet." A few days later when I was passing his house I had a sudden desire to see the place where he lived his isolated life, and, since I was soon to leave, to say goodbye to him.

I walked quickly into the damp old house and up the dark staircase.

It grew darker as I climbed and entered his room. He had already lit a candle. I could see a bed in one corner, low on the ground — virtually a pallet — and an earthenware stove on which he was grilling two apples. By the window there was a table covered with papers; the armchairs were scattered with books. The severe face of an old lady looked down from the wall — his mother, perhaps. He hesitantly stretched his arm towards me and asked me to take a seat. He looked very thin.

I find it difficult to remember what we talked about. He apologised for his room being so cold, he asked after my son and about our coming journey . . . I was watching his lips: not once did they tremble. I pointed to the drawers of his desk. Was his book in there? He nodded vaguely. Somehow, I don't know how, he must have been dimly aware that I didn't believe him . . . I talked, constantly on the verge of tears—but my eyes must more surely have communicated to him how defeated and bitter I felt. We remained silent. Then an extraordinary thing happened. His face, which had always had the expression of someone who lives only for himself, and his own ideas, changed dramatically and darkened over. It was only for a few seconds, but I saw it register that most human of griefs, the pure, intense suffering of someone who realises they are being abandoned. Then quickly he regained his normal obstinate tranquillity, the mark of his unapproachable superiority.

For the next two days my little apartment was cluttered with trunks and boxes. They seemed to me like so many coffins, filled with my dreams and hopes as well as my books and furniture. My husband wrote claiming that he needed to have me with him, disavowing his feelings for the poor dead woman. Perhaps he had finally realised that she had loved the physiologist all along, and had allowed his jealousy to suffocate what was left of his love for her. For one brief moment I had tried to seize my freedom. I had succeeded only in riveting my chains more securely.

PART III

TWENTY

Surprisingly, for the first time in my life I felt completely emotionally independent. During our life in Rome I had always had some misgivings — partly because of my fear of him — about trying to assert my independence by denying my obligations towards the man I was bound to by law. Now I felt calm and detached. When I arrived at our lodgings there were signs that my husband had been particularly considerate of my needs: new magazines and books were laid out for me on the desk. He offered me a timid smile. I took it as a warning that once again he was going to try to make me love him. He seemed impelled, apparently, by a strange mixture of feelings. On the one hand he was ashamed that his secret passion for my friend had come into the open, giving me the opportunity to tell him that I did not love him; on the other, he wanted the past forgotten, and hoped to achieve this by making me consent to a new sexual relationship with him. Yet he lacked the perseverance needed to give me time to respond to such an approach. He was too embarrassed, too incompetent. It wasn't long before I discovered that his new good intentions were more of a burden to me than his old domestic tyranny.

I was partly protected from his new desires by the demands of his job, which wore him out. Determinedly I insisted that he recognise that this part of his life had nothing to do with me. I suspected from the start that he would be an even more brutal taskmaster than my father, and my first impressions when I arrived home confirmed this. Moreover, since the workers knew my husband's origins, they didn't have the same instinctive fear of him which they had had for a strange manager from a different region. They disliked my husband therefore even more intensely than they had my father. Indeed, when I met the militant young men in the Worker's League, I realised that they found my husband ridiculous. And this gave them a strong weapon since it is hard to obey those you can turn into a figure of fun.

I was disturbed by the idea that they might be hostile to me too. Yet what could I do about it? Perhaps become involved in their struggle . . . by founding a school where I might educate the women whose ignorance contributed to the high infant mortality in the town, or teach them to read and write . . . but unfortunately I hadn't the courage to present my husband with such a scheme, and I had no confidence that I might find anyone in the area able or willing to help me with it.

So my life entered a new phase. My sister's marriage triggered off the first painful crisis of this new period of my life. I don't know why, but in the preceding months I had been playing with the idea that she and her fiancé would break off their engagement. Perhaps I doubted whether their love was good for them, perhaps I was jealous to see them so happy; or perhaps I was afraid that her love was like mine—an illusion, mere wish-fulfillment. I'm not sure. In the weeks after my return, she and my younger sister were preparing her trousseau, and they both seemed very happy. My eldest sister, in particular, was eager to take her life in her own hands and make something of it. I remembered our mother and wondered if she had been like that too, full of trust as she abandoned herself to the belief that love would never end.

My sister was married at the town hall one evening. The only family witness was my brother. Her fiancé refused to have my husband at the wedding, and so I was not allowed to go either. And Father refused his consent right to the end. He also refused even the smallest dowry. Yet when it dawned on him that this beautiful, tenacious girl who had inherited so many of his qualities and had been a surrogate mother to his children for so long was really leaving him at last, even he had to shed a tear. I cried too, in the darkness of my bedroom; I cried because the step she was taking was irrevocable, because our family was already inextricably enmeshed in a chain of failures — hadn't they been disastrous enough without adding another...? At least, that is why I thought I was crying. But in reality my tears must have been a desolate lament for my own isolation, for the state of mind which prevented me from feeling close to my sister in her happiest moment, and which made me feel unfit to join the celebrations, keeping me apart from the cheerful company of those loving and optimistic people...

As I lay there in extreme distress, I felt suffocated by an inexplicable inner turmoil. I longed for tenderness, for someone who would soothe me; I longed for poetry, for colour, for all-enveloping sound. Half asleep, I fell into a spell-binding dream of ecstasy, an ecstasy I had never known. I shook it off finally, but it took me some time to realise where I was. Now, in a frenzy, I went to my child, clasping him in my arms. He didn't seem surprised, but I felt he wanted me to respond to him, to smile.

I tried to smile, but he shook off my embrace and stared at me, anxious and questioning... Why did I communicate my unhappiness to such a small child, and demand of him something he could not give? Why did I so ludicrously demand from him the love my life had always lacked? At that moment I felt that everyone I had known, including my mother, my sisters, and my brother, were like passing ghosts who had never really known me at all, had never discovered what deep feelings I had, or how serious I could be. No one had ever offered me anything to help me grow, no one had ever spared me a tear; and I had never done anything for anyone either, I had never shown affection, helped others achieve anything, or given anyone any sympathy.

. . . And I knew that it was the strength of my feelings, so rigorously suppressed, which now weighed me down, suffocating me in retaliation . . . I was certain that those feelings were still there completely intact, and so forceful, that if I let go, my rebellious scream of frustration would fill the uncaring silence of the days and nights.

But rebellion was out of the question, so why grieve? It was spring time, the countryside looked lovely, I was with my growing son, so why grieve for the past? Why recall lost faces? Why imagine that people I had never met were speaking to me in sympathy or in anger, making my heart beat faster? And why, as I waited for my husband every night in bed, mentally distancing myself from him, did I feel my blood pounding with the anguished conviction that I was depriving myself of something that was my right? After the anguish I had experienced in this town I was still stubbornly determined to win through. I still wanted, as fiercely as ever, to have known sexual ecstasy. I still believed that the bliss when two bodies intermingled could create new life and help people achieve full human dignity and fulfillment.

The tranquil woman without desires that I had felt myself to be just a few months earlier seemed a remote, incomprehensible creature. Long ago, she had tried to understand what it meant to be human; now she seemed completely detached from me. The meaning of existence was only too eloquently and irresistibly being unveiled to me now, in the great spiritual desert I had allowed to grow around me. It was harmony, nothing more, the combined gratification of every need, intellectual and sensual, of the heart and of the soul . . .

My husband, tired and irritable, came into the darkened room. He turned on the light, moving around without looking to see if I was awake or not. I closed my eyes tight, then felt his heavy weight beside me. Out of the silence I heard him murmuring endearments as he tried to communicate his passion and arousal; then he took hold of me . . . My head sank back against the pillow . . . All I could feel was outrage and frustration. My hatred for him and for myself made me feel sick. And once again I felt the sudden shock of fear that I was really going mad.

He slept. I lay awake, listening to his heavy breathing for hours. Thoughts turned over and over in my mind, they seemed to tear at my flesh, making my head burst with pain.

Was this to be my entire existence? Was I merely to be used as an object of pleasure, sensually debased in a relentless round of days and nights, until I died?

Weeks later, my father finally left for Milan, never to return, and with him went my younger sister and my brother. My eldest sister and her husband went to live in the Veneto. Not one member of my family now lived close to me. At Easter we moved into the large, pleasant house papa had vacated. The house was surrounded by a large garden, and there some of my poor father's personality seemed to live on. That tangled greenery, the neglected but lovely collection of shrubs and trees, revealed how much he needed beauty, how strongly he wanted to express his individuality, how deeply he loved simplicity. He had given to that garden more than I had ever given to anything. How many confused speeches he must have made, with only his pride to support him, before that mute audience of flowers! Time had been too powerful for him too. He had ruthlessly created a factory, giving it all his thought and energy, and had used it to transform a whole community, jolting them out of their traditional inertia and widening their horizons. But his commitment had gone stale. He had become isolated, with no friend to respond to his ideas or argue against them; and even his hope that the cultivation of nature might produce the rewards which love for his fellow man had never earned him had been in vain.

My son became the happy king of his grandfather's old home. He played in the sunshine most of the day, while I read or daydreamed. I dressed him in a tunic of unbleached linen which reached his knees, and with his shining face and dark blue eyes glowing beneath his golden curls I thought him a miniature Siegfried. He was my only companion. When he burst into my room, throwing the doors open to the sunlight, he compensated me as no one else could for my regular, punishing contact with my husband's family. After a time I forgave my mother-in-law her irritating exclamations of surprise whenever she saw our house and its garden and orchard. "It's paradise," she would say. "You can live like a queen here! Well, my son, at last justice has been done!" But my sister-in-law, since the doctor had died, was more bitter and spiteful than ever: I was convinced that she could tell how unhappy I was and must have been pleased, but she pretended that like the others she thought me content.

My husband was patently overjoyed at finding himself such an object of admiration; his family almost worshipped him! I continued to find him a relentless source of incredible irritation: at the table, in the garden, in the street, I would suddenly become aware of some new and intolerable mannerism.

The monotony of our routine was sometimes interrupted by the visit of an important client or supplier who had to be invited to dinner. When they left they congratulated us on the cultivated atmosphere of our home. If my husband tried to thank me afterwards I cut him short, not wishing to hear. He was hurt by this and fell silent until he could retaliate with mockery, sarcasm, or derision. My child listened to him, shocked — sometimes he pressed my hand to show me I had his tacit support. I felt both happy and distressed to realise what little confidence he had in his bad-tempered, argumentative father.

One evening everyone went out, leaving me alone at home. I put the child to bed, then sank into a wicker chair in the garden. My gaze was instinctively drawn to the gloomy vault of star-strewn silent worlds. But I wasn't tempted into speculation about the mystery of the universe. I was immersed in a more urgent and particular human anguish: the fear of dying soon in such hostile and alien surroundings and leaving no trace of my existence behind me . . . The immensity of the sky only reminded me again that I was in chains, yoked to a pitiless life which rendered me incapable of anything other than continuous depression . . .

I jumped up to look at my sleeping son. Fearful as I was, he at least was peaceful and trusting . . . If only I could save him, my treasure, from a future like mine! If only I could be certain that through all his life he would be as happy as he was at this moment, enjoying the serene sleep of childhood!

As I watched him I imagined that he was asking my forgiveness. I pressed his little hand to my lips. I had nothing to forgive. Indeed, one day he might be justified in asking, "Why, my poor mother, did you make such a sacrifice of yourself?" I was tormented by remorse. What would his life be like, growing up with two such parents? Although he was the only person in the house capable of a spontaneous smile of pleasure, even that was now becoming a rare event.

He respected my need to read and study: I was the only person who gave him any notion of what it meant to live for ideas. But perhaps he was also aware that life can play strange tricks. I was, I had to confess, becoming inclined to treat him badly as a way of relieving the torment I endured in my bleakest moments. Either I demanded too much of him, forcing him to work and refusing to let him play, or else I neglected him, leaving him to play in the garden or to run to the factory, or to amuse himself by colouring pictures or painting newspapers which I spread on the floor, while I ignored his real demands. I lacked the consistency of a proper teacher, and wasn't relaxed enough to guide him through his own experiences. Nor did I feel especially interested in what his real needs were and how they could be satisifed. There were times when, knowing this, I hated myself. I had decided to sacrifice myself for him and put my own needs second, yet I found I wasn't able to dedicate myself to his intellectual development even though I kept him with me so much. The thought made me utterly wretched.

. . . And then I discovered that this was how my mother had felt about her relationship with her children! One day, I opened a small box of her papers my sister had given me before she left for the Veneto, and I went through them — I had never before had the courage to do so. I found letters from relatives, shopping lists, various notes and copies of letters written to her parents, her sister, and her husband. Some poetry from her younger days was there too: it was sentimental and romantic, but nonetheless had the ring of tragic sincerity. There were also notes which she had written during her breakdown, before she went to the asylum, in which she expressed how she felt as a mother.

As I was going through them I found a letter which made me gasp. It dated from Milan, and had been written in pencil at night. By now it was almost illegible. Mother was informing her father that she would be arriving the next day: her bags were packed with the few possessions she had, she was in the nursery, preparing to embrace her children before leaving them . . .

"I have to leave . . . I'm going mad here . . . he doesn't love me any more . . . And I am so unhappy that I no longer even love my children . . . I have to leave them, I have to leave . . . I'm sorry for my children, but perhaps this will be better for them . . ."

The letter was unfinished, and it was clear that she hadn't rewritten it or sent it. She had lacked the courage to carry out a decision that she must have reached in some moment of lucid despair. Perhaps she had feared poverty, or believed her heart might break if she left her children and the man with whom she had shared her youth. Once she had loved him — had she loved him still when she wrote that letter? Since she stayed it must have been for our sake, from a sense of duty and a fear that one day we would accuse her of abandoning us.

I had no inkling that my mother had ever been through such a crisis. In Milan, however precocious or intelligent I had been as a child, I had seen nothing. How I wished that I had been older then, when she was still in full possession of her faculties and still had enough vigour to struggle for her rights against the fatal, seductive power of self-sacrifice! If I had been able to catch her unawares and if she had asked me, "Daughter, what should I do?" surely I would have answered, in the name of my brother and sisters as well, "You must leave us, mother, leave us!"

Yes, surely that would have been my answer. I would have said, "You must follow the demands of your own conscience. Put your self-respect before anything else. Be brave. Even when you are far away, continue to resist, work, and struggle. And look after yourself, too. One day we shall recognise how tormented you were at this moment, and then we will make up our own minds about your decision. In the meantime, spare us at least the spectacle of your slow decline into painful, inevitable disaster!"

But we had had no understanding of her suffering, and she had been left to go mad. If she had gone away, even if father had refused to let us join her, we would at least have had the benefits of her experience as an independent person ten or twenty years later, even if that experience had exhausted her . . .

Why do we idealise sacrifice in mothers? Who gave us this inhuman idea that mothers should negate their own wishes and desires? The acceptance of servitude has been handed down from mother to daughter for so many centuries that it is now a monstrous chain which fetters them. Every woman, at some point in her life, realises how much she owes the woman who gave her birth, and at the moment of recognition feels intense remorse, aware that she has never fully recompensed her mother for the damage done to herself in doing good for us. But as soon as she becomes a mother herself she stands her wish to repay this debt on its head: she denies herself in her turn, providing a new example of self-mortification and self-destruction. Yet what would happen if this dreadful cycle was broken, once and for all? What if mothers refused to deny their womanhood and gave their children instead an example of a life lived according to the needs of self-respect? Perhaps we would begin to learn that parents' duties start long before their children are born. Perhaps if we realised that relationships founded on domination and seduction originate in selfishness, we would put more emphasis on the responsibilities involved in parenthood. It is after all a remarkable phenomenon for a couple to feel assured that they possess the capacities to create and maintain a new life in health and strength. It is an act which requires great humility. Wouldn't a recognition of this offer children a better future?

Children should be grateful to us for being who we are and for wishing that their lives should be happier and more enjoyable than our own: they shouldn't feel indebted because we give birth to them unthinkingly and then react by renouncing our own identity.

These thoughts kept me awake the night after I had read my mother's papers. They reminded me of the problems of conscience I had grappled with in Rome, but they seemed much more urgent and more telling. And the things I became aware of that night grew stronger and stronger during the following days and weeks.

I began to feel that I had formulated a law of my own. It might cause me distress, but by now it was a part of me. In time it would surely become instinctive and would force me to act. When the time came I would follow it as effortlessly as swallows follow changing currents in the spring air.

I became much calmer, but only outwardly. At times I was so possessed by my new ideas that they became abstractions, devoid of any real significance for myself; they seemed like obvious and natural truths, which as yet had no connection with the way in which I and everyone around me lived.

The only person to notice any change was our maid. Although she rarely spoke to me, she used to watch my changing moods, and sometimes the intense expression on my face surprised and frightened her. Everyone else regarded me as if I was still a precocious child, but she tried to give me advice, entreating me to work as I had done before, to hope, to have faith in the future.

I was moved by her concern. Her simplicity and affection for me seemed to have developed into a strange intuitive awareness of my state of mind, perhaps as a result of our constant companionship over the past years. Or perhaps the few words I had spoken to her aroused her curiosity, perhaps my increasing distress and the inconsistency of my statements had suggested a train of thought which had allowed her to enter into the melancholy prison of my present thoughts.

Yet it was freedom I wanted. I thought that if I could achieve that I would be able to influence everyone who longed for liberation, by sharing my happiness, energy, and hopes for the future with all those who had not yet realised that they too could change their lives, who still thought that they were born only to suffer!

My emotional life was increasingly intense: it rose with the dawn and took wing at sunset. I felt capable of the most sublime poetry. Every thought was an eruption into brilliant sunshine, an ascent among icy peaks or a walk amid exquisite flowers. I experienced moments of perfect joy — I was simply happy to be alive, as if the spring winds had come to remind me that new leaves were just unfolding. I decided that no work of literature could have any lasting value unless its language unmistakably paid homage both to humility and to self-respect. Time might go by, our illusions and certainties might change, even our desires might be transformed, but our reactions to the force of love and pain would never change. We would always have to face the challenge of transforming our existence once more, we would always be humbled by the recognition that even in those places where we believe ourselves completely isolated we find sympathy and companionship.

Tension between my husband and his employees became as acute that autumn as it had been with my father the year before. The factory was making considerable profits, and my husband, as manager, was paid a sizeable percentage of them, but workers' wages were kept low and discipline was harsh. I thought this totally unjust. I felt ashamed by my powerlessness and depressed by my inactivity. Groups of workers passed our garden gate on their way to and from work, and they laughed at me in contempt. Much as I resented their impudence, I felt that they were more deserving of respect than I. Afraid to leave the house, I wandered instead through the garden for hours upon end, like a ghost. Just like my mother . . . My life seemed to be just what hers had been. Was I travelling in the same direction?

I became increasingly unhappy, and was permanently exhausted. For a time I worried that I might be pregnant again. My wave of terror at the thought was a real indication of my misery. I began to wish that I could run away and leave that house behind me.

I asked my husband to let me go and stay with my brother in Milan. He had refused this once before, but now he agreed. My fears about being pregnant vanished. But he had guessed why I was so worried, and the atmosphere between us became unbearable. We parted without exchanging a word, but nonetheless I felt threatened by his silence.

Once more I became immersed in city life, this time the city of my childhood. It is not that I searched the streets and parks for the girl I had been fifteen years ago, but I was fascinated to find that the place was still so familiar. In the evenings the misty squares and lines of street lamps along the deserted ship canal looked just as I remembered them. It was here that I had had my first education from my father, learning to respect, to worship even, collective human achievement.

As a child my father had taught me, albeit confusedly, that urban man conducts an unceasing and magnificent struggle against the limitations and insufficiencies of nature. The walls of a city might make it to some extent a prison, but men still feel more powerful and free within them than they do beneath an immense starry sky, in the mountains, or by the sea, where they have to confront the indifference of the elements. They can only affirm their own power by ostentatiously parading in their cities the most recent proof of their inventiveness.

I was aware that in Milan and Rome, just as in the country town I lived in, the motivation for all this human effort was selfish individualism. When I watched people in crowds I noticed how they rushed past each other without giving any sign that anyone else existed. But when I visited the vast workers' suburbs, looked over their new schools, and attended public meetings, I also realised that within the close-knit and chaotic web of a city an enormous change was taking place and a new consciousness was being produced. This consciousness, still confused, contained nonetheless a vision of the future which originated in feelings of reciprocity, in contact between past and future, in realisation of the continuing importance of solidarity. Only a city can create this. The people who articulated this new vision with such gentle persistence were few. But I felt that their ideas were similar to those of my old revolutionary friend in Rome. And I envied them, just as I had envied her, their powerful altruism, which I felt sure was strong enough to propel even a modern industrial city forward into a new phase of change.

My youngest sister took me to visit people who were planning to live in revolutionary communes. It was obvious that she wanted to be involved too, even if only in a small way, and this made me anxious. Yet I could understand why she reacted against the prospect of being merely a sterile and ignorant observer of other people's lives. She had had a depressing time in Milan. Father had left her on her own too often with nothing to do. He was now so restless and frustrated that he was always away. My brother had a factory job and a girl friend, and hoped that soon his wage would support them both. He attended courses at the People's University, where he had made many interesting friends, and as a result he neglected his sister. "But what can I do?" he asked me, "She needs a friend of her own age." She listened intently, wide-eyed, to our conversations. It was true that she had no real companionship, no friend who could care for her and offer her the enthusiasm she would need for a more active life. As a result she had no focus except her own emotions, and I was alarmed by the speed and ease with which she passed from the deepest misery to intense excitement. She still had all the freshness of a young girl, yet all the same she feared always that she would be the chief victim of our parents' disastrous marriage, doomed to carry their irremediable conflict within her for the rest of her life. She would ask me why I couldn't be with her more often, staring at me as if I held some key to her future.

Her anxiety made me feel afraid for her, but I also felt enormous pleasure when I was with her. I thought she showed a keen awareness of the problems with which life had confronted her, and I felt that I had at least contributed to her insights. It was impossible to predict whether my brother or my sister would find real satisfaction in their lives, but when they told me about their particular anxieties and their hopes I was aware that they were representatives of a new generation. My sister, like many modern women, would have to break through barriers she had made for herself and that others had made for her if she was to become a full personality, in possession of her own identity; my brother would only be able to achieve knowledge of himself if he could find a woman who understood herself and her own desires, and on the basis of this could offer him real recognition.

There was no guarantee that either would find partners with whom they could share their enthusiasms and their suffering. I sometimes thought that if I could once meet a happy couple before I died I would count myself lucky. But then I would remember the editor's daughter and her fiance, whom I had met that day in Rome just before my Norwegian friend died; I felt convinced, remembering them, that such couples did really exist, and, remembering them, I would remember others. But if the thought of them reassured me, I became increasingly uncomfortable when I contrasted their lives with the squalid conditions I had allowed myself to sink into and realised the stagnation of my own development. The emotions which then tore my mental life apart were not those which any poet has ever been able to express.

This visit to my family was only an interlude in my life, but by the end I felt ready for anything. I was eager, strong again, more than ever convinced of the usefulness of the ideas I had been brooding over during these months of isolation. I was sure my ideas really were creative, and felt certain that there must be people who didn't carry the blood of incurable conflict in their veins — even if I and my brothers and sisters did. Such people could unite in common action because they felt secure about their future, and this security was reinforced by a memory of loving parents and by a belief that they themselves could be the same.

Yet at the same time I thought that such experiences would only be widely shared in some future society, although I was puzzled by my absolute certainty that such a future might exist. Had it been generated by a childhood and adolescence in a home where my parents no longer had any mutual understanding? Had their conflict aroused by curiosity? Despite many obstacles, this curiosity had developed my own capacity for logical and abstract thinking. Sometimes when I looked at myself from the outside I admired myself for the course I had taken. I thought I was a privileged bearer of a new sort of truth, which manifested itself through my suffering. But if this was true I should be able to produce something which others, who suffered like me, would find useful, and I very much doubted that I was capable of that.

TWENTY-ONE

My husband seemed rather embarrassed when he met met at the station. As we drove home in our carriage he concentrated mainly on the child, and when I went into the house I was surprised to see how frightened our maid was looking. But because my mother-in-law and sister-in-law were there I had to try to be polite. They had prepared a welcoming party for my son, and he was so bored by it and so restive that I had to join in too. When I glanced towards my husband, I was astonished to see that he looked unmistakably older. His face was a pallid, emaciated mask, showing signs of grave illness. Was it really only a few weeks since we had parted? It seemed like years. And I felt more than this: I felt he was now so distant and estranged from me that we might never have been part of each other's lives.

When we were alone he told me that while I was away he had been ill. He talked about it a great deal, but what he said was very confused. He claimed it wasn't serious, just the return of an old infection from a long time ago, when he was in the army...

I had a flash of memory, of something I had heard before ... But where? In the city? From the woman doctor?

"It is nothing very important," he repeated. "Don't let it worry you." He had been ill in bed for a few days, and the doctor wanted him to continue to rest, but that was impossible. Anyway, he was better now.

As he told me his story he kept swearing under his breath —usually a sign that he was apologising for something. I listened in silence, unable to make out what had really happened. Standing up, he took me in his arms with a respectful hesitation, very unusual for him. He searched for my lips; instinctively I bowed my head. He placed his lips on my brow, murmuring "You're a good woman...too good...I don't deserve you...!"

When we went to bed that night I could feel his desire mounting passionately as he lay beside me. Once more I remembered that conversation long ago with the woman doctor in Rome, and her bitter smile. And then I was overcome by a savage and irrepressible impulse to defend myself. After a moment he turned away. I trembled as if in a fever.

The next day the doctor from a nearby town came and talked vaguely about my husband's need for rest and treatment, looking shiftily at me before he left.

The maid still watched me strangely, or, rather, had a strange way of not looking at me. Finally she let slip that a few days after I had left, the master had gone away too, and that when he returned he was ill. I didn't question her, but she added, "That's all I can tell you..."

She had no need to tell me more. I could depict the scene clearly enough for myself. One day, an irritable man knocks on the door of a brothel...I pictured his family's shame, their decision to hide it from me, their lies... Did anything in all this surprise me? No. In a sense it was like looking at a drawing which I had watched from the beginning and which was now finally shown to me, complete and perfect.

And I said not a word to him. Even if I had wanted to, my lips would not have opened to allow the words to pass. I told the maid to prepare a bed for me in the room next to my son's. That night, before he went out to make his final round of the factory, I told my husband what I had done. He turned paler still, but he must have been expecting some reaction. Pretending not to take it very seriously, he grumbled, "Well, as long as it's only for a few days!"

After that I was filled with utter disgust whenever he came into the house. He put on a show of being an impatient victim, although at the same time pretended not to find my new sleeping arrangements at all surprising. Yet I knew that he went to his sister for advice about our relationship and sometimes tried her advice out on me. When he wasn't complaining about his illness, which was more serious than he had expected, he moaned at me about the Socialists, and how they were attempting to provoke a strike. Sometimes, when he came home and found me bending over our child, absorbed in reading him a story or describing a picture, his lips would narrow vindictively as he spat out some witticism... "Are you trying to make the boy as literary as yourself!"

I was trying to understand my son better. Our intimacy seemed to increase the more his intelligence developed, and he began to have thoughts of his own. He sat at a small table working at his exercises while I wrote or read, stopping only to answer his questions. We spent many peaceful hours like this. But when he left me to go to play I seemed to grow tense.

In those days I was reading Amiel's *Intimate Journal,* a book which gave me strange pleasure. I began to have hallucinations, in my work-room, among the shrubs in the garden, in the middle of the road, or even on the sea shore. I thought I saw my mother, a young woman standing by my sister's cradle, as she decided to accept her terrible fate; and the "prophet" bending over his desk, writing down the message of bland pessimism woven from repressed tears and screams; I saw a famous writer I had admired in childhood, whose twenty-year-old son had just killed himself—a victim, perhaps, of parental conflict. They were all blood-stained symbols of the delusions of sacrifice, terrible examples of the punishment in store for all those who deny their own feelings.

But wasn't I one of them too? After all, I had never yet been stirred to action either by reasoned argument or by the intensity of my own feelings. I was still living with a man I despised, who didn't even love me. To the rest of the world I wore the mask of the satisfied wife, and so I partly helped legitimise ignominious slavery, and sanctified a monstrous lie.

And now, with the ultimate cowardice which has defeated so many women, I began to think once more of death as a means of liberation. I was prepared to leave my son so that I might die, but I wasn't courageous enough to leave him so that I might live.

A wave of madness swept over me. In the evenings I just managed to tolerate the usual conversations with the whole family, but if I was left alone with my husband I felt overcome with humiliation each time he looked at me, each time he tried to make amends. I allowed myself to be drawn into arguments, sarcastically criticising his complaints about the crisis in industry and the attitude of the workers. My voice rose sharply; I began to lose the sense of what I was saying. Then a little voice would interrupt: "Mamma!" and a moment later, "Mamma, come here!" I would control myself and go into my son's darkened room. Seeing my shadow in the doorway he would call again, more quietly, "Mamma!" When he sensed that I was near his bed he would stretch out his arms, clasp my neck, and pull my head down next to his. Silently he stroked my eyes and cheek with warm, trembling fingers. What did he want? To make sure that I wasn't crying, that his papa wasn't making me cry? Once more I heard him whisper, "Mamma," and I pushed my face into the bedcovers. But soon it was bathed in tears, his and mine... Deep within me I was begging his forgiveness, and I stayed there for a long time, awaiting the blessing of sleep for him and for myself the coma of the depression which always followed such crises.

One day a telegram arrived from Turin. My uncle, Father's elder brother, was dangerously ill. He had always been very fond of me, despite everything, and when things had been difficult in Rome he had helped us with gifts and loans of money.

He was a very different person from my father, much more the typical hard-working bourgeois. He had his principles, conventional and limited though they were, and if he was a complacent man, he was also extremely kind. I had seen a lot of him when I was a child, and although we had grown apart since then I was always pleased to see him. Portly, pink-cheeked, crusty, he still enjoyed having his nephews and nieces around him.

I hoped to get there in time to see him once more. I was also afraid that if he was very ill he might no longer recognise me. My husband made arrangements for me to travel that same evening. After skirting round the subject for a time, he began to instruct me as to how I was to behave to my rich uncle and his family; I felt he was killing off all my spontaneous feeling for my uncle, and bitterly I wondered once again if life was always going to be like this.

I travelled all night, thinking the journey would never end, and when I arrived in the smoke-filled station next morning I was met by my father and my aunt. They asked how I was; Father complained about the state of the railways; my aunt reproached him with not having kissed me... It was a long time since I had felt my father's arms around me!

My uncle had died during the night. He had been one of the few people to whom I still felt deeply attached by family solidarity, and he was gone. I felt empty, but also liberated. Like many young people, I felt suddenly that the old order was departing so as to allow me to live and dream in my own way.

I spent three days in Turin, saddened by seeing the greed of his nephews and nieces and other relatives who had gathered round the corpse. It was a great relief when my father took me off to walk with him through the peaceful streets of his beloved birthplace.

He seemed tired as he talked, and we both felt our old affection returning, though we were both surprised by it, as if we expected that at any moment it could vanish again. We were after all completely independent of each other now, each following our own misguided path. We could neither really complain nor offer guidance to each other. Nor were we able to imagine any longer that we would ever again turn to each other for support, or remain loyal to each other whatever the outcome. So we confined ourselves to gathering up the threads from the past, concentrating carefully on the feelings and characteristics we still had in common.

It was he who told me about the provisions of the will. I was to have 25,000 lire; my brother and sisters, 5,000. I almost resented this, feeling an urge to divide my share with the others, and indeed felt peculiarly ashamed of myself, as if the possession of money for which I hadn't worked, or of any privilege, however small, diminished me. I felt undeserving, not just in relation to my own family, but also to those who worked to earn their own living with energy and determination, and were in this sense my true brothers.

Nonetheless, once I had overcome this acute and complicated sense of disappointment, I couldn't help thinking about the practical effect the money could have on my life. It meant that I would acquire some financial independence. It wasn't a large amount, but it would support my child, even if I had to work to support myself.

There was a clause in the will delaying its execution for six months.

I wrote to my husband, telling him when I would return. I felt confident that now I could make more demands on him. I could travel more, take holidays, buy books for myself and my son without always having to ask his permission...

In the midst of my vague plans I constructed a strange fantasy. I had a lover somewhere else in Italy. I visited him from time to time and took my fill of pleasure and delight. Then I returned home, to the gloomy house I was not able to leave because of the strength of my maternal feelings. Thus nobody was betrayed by me. My husband already knew how much I despised him. My needs would be satisfied, and I would also be given the strength to carry on, to tolerate my existence...

What madness! I let my imagination run wild like this, but even though I wasn't sure what I *would* do, I knew what I could never do. In a sense the future already lay within me: whatever the solutions to my problems, by now they were so clearly formulated at some level that they felt almost like destiny.

It was morning when I arrived home. My son was playing with his puppets, and I sat down on the carpet to join in his game. My husband, sunk in silence, was reading the newspapers. We didn't exchange a word.

My sister-in-law arrived, mawkishly cheerful. I was in no hurry to give her the news she was waiting for, and after a time, unable to contain herself any longer, she burst out, "So we're rich, are we?"

I bent my head even further over the puppet theatre. My son was so absorbed in the performance that he hadn't heard her. Her shrill voice continued, swamping the dialogue I was speaking for the little characters. "And now our dear little boy has another fortune laid in store for him. Oh, I can see that he'll own the whole town one of these days!"

Now his dear blue eyes were staring straight at me: they seemed to be saying, "Go on mamma, don't listen to her. I'm listening only to you; you are the only person in my life..."

Oh yes, go on. But that night, as I was going to bed, exhausted, my husband came to my room. We had a terrible struggle before I was finally left alone in the darkness, wishing that I could die.

The next morning I said quietly to my child, "Perhaps I will die, you know. But if I do, don't cry for me: just remember me."

Death!

I felt as if a hard, heavy lump was growing in my brain.
Suddenly I had a ghoulish thought. One day, perhaps, *he*, my
husband, might *disappear* . . . After all, people can die, vanish
like a breath of air. And life goes on. We go on meeting, seeing, speaking to other people who never even mention their
names . . . As if they had never existed . . .

Had I died this would have happened to me . . . And what
would have become of my son?

But now, if *he* went . . . my son and I would be alone . . . I
would wander round the house — it would be my house, no one
else's. I could walk round the garden, through the streets . . .
the sea would still be there, and the villages in the distant hills.
The world would be rich and spacious, and my son and I
would be free, free . . .

It was a daydream from which I awoke with a start as I
heard my son calling to the maid. I was astonished that I felt
no horror at what I envisaged. I heard the garden gate open as
my husband came in. It was midday. He came close, and I felt
him looking at me, so I turned away. Throughout the meal I
concentrated on my son. Alone for a moment with my husband afterwards I turned to him, feeling my face go rigid: "I'm
going to lock my bedroom door in the future!"

He slammed his fist on the table. Then he got up, paced
the room several times, and sat down again in a fury.

"Do what you like!"

He stood up again abruptly and went into the garden. But
he came back almost immediately, spitting out a flood of
obscenities. Bending slightly I held my child to me, as my fingers mechanically followed the lines of the book he was reading. Then to interrupt the flow of insults I looked my husband
full in the face. I told him that there was only one way out, the
one I had suggested a year before — separation.

His face grew livid. All right, I could go, I could go. He
would soon find another woman to replace me!

Calmly I went on, "Do as you like. But not with my son in

the house. He will come with me to my father's house until we've reached some legal agreement."

He was standing by the french windows which opened on to the garden. He raised an arm, then let it drop. His face was swollen with anger.

"Our son?" he exclaimed, "Just you try!"

He was shouting so loudly that his voice must have been heard in the street. I felt my child shuddering, and as he choked back his sobs he clung to me.

"As for you, get up! You're coming with me to the factory. Up you get!"

The trembling little voice objected: "I have to do my homework . . ."

My son's pure blue eyes met his father's stormy, terrifying gaze. There was a moment's silence, during which I didn't move, aware of nothing but the pressure of a small, damp hand.

I heard the door slam and footsteps retreating over the gravel.

The two of us were left alone in the house for the whole sultry afternoon . . . With a broken-hearted gesture my child dried my slowly dropping tears and asked, "What was papa talking about? What did he want? Why does he always shout? Why does he make you cry so much?"

"I have to go away, my son; I have to leave here . . ."

What was I saying? I could tell how much I was disturbing my child by the violence with which he grasped my shoulders.

"Mamma, mamma, I'll come with you, won't I? Say I can, please! . . . I don't want to stay here with papa, I don't want to leave you . . . I don't want to, mamma! You will take me with you, won't you? . . ."

And he flung himself into my arms, bursting into floods of tears which seemed to seep through my skin, sobbing like an adult, as if he contained all the grief in the world. Oh, my son! And I held you and wept with you, sharing in your despair. I felt as if I had taken you back into my womb and was expelling you for a second time into the world, in a never-ending spasm of pain and joy and in fearful acceptance of the domination of our everlasting bond . . .

I wrote to my father to let him know what I had decided. Then, sadly, I re-read a book I had consulted in Rome a year before. It stated, simply and clearly, my legal position. I suppose I already knew it, but only then, as I applied it to my own case, feeling myself a total prisoner and the law my prison gates, did I realise how truly monstrous it was. It was almost incredible, but according to the law I had no existence — except as someone who could be cheated of her rights, of everything she had: her property, her work, her son!

Days of terrible tension followed. Although I now felt myself gathering all my strength for a final effort, I still couldn't bring myself to go through with my decision. It wasn't that I was afraid of my gaoler's anger any more. I was simply unable to suppress the anguish I felt as a mother losing the one person who had brought happiness into my life. Sometimes I felt nothing — no rebellion, no resignation even. But repeatedly I had the same argument with myself.

"You don't love him, and he doesn't love you: you are like two strangers. You only stay out of a sense of duty."

Then: "What good has your sense of duty ever done you?"

And again: "This is your last chance."

The logic was undeniable. In Rome, a year earlier when I had rebelled, it had been almost on impulse, and even I had been surprised at myself. But I had now spent a year in torment and my mind was made up. I had glimpsed the abyss, and had decided I must leave or die. I had been finally driven by fate, coincidence, or some logic I didn't understand to show the man whose slave I was how much I loathed his embrace. It had taken me ten years. I felt ashamed of myself. Those hours spent wrestling with my conscience had never once impelled me to break the chains that bound me. I had left it to my body to rebel, to cry out, to fight for its freedom. It was to my body that I owed my liberation.

Sometimes when I thought about leaving forever, escaping that life based on lies, I thought that perhaps it would be even more beneficial for my son than for me. I would certainly suffer terribly without him, and I hated the thought that he might forget me, and that I might die alone; but I would never again feel self-disgust, and never again would I lie to him. His life would not be overshadowed by my cowardice.

Yet how could I condemn him to stay behind? Why should the law insist that my son be bound to his father? I had been responsible for him until then. Why should I not still be allowed to look after him and take care of his education?

It was an appalling dilemma. If I went away, we would certainly be separated, and he would be little more than an orphan; yet if I stayed I would be an example of humiliation to him for the rest of my days. And he, like me, would grow up in the company of a mad mother and a criminally indifferent father.

My child came and stroked my hair, already turning grey. I responded passionately: he was mine, and I wanted him more than anything else in the world. Even if it meant damnation for the two of us, I wanted him to myself. It was unimaginable that he might grow up without me, giving pleasure to others but not to me.

Once I asked him, "Would you rather go to boarding school than stay here with papa?"

I had never liked the idea of his being shut up in a school like that . . . But if it came to a choice . . .

The little one nodded. But later that day he turned pale whenever I spoke to him. "What did grandfather say when he wrote to you?" he wanted to know. "Is papa going to let me come with you to Milan?" By now he was openly suspicious. Yet whenever he saw me in despair after a quarrel with his father, or staring into empty space, he forgot his own pain and comforted me, telling me he loved me very much and would never love anyone else.

"And will you always remember me?" I asked. "Even if I die? Even if I go away and leave you?"

"Yes."

I knew that he answered truthfully, that he wasn't, as I was, searching through a labyrinth of emotions for something which would explain all this. It was simply a promise he made to himself. It might lie buried for a while, but in the future it would give him strength.

I spent nearly two weeks like this, swinging from despair to rebellion and back. Rumours about us were rife in the town. Everyone knew about my husband's infection, and they assumed this was the reason for my anger. His mother came to talk to me about it, in tears: "You poor thing. But you don't know how many other women are in the same state as you — there's so-and-so and so-and-so else. . . ."

My sister-in-law came too: "Well, it was only human weakness, you know, from his time in the army." One evening when she was there my husband tried to hit me, and she restrained him, pulling his arm and saying, "Don't put yourself in a compromising situation. Can't you see that's what she's waiting for? . . ."

We wasted hours in incoherent, exasperating argument. It exhausted me. I longed to be a little girl again, able to cry myself to sleep. I have no idea what gave me the strength to resist him. Finally I asked to be allowed to go away to consult my father and have some rest. Perhaps if we were away from each other we might begin to see things differently.

But none of his family could accept my point of view or agree to what I asked. They threw in my face my father's affairs, my mother's insanity, my atheism, all the things that had been brought up in the past . . .

Yet they seemed as frightened of me now as they had been

at the beginning. Once I thought I glimpsed amazement, respect even, in the way my husband looked at me — after I had made a wild speech about my absolute inner certainty, which would stretch beyond the grave . . . Momentarily I felt hopeful. Perhaps these ten years hadn't been wasted, perhaps he wouldn't make our child suffer for the damage I had done him. After all, he still pleaded with me to stay for the sake of our son. If he loved his son so much might he not realise that it really was impossible for the two of us to live together, and give in? He was still a young man. He could make a new life for himself. If he really felt such pain at the thought of losing me, might not this pain do him good, help to make him a better person? . . .

At last he told me one evening that I could go to Milan for a time if I wanted to, but that I couldn't take the child. Meanwhile, that same morning, a letter had come from my father, promising to intervene as best he could to help me win custody. But he was worried that the tension might be bad for me, and urged me to leave.

I was still thinking about what my husband had said, when he started to roll his eyes and groan inarticulately. I went to him and shook him. His eyes were glassy. I couldn't tell if he had really lost his senses or was just pretending, but I poured a glass of brandy and forced him to drink it. He slowly recovered and thanked me. Then suddenly he fell to his knees, clasping my legs as he cried out, "Don't leave me, don't leave. Can't you tell how much I love you?" as if delirious. I tried to calm him but he only pulled me towards him murmuring incoherently.

I felt utterly distant from him, entirely separate. I despised him for his cowardly reliance on male strength. How could he use his sexual desire as a means to keep me?

Resolutely I said, "I'm leaving tonight . . ."

By then he had regained his self-control, and, quickly concealing his humiliation, he nodded. All right, I could go; but not the child, he would stay. When I was away from them I would realise that I couldn't live without my family . . . and if and when I returned we would make new arrangements about living together.

He went to his room. I stayed at my child's bedside, not wanting sleep, feeling nothing, thinking nothing. I was waiting — for what, I don't know: light perhaps, or warmth. Anything that would make me feel alive. I needed all my strength.

My son breathed quietly, and as I listened to him I realised that I would never hear that sound again. I heard a clock strike in the distance and started from my chair. But how slowly the hours passed! Perhaps my father would be prepared to use force to help me get my child back. The future seemed dark with problems, confusion, pain. I thought I saw my son's face in the centre of it all. Surely one day, in the street perhaps, just as he was passing a turning, I would suddenly catch sight of him. Surely he would always be watching out for me. And then people change, laws change. Surely if someone is determined enough, obsessed enough, they can persuade the most obstinate . . . until death!

Death! I shivered at the word, as I had done that night so long ago! But I had overcome all desire for death, even death for the man who was my enemy. I didn't hate him anymore. For me he had become nothing but a shadowy figure who accompanied the spectre of the law through that incomprehensible, decisive night.

I lit the lamp and covered it. There was a rustle from the bed. "Mamma?" I moved to him, took his hand, and he went back to sleep. I stayed there, motionless, hardly daring to breathe.

It was midnight. I had three hours left. My knees began to tremble, so I sat in the armchair. The night air made me cold, and I tried to warm myself, closing my eyes and taking my hand from the child's so as not to pass the cold on to him. Suddenly I felt my strength ebbing. I seemed to be falling asleep. I was so tired: would I really manage to leave?

Three o'clock struck. I leapt to my feet, put on my coat,

and went to the door. Then I turned back to the bed and woke him up. "I'm going now," I said quietly. "It's time I went. Be good, love me, remember, I'll always be your mamma..." and I kissed him hesitantly, unable to cry. Then I heard him saying sleepily, "I'll always be good... Send grandfather to fetch me, mamma... I'll stay with you..." He turned peacefully towards the wall. It was then that I knew I would never return. I felt urged on by something outside myself, pushing me forward to a different life. And I knew that no future pain could ever equal the grief I felt at that moment.

Without knowing how I got there, I found myself on the train. The carriage, jolting forward, jarred inside me as if something was being torn from my body. As I gradually realised that this iron monster was finally taking me away, the events of the past months seemed suddenly inexorable, inevitable. I had gone to the train like a sleepwalker, and only now was I aware of what I had done. It was a terrible moment!

How could I have done it? Perhaps my child had not really gone to sleep after I kissed him; perhaps he was calling for me even now... I felt as if I had practised a terrible deceit. Shouldn't I have woken him properly and told him I would never come back, that I didn't know if he would ever be able to join me? Perhaps my husband was with him now, standing by the bed and lying in his turn, with the promise that I would return soon. Perhaps my son believed him, or was afraid to ask too many questions... And what would he do tomorrow, and the day after? Would my life be filled with these appalling, unanswerable questions from now on, forever?

How could I have done it? Why hadn't I been stronger? Yet I felt as if I had just had an operation to remove another person from my body — in order to save us both...

I don't know how long that awful journey lasted. At every station I had a dreadful impulse to leave the train and wait for another which would take me back. And then when the train moved forward again I began to think of suicide — it would be so easy, just through the door. Death would be instantaneous.

When we arrived in Milan I once again felt propelling me that power outside myself. Sad and determined, I set out, through the smoke and crowds, away from the station. I strode onward, lost and unhappy, into the noisy streets, where the morning sun was dispersing the mist.

TWENTY-TWO

A whole year has passed since then.

And I have never returned. Nor have I seen my child again.

My presentiment was right.

For a long time I preserved the illusion that my child would be allowed to come to me. For the first few days I rested, taken care of by my sister, who, although very anxious, asked no questions. Then, as the weeks went by, the correspondence between my husband and myself became increasingly violent: my father wrote to him, and finally we communicated only through lawyers. My husband was obviously surprised by my determination; he had felt sure I would return because he held our son as a hostage.

The child enlisted the help of the maid and sent me notes, spelling out, uncertainly, his love and distress: "Mamma, I wish I could run away from here, but I don't know how to. Everyone says horrid things about you, but I love you. I won't forget you in a hundred years. What are you doing? When are you going to send somebody to fetch me?"

My sister had given me a little room in her house, and I stayed there for a long time, barely noticing how time was passing. I read and re-read his notes, those outpourings of a stricken little heart. At night I hid my head and hands under the bedclothes, stifling my cries of pain . . . I called to my son, talked to him . . . I sprang up from the bed, determined to join him, whatever humiliation, corruption, or subservience lay in store. I didn't care so long as I could see and touch my child again.

But something inflexibly prevented me. A voice, speaking neither from my mind nor my poor, wracked body, told me that the step I had taken was irreversible. I had put an end to self-delusion, and I *must* endure this present anguish if I was not to die of shame and self-disgust. This inner command was terrible!

For months I prepared for death, as if suffering from a terminal illness. Secretly I was convinced that my husband would never make any concessions; his desire for revenge was inexorable. Instead of threatening letters he now sent me mocking notes, reminding me I had no legal grounds for separation. My father grew tired of negotiating, and withdrew. He had always warned me not to hope for too much. My husband then refused to authorise payment of my uncle's legacy to me. Finally, even the lawyers gave up. I must, they said, remain the property of this man, and should count myself lucky if he didn't force me to return to him. Such was the law.

My husband dismissed our maid, so I received no more letters from my son. I heard that a young governess had been employed, and I wrote to her, but received no reply.

There was nothing anyone could do for me.

I wished I was dead.

In a way I was dead. I had nothing left except my memories.

Time passed. By now my child must have developed a different picture of me. Other people would be influencing how he looked and what he said. But my picture of him would never change, and I found it hard to accept that my experience of motherhood had ended when I kissed him goodbye.

It was months before I noticed, with some surprise, that I really was alive, that nothing really essential had died inside me, and that the old questions were still there, waiting to be answered. Sometimes I saw children in the street who reminded me of my son, and sometimes one of them would return my gaze uneasily. But none of them seemed to need me. Yet on other occasions, walking in the early morning or at dusk, I would be passed by a child who would stop me with a sad, quiet question. It seemed to comfort these children when I talked to them and embraced them. Where did they sleep? How did they live? . . . I was disturbed by the thought that they and their mothers wandered aimlessly through the outskirts of the city. In spite of my own preoccupations, I felt concern.

One morning my sister took me to a clinic for poor children started by a group of women. I offered to work there on a voluntary basis two or three times a week.

My first visits were discouraging. The children were so different from my own beautiful, healthy child. They all seemed to be victims of ignorance, filth, hunger, and violence. I felt I could not bear to see such misery endlessly repeated . . .

But it was when I realised that *other people* also lived, although they suffered, that I began to live again myself. And when I did so I began to hope again, if not for myself, then at least for others. When I discovered that in spite of everything I still had confidence in a better life, a better future, I wept with joy.

I rented a room near my family, and when I wasn't teaching, which is how I now earned my living, or at the clinic, I sat at my desk and wrote articles. I made vehement appeals to the rest of society: others had made them before me, but I tried to infuse them with my own tears and blood. Gradually these articles began to sound somewhat frantic, because the magazines which used to publish what I wrote rejected them all.

Yet I still feel that the fire of justice is inextinguishable, and that what I ask for is not recognition, but only to be listened to. At dawn and at dusk I look from my window and see the crest of the Alps rising above the pink clouds. Sometimes I hear the sound of the dead march as a funeral cortège makes its way to the cemetery. I feel that when I look life and death in the face I am no longer afraid of them. Perhaps I even love them.

Everything in the sky and on earth seems in constant flux.

Everything seems to merge and become confused. Yet one thing is clear. I feel at peace, *in harmony,* and if I were to die now I would feel no remorse.

I feel at peace with myself.

Yet I have no hopes. Tomorrow I might discover a new reason for living, a new dimension to life which might seem like rebirth, but I don't expect to. Tomorrow I might as easily die . . . and writing this will then have been the last evidence of my existence.

It is a book for my son.

My son! His father probably believes him happy, offers him toys, books, and teachers, surrounds him with every luxury. He wants him to forget me or to hate me.

I would rather have him hate me than forget me.

He will be brought up to respect the law, useful as it is to those in power, to love authority, order, and comfort . . . I often look at his portrait and see my own grief reflected in his eyes, his father's harshness in the curve of his lips. But then I think: he is my son, and, being my son, he will be like me. I want to take him, hold him, absorb him completely so that after a time I would disappear and he would become entirely *me.*

One day he will be twenty. Will he leave home then to find me, or not? Will fate be kind? Or will he already be in love with another woman by then? Will he remember how I stretched out my hands to him, calling, calling his name?

Perhaps by then I shall be dead and no longer able to tell him the story of my life, the progression of my feelings . . . or to tell him how long I waited for him.

So I have written it all down here: so that one day my words will reach him.